PANAMANIAC

by Robert Rahula

ALSO BY ROBERT RAHULA

NOVELS:
Messieurs
Island of Misfits
Day Another Paradise In
One Last Fling
Bathhouse Stories
Conversation in a Belgian Bar
All the Yage in Reno
Exigent Circumstances
Uninvited Guest

POETRY:
Trigger Points
Dentro Del Corazón Bloqueada
Camino
Migration
I Sing the Body Politic
Wonderland
From Whose Bourn
Poemas Españoles
Expat Poems

ANTHOLOGIES:
Half Life
The Essential Dan Landes

Panamaniac

© 2015 Robert Rahula

All rights reserved. This book or any portion thereof may not be reproduced or used in any manner whatsoever without the express written permission of the author except for the use of brief quotations in a book review.
www.robertrahula.com

This is a work of fiction. Characters, organizations, businesses, products, locales, and events portrayed in this book either are products of the author's imagination or are used fictitiously.

First Printing, 2019

ISBN 978-1-7329708-0-9

Alma-Gator Press
Barcelona · Madrid · La Chorrera

for H.P.

He whose desires have been throttled,
who is independent of root,
whose pasture is emptiness,
signless and free –
his path is as unknowable
as that of birds across the heavens

-Dhammapada 93

PROLOGUE

When we last saw Ricardo, (see, "Ricardo's Epiphany" in the book *Messieurs*), he was fifty-six years old, living alone in Hamburg, New York, working as a probate lawyer for a small law firm during the day and writing short stories at night. Apart from visiting the brothels in St. Catherines, Canada, or the gay bathhouses in Buffalo, his life was not very satisfying. A few years have passed. He is about to turn sixty-two, the age when many men start to think seriously about retirement. Ricardo is thinking seriously too. He would like to leave the states, but he knows that his particular interests require special accommodations.

Chapter 1: Summer Wedding

Ricardo was at a wedding. Generally he liked weddings, as long as they weren't his own. But this one was outside, under the hot August sun. He was sweating, standing there beside Eve. He knew the groom, and the bride was a friend of Eve's. Like most weddings, it started late. The minister was droning on.

Dear friends, on behalf of Jim Pategante and Susan Seligman, I welcome you all here today for this marriage ceremony. We are here today, on this beautiful sunny day, to encourage and celebrate the covenant that these two people, Jim and Susan, are going to make, and we are here to share in the joy that Susan and Jim experience as they pledge their love and commitment to each other.

Yeah, Ricardo thought, I bet Jim is just all atingle with joy right now, just flush with happiness... yes, flush is the right word, as he flushes his single life down the toilet. I bet he just wants to get through the ceremony without fucking it up.

We rejoice in the manner God has led them to each other and brought them to the place where they now stand.

Oh God, Ricardo thought, he's going to do a religious wedding. Jesus fucking Christ. It's bad enough we have to stand here outside because these idiots thought it would be romantic to be married underneath the large pine tree at this park, i.e., they were too cheap to rent an air-conditioned hall, and while <u>they</u> are in the shade of that pine, <u>we</u>, the obligated audience of friends, or friends of friends, are standing in the sweltering sun... that's bad enough, but now we have to listen to a fucking religious preacher.

> *In the Bible, Paul wrote beautifully about the power of love in his first book of letters to the Corinthians, chapter thirteen, where he said: If I speak in the tongues of men and of angels, but have not love, I am a noisy gong or a clanging cymbal. And if I have prophetic powers, and understand all mysteries and all knowledge, and if I have all faith, so as to remove mountains, but have not love, I am nothing. If I give away all I have, and if I deliver my body to be burned, but have not love, I gain nothing. Love is patient and kind; love is not jealous or boastful; it is not arrogant or rude. Love does not insist on its own way; it is not irritable or resentful; it does not rejoice at wrong, but rejoices in the right. Love bears all things, believes all things, hopes all things, endures all things. Love never ends; as for prophecies, they will pass away; as for tongues, they will cease; as for knowledge, it will pass away. For our knowledge is imperfect and our prophecy is imperfect, but when the perfect comes, the imperfect will pass away. When I was a child, I spoke like a child, I thought like a child, I reasoned like a child; when I became a man, I gave up childish ways. For now, we see in a mirror dimly, but then we shall see face to face. Now I know in part; then I shall understand fully, even as I have been fully understood. So, faith, hope, love abide, these three, but the greatest of these is love.*

Ricardo looked over at Eve. She didn't seem uncomfortable in the heat. In fact, she looked lovely, but she always looked lovely. Eve always dressed in a classy vintage way that Ricardo liked. A dark jacket with a white blouse from that Ann Taylor store she always shopped at. Conservative skirt, but the fit contoured her body so well, and Ricardo knew what lay beneath. He hoped she would agree to leave the reception early and stop by his place so they could have sex before she had to rush home.

Eve must have sensed he was looking at her. She turned to look at him, took his arm and leaned up to his ear. "Doesn't she look beautiful?" she whispered, nodding toward the bride. "Absolutely," Ricardo replied. He looked over at Susan. Susan was always a bit provocative. It was a pretty wedding dress, but she had picked one that didn't cover the tattoos on her back. Plus, she had tied her black hair back, which exposed the tattoos more. She was short but with large breasts. What the personal ads refer to as "curvy". The kind of girl who you just knew would pork out in about five years, but for the moment, quite hot. Ricardo remembered meeting her one time, at some party at Jim's about four months ago. She was drunk, but not so drunk that she wasn't aware that she and he had been flirting with each other while Jim was attending to the other guests. He kept staring at her, letting his eyes dart from her eyes to her halter top, then back to her eyes. She met his gaze and held it, smiling. Occasionally she would come around with hors d'oeuvres, and not walk straight up to him, but come from the side, so she could lean into him, pressing her side against his and asking, "Care for a tasty-bite?" He liked her boldness, her drunkenness, and her smell. Something like lilac, but muskier. At one point, she went into the extra room where the guests had stored their coats, and he followed her in. The light was off. She was just standing there facing him when he walked in. He let the door close behind him and walked up to her. He placed his fingers on the top of her halter top and started to pull it down inch by inch, but she tightened her arms on her sides so her nipples would not be exposed.

"Aren't you a friend of Jim's?" she asked with a teasing tone.

"One of his best friends," Ricardo replied. "One of his absolute best."

She laughed, and then said, "Then you shouldn't be doing this."

"Why not?"

"Because you're his friend."

"Oh." Ricardo couldn't think of a retort to that, even though his brain was telling him that one thing had nothing to do with the other. So he leaned down and kissed her. She kissed him back. He felt her tongue glazing the inside of his lips. Then she laughed, broke away from him and slipped out the door.

"Have you ever met her?" Eve asked him.

"Who?"

"Susan, the bride."

"Hmmmm, no, I don't think so. Jim talks about her all the time."

Actually, Jim rarely talked about her. In fact, Ricardo hadn't even talked to Jim in about two months. Jim hadn't sent Ricardo a wedding invitation either, but Susan had invited Eve, and so Ricardo came as her guest. He still saw Jim occasionally around the office. Ricardo made a mental note to try and be nicer to him. He looked over at Jim. The preacher was talking directly to Jim now.

Jim, the woman who stands by your side is going to be your wife. She will look to you for comfort, for support, for love, for understanding, for encouragement, and for protection. You must never take her for granted, and you must always stand by her for good or ill.

What a crock of shit, Ricardo thought. She'll look to you for comfort and support alright, constantly, until she gets bored and finds someone else who's more comforting or more supportive. And you'll do no better, Jimbo. You'll be taking her for granted within a week of the honeymoon.

Ricardo felt his lips purse up a bit. Well, that was a bit harsh, he thought, but still... It took two to de-tango, and people had no shortage of de-tango-ments. People loved each other when it was convenient. He thought back to his two marriages. Two more opposite women he couldn't imagine, yet he married both of them. Actually, as he thought about it, there were some commonalities. Both had been stuck in bad relationships when he met them. Ricardo guessed that their marrying him seemed somehow like a way out. It was funny how some women got into those abusive relationships, then looked for someone to rescue them, then resented being rescued. He wondered if Susan had been entangled with someone else when she met Jim. It seemed like most people just leapfrogged from one relationship to another, finally settling for the most comfortable lily pad.

Ricardo glanced around at the crowd. Almost all couples. All of the women were intently watching the ceremony. The men all stood there, eyes glazed over. Some of the men were discretely checking their cell phones. But Ricardo realized that if someone glanced over at him and Eve, they would see the same thing: a couple, the woman enraptured by the whole concept of the marriage ceremony and what it means, and the man dutifully, and quietly, standing by her side.

Ricardo did all those dutiful things too, for the same reason all men do them: so they can get to the sex, the intimacy, the flesh, those trembling wet desperate moments that give life its only meaning. That's what Ricardo believed, at least as far as he could figure out. And he was still trying to figure it out. Even at sixty-one, he was still trying to figure it out.

Now the preacher was talking to Susan.

Susan, the man who stands by your side is going to be your husband. He will look to you for comfort, support, love, understanding and encouragement. You must never take him for granted and always stand by him for good or ill.

Clearly, this preacher was a cheerleader for that type of committed monogamous relationship that churches always espoused. Ricardo wondered if anyone ever achieved that type of relationship. He certainly didn't in his two marriages. Maybe that type of relationship did exist for some people, but Ricardo knew that it just didn't exist for him. After his second divorce, he came to the conclusion that the whole business of marriage was simply incompatible with his personal proclivities, meaning the pleasure he got from sex with other people. He had kept his affairs hidden from both wives of course, but that meant that the whole "being-committed-to-marriage" business was a lie. The only reason he didn't cheat more during his marriages was that it required such an effort to conceal the affairs. After his second divorce, he tried dating again. But even dating, which women saw as a test drive for marriage, required this feigned commitment. He just couldn't do it. Well, he did it, but he felt like such a hypocrite. So after a while, he made the decision to confine his relationships with women just to prostitutes. It was a deliberate choice on his part. He stopped dating, stopped going to parties or events to meet people, stopped accepting introductions from well-meaning friends. He just redefined his social life around prostitutes. He was making decent money in a small law firm doing probate work in upstate New York, so he could afford to drive across the border several times a month to St. Catherines in Canada, to visit the brothels there. The sex was good, and best of all, there were no entanglements. No prostitute ever wanted to possess him, nor ever asked him to account for where he'd been the night before, nor ever forbade him from seeing other women (or other men, for that matter). No prostitute ever wanted to parade him in front of other women, to show they had secured a mate. Ricardo thought the business of prostitution was the most honest straightforward human relationship that he ever had. Everything was transparent and above board. Everything was professional and respectful, and above all, discrete. Love, of course, could still creep into the picture, but love was easier to manage in a brothel. There was one young woman, named Haley, up in St. Catherines, whom he almost fell in love with. For almost a year, he would visit only her. As long as he only saw her in the brothel, they had the perfect life, each pretending for an hour or two every other week, that they were the only lovers in the world, passionate and committed to each other. She was skinny like a boy, and had small breasts and the palest skin, but treated him so tenderly and lovingly. But then Ricardo started having feelings towards her. And as the months went by, Haley acted as if she had feelings towards him. Maybe that's what made the sex so good. It certainly was a beautiful time in his life. Then he made the mistake of trying to take the relationship out of the brothel, trying to take her out to dinner, trying to get to know her, to get involved in her life. It was a fatal mistake. Outside of the brothel, the realities and difficulties of real relationships came up. There was, after all, the age and culture difference. She was nineteen. He was fifty-six back then. He had nothing in common with her, nothing to talk about, and relationships—real relationships—outside of brothels, have to have some commonality to survive. His "affair" with her soon came to an end, and Ricardo started frequenting other brothels. Ricardo never did find another prostitute as sweet as Haley, but that didn't stop him from looking. When he had the money, he'd make the ninety-minute drive to Canada. When he didn't have the money, he'd head over to the local gay bathhouse in the neighboring city of Buffalo, New York. The sex with men was different, but it was still sex, and still discrete. Ricardo didn't think that his need for regular sex, whether it was with a female or a male, was any different than any other man's. It was just that other men seemed to throw in the towel as they got older. They got married and gave up sex. Either the routine wore them down, or the living with just one person wore them down.

Ricardo wasn't sure. He just knew that every married man he knew always bitched about their wives and alluded to the fact that the wild days were way in the past. Ricardo didn't want to be one of those guys. So, he kept his business discrete and continued to patronize brothels and bathhouses.

> *In Genesis 2:22 it says, "the Lord God made a woman from the rib He had taken out of the man, and He brought her to the man." Jim, you must always hold Susan very close to your heart, and love her in sickness and health. In Genesis 2:18, The Lord God said, "It is not good for the man to be alone. I will make a helper suitable for him." Susan, you must be a true helpmate to Jim at all times, helping him with every burden of life.*

Haley seemed a long time ago. He still remembers her body, her small breasts and shaved pussy, and especially how she would lock eyes with him when she was giving him head, but all his images of her were more like snapshots, frozen in time.

The pictures in his head of his two wives had that same quality, like old photographs you find in a drawer, old photographs that might evoke a certain sadness. His whole life as a married man—a twice-married man—seemed even more removed, light years removed. After his second divorce, he enrolled in law school and managed to graduate. He had moved innumerable times since then, and had lost track of both wives. Hell, they could be dead for all he knew. He finally settled in Hamburg, New York, drinking heavily of course, tried rehab twice, but finally decided he needed to drink to keep his sanity. He took a job doing probate work, and even though it was monotonous, he discovered he was good at it. He used to joke that the only people he could stand were his clients, who of course, were dead. Somewhere along the way, he started writing short stories, and then some of them started getting published. Finally, a publisher contacted him about doing a book, and he combined three of his short stories into a book called *Messieurs*, which sold reasonably well. Not enough to live on, but enough to get him wondering how he could find a way to just write full time. He had been thinking about his for a while. More accurately, he had been obsessing about this for a while.

> *Jim, since it is your intention to marry, join your right hands and declare your consent. Do you take Susan to be your lawful wedded wife to have and to hold, from this day on, for better or for worse, for richer or for poorer, in sickness and in health, as long as you both shall live?*

Eve, of course, was a whole other story, the recent exception to his no-dating lifestyle. She worked as a paralegal in another law office down the hall. She had been married for eighteen years but was in the process of divorcing her husband or separating from her husband, depending on what day it was. She and her husband had been living apart for about two years, but evidently neither one of them could pull the trigger. They just kept dragging it out. Ricardo tried to stay out of it. Eve would come by after work for a quickie before she had to get home to be a dutiful mom to her two teenage children. As long as she was technically married, she said, she didn't want her kids to know she was "seeing" anyone. Normally, this would be way too much drama for Ricardo, but the sex was so good, he put up with having to accommodate himself to her schedule. Sometimes, she would send him a text saying *I only have 30 minutes* and he would leave work early to prepare his apartment so that all was ready when she rushed in a little after five, pulling off her clothes as she made it from his front door back to the bedroom, where he would have dildos and lubricants all lined up on the night stand. Eve loved to fuck, and more, she loved to be eaten out. If he shoved a dildo aggressively in and out of her pussy while he sucked on her clit, she would

sometimes squirt when she came, covering his face with a
sticky, wonderful, girl-cum. She would act all embarrassed
about that, but he loved it.

> *Susan, do you take Jim to be your lawful wedded
> husband, to have and to hold from this day on, for
> better or for worse, for richer or for poorer, in sickness
> and in health, as long as you both shall live?*

Ricardo checked his watch, and again wondered if he
would have enough time to get Eve back to his apartment
after a brief obligatory appearance at the reception.

Chapter 2: I Left My Heart

A month had passed since the wedding. It was now late September, on a Thursday evening. Eve had just left Ricardo's house after an intense after-work love-making session. Ricardo lay naked on his bed, completely drained. She had done that thing he loved so much: she let him fuck her until he almost came and then took his cock in her mouth, sucking him hard and twisting his balls until he came in her mouth, but not swallowing, but rather crawling over on top of him and forcing his mouth open with her tongue and forcing all of his cum into his mouth. Then they both licked and kissed each other hard, both swallowing his cum. There was something about that act that connected him so deeply to Eve, that made him feel so trusting of her, so one with her. She had other tricks that he loved, but this one was the best.

Afterwards, she showered quickly, then dressed even more quickly, all while he lay on the bed unable to move. She kissed him goodbye, saying she had to run to fix dinner for her kids, but that she would see him tomorrow at the office. After he kissed her, he said something he had never said to her. "I love you." She looked at him, smiled, and said, "I know." Then, she was gone.

Ricardo lay there for about twenty more minutes, just floating in some post-coital bliss, but gradually feeling movement come back into his body. He started thinking about love, about the quality of love, about the flesh of love. Then he suddenly realized that "that feeling" was coming over him. He needed to write. He jumped out of bed, grabbed his bathrobe, went to his writing desk, turned on his laptop, and started to type. The following words flowed out of him...

Samuel got the news three hours before the doctors cut him open. The morning nurse, the one who usually brought him breakfast, came in, empty-handed but all excited, to tell him. "Mr. Francisco, they found a heart for you. They're on their way with it now. We've got to get you ready for surgery. Sorry, no breakfast this morning." She grabbed his glass and the water pitcher from the table beside his bed. "And no more fluids until after the operation. Sorry."

Samuel could scarcely believe it. He'd been lying in this same hospital bed for almost three months, hooked up to several machines that were keeping his dying heart alive. Up to three months ago, he had been getting by on various medications, but then he collapsed in his apartment and they had rushed him to the hospital. He hadn't been out of the hospital since that day. Initially, there were many consultations with specialists—doctors who came in with the unanimous opinion that only a heart transplant would save his life. When they first explained what his life would be like with a transplanted heart—the lifetime of medicines, the side effects, and the limitations on his lifestyle—he was against it, but finally his family doctor convinced him.

"Sam," he said, "the life you've enjoyed for forty-five years is over. It's gone. With a transplant, you have a chance of living outside of this hospital, but if you don't have this operation, you will never leave this building alive. This hospital has the best equipment in the world, but your heart muscles are so dead, that even these machines can't keep you alive more than six to eight months. Look around this room, Sam. Do you want to die here?"

So, he relented. He signed volumes of papers, got on the waiting lists, watched endless "educational videos" for transplant patients, and waited. At first, there were daily visits by relatives and friends who had heard the news. Almost all of them put on a simplistic optimistic face. "You'll be out of here in no time," they would invariably say. But as the weeks wore on, the visits slowed, and even the forced optimism evaporated. Sam had almost given up hope. Recently, he even considered telling the doctors to take him off the list, to pull all the tubes and wires out of him, and just let him die. But when that feeling came over him, he would tell the nurse that the pain was worse, and they would increase his pain medicine, and he would drift into a blissful reverie of how his life used to be.

"Who's the donor?" he asked the nurse.

"Oh I don't know," she said, "some traffic accident on LaSalle early this morning, three cars and a bus. That's all I know. I've got to go and do charting. Bobby will be here in a minute to start prepping you." And she rushed out of the room.

She probably was not supposed to tell me that much, Sam thought. There were strict protocols against knowing anything about organ donors. However, he thought he might have a few minutes before Bobby showed up, so he opened his laptop, and went to his news tab. There it was: a fatal traffic accident on LaSalle. One person killed, a certain Keith Thompson, a food columnist for a local paper, sideswiped by a teenager who had just gotten his driver's license. But then Sam heard Bobby pushing a cart and opening the door, so he stopped reading and closed his laptop just as Bobby walked in.

It wasn't until a month later that Sam started thinking about Keith Thompson again. He couldn't think about anything for the week after the operation—there was simply too much pain and too much pain medication. In fact, he didn't remember much about that week. But eventually, they eased back on the opioids, and by the end of the second week, he could move around without too much discomfort and had started rehabilitation therapy. There were a couple of scares with infections, but the doctors all exclaimed how pleased they were—there did not seem to be any issues with tissue rejection. His new heart was adapting well. By the end of the third week, Samuel was back at home, going to therapy four times a week, and happy to be alive.

It was some notice in the paper that caught his eye and started him thinking again about the man whose heart now beat in his chest. Something about a charity fund started in Keith Thompson's memory by his wife. Samuel started wondering who Keith Thompson had been.

Samuel knew that there were good reasons why patients are never told who a donor is. There are enough emotions associated with getting a transplanted organ such as "why did someone else have to die so that I could live?" without complicating the issue with real information or images of the real person. But Sam couldn't help himself. He started digging deeper into the internet stream of information and found articles, old Facebook posts and Pinterest photos of Keith Thompson. They were easy to find because Keith had worked as a food editor for the local newspaper for many years, so there were many internet articles that had at least his byline on them. Gradually, Samuel began to build up a picture of Keith Thompson's life, what he looked like, what he wrote, what he believed in... who he was.

Keith had been married for fourteen years and had an eleven year old son. He wrote the local food column which meant he reviewed new restaurants in town or wrote about recipes when there were no new restaurants. Sam read all of the old columns he could find. He discovered that he liked the way Keith wrote. Keith Thompson obviously enjoyed food, but wasn't pretentious or pampered about it. He would give a good catfish dish at some local hole-in-the-wall eatery the same nice write-up he would give the fanciest restaurant in town. In fact, he would gently reprimand the fanciest restaurant if they started putting ambience above the quality of the food. Sam printed out all the columns he could find, kept them in a binder, and made a point to try each of the restaurants to see whether he agreed with the review. It started out as simply a homage to the man whose death had given him life, but Sam found he enjoyed trying new dishes in new places.

As time went by, Sam's life returned more and more to normal. He went back to his old job in the post office. Sam had been a front desk worker for the post office for years, but it was an indoor job, and his doctors urged him to find something that involved regular exercise outdoors. The union helped negotiate a transfer to a walking route, but one that involved carrying less weight than the regular routes. They found a route for him on the edge of town, where the houses were a little further apart. Sam discovered that the people there were more friendly than the customers that came into the post office all hurried and rushed. As Sam got to know the route and the customers, he would often stop and chat with them when he delivered their mail. In the early months, when he was still recovering from the surgery, he told himself he was stopping to chat in order to rest for a few minutes, but he found that he enjoyed chatting with his new customers. Most were retired older folks eager to share photos of their grandchildren or talk about all their ailments. At one time, Sam would have found such medical recountings irritating, but now he sympathized. He too had his good and bad days, and would point out to the elders how each doctor visit, each new medication, was like a new lease on life, and how they should make the most of every day. To the more religious customers, Sam would quote a biblical verse he had heard as a child that referred to everyone's days as being numbered and no one knowing when their number would be called. They nodded in agreement.

The one thing that hadn't changed in Sam's life was that he was still single. He had had a girlfriend years earlier, before the first signs of fatigue had appeared, those first indications that his heart was having trouble pumping enough blood through his lungs to re-oxygenate the red blood cells. She and he had been dating for many years, but as his illness progressed, they had split up. During the long months he lay in the hospital bed, Sam always felt betrayed by this woman, that she would leave him in his worst moment of life. But somehow, after the surgery, Sam came to accept that the separation had been inevitable, that there was simply not enough love or commitment in that relationship to survive *the stress of a partner having a catastrophic condition. He had never thought of it from her perspective, how difficult it was for her to be in a relationship with a bedridden patient who might die any day. They had been a fun good-time couple, and Sam was grateful for those memories.*

But as his health improved, Sam began to hope that a new love might enter his life. He started keeping his eyes open. He would linger around the waiting rooms after the cardiac rehabilitation support groups ended to see if there were interesting-looking family members or friends of friends who might be there. He would chat with the nurses when he went in for his frequent evaluations. He would take note when any new customers moved onto his delivery route. But no one crossed his path that struck his fancy. It began to dawn on Sam that his access to women, his opportunity to meet them, had been severely reduced by his transplant operation. Before the operation, he had been a regular at the bars and at parties. Most of his friends drank heavily, or at least regularly, and Sam had been right there with them. Consequently, with friends at parties or at bars, there were always opportunities to meet women. But one of the post-operative conditions of heart transplant surgery was no alcohol, and almost all of Sam's old friends slowly drifted away when he couldn't (or wouldn't) join them at the bars or parties. Sam realized that most of them had been simply good-time buddies, just like his old girlfriend. He needed new friends, ones who shared his new-found realization that life is short. He joined a cooking group that he found on an online "meet-up" website. He started doing some volunteer work helping to clean up a local park. And he made new friends, and they were good people, but they often were couples or other men, or other women who didn't strike that particular chord in him. Occasionally, he would go out on dates and he would have a good time, but no relationships ever developed.

And so, the days went, one after another, and a year passed, and more, and then one day he realized that exactly two years had passed since his surgery.

It was midday, and Sam was thinking about where he was going to eat lunch when the realization hit him that it was the two-year anniversary of his operation. Well, he thought, I need to pay my respects to this date. Usually, on nice days like this, when he brought a sandwich, he would go to the park to eat his lunch. But today he decided to walk over to the Sabana Cemetery. They had picnic tables under some oak trees. He made his way over there thinking about the past two years and all the changes that had occurred in his life. He was simply not the man he was before the surgery. He was exercising and eating right; his blood pressure was normal, and he had new activities and new friends. He had to admit that the surgery had given him a new lease on life, or at least a new appreciation of life.

When he got to the cemetery, he was glad to see there were not many people there, and no one at the picnic tables. On certain days of the week, the cemetery had many visitors, perhaps because it was the only cemetery in this older section of town. Sam was glad to have the picnic tables to himself. He ate his sandwich and listened to the birds in the trees above him and watched the branches sway and felt at peace with the world. It wasn't until he stood up that he saw the green sweater lying on the seat on the other side of the table. He threw his trash in the nearby trash can and walked around to the other side of the table and picked up the sweater. It was a woman's sweater, lightly embroidered. It had a slight scent on it that almost smelled familiar. He looked around. About 1000 feet away, he saw someone kneeling by a grave. On an impulse, he took the sweater and walked over to the person.

As he approached, he saw it was a woman. She was still kneeling facing the grave as he walked up.

"Excuse me," he said, "someone left this over by the picnic table and I..."

She stood up and turned around and looked at him, and smiled. She was beautiful, in an oddly familiar way, perhaps the most beautiful woman he had ever seen. He suddenly lost his train of thought.

"and... and I... I wondered if it might be yours..."

She smiled at him. "Yes, thank you, I wouldn't want to lose that." She reached out her hand and Sam handed her the sweater, still staring at her face.

"I'm sorry," he said, "I don't mean to stare... You just look so familiar. I... I try to come here for lunch when I can, because it's so peaceful, but I've never seen you here before."

"Yes," she said, "it is peaceful. Sad, but peaceful." She stuck out her hand. "My name's Claire."

"Oh sorry, I'm Sam." He shook her hand. It was soft and warm. Sam felt an overwhelming tenderness come over him. He felt his face flushing. "I... um... I'm the mailman for this area, that's why I can stop by here for lunch."

She smiled. "Yes, I sort of figured that when I saw the uniform." Sam liked her smile. He liked her eyes and the way she kept looking at him. He realized he was smiling back at her.

"I like it here too," she said. "Usually I'll come by on the weekends. I used to bring my son here, but he said it makes him too sad so I don't push it unless he wants to.

"Are you, are you... I don't know how to ask this... are you visiting a grave?" Sam asked.

"Yes," she said. "My late husband."

"I'm sorry."

"Thank you. It was so hard to accept at first, but life moves on, you know. I have to think it's all part of some grand plan. What's that saying, 'to those who listen, the fates guide...'"

Sam finished the quote for her. "And to those who don't, the fates drag."

She looked startled. "How did you know that?"

"I don't know. It's an old saying, isn't it?"

"Yes, I guess it is." She looked down and was quiet for a moment.

Sam didn't want to have the conversation stop. He wanted to get to know this woman.

"Uh, how old is your son?"

"He's thirteen now."

"That's a difficult age."

"Tell me about it. He's a good kid, smart as his dad, but sometimes he's a handful. I never thought I'd be raising a teenager alone."

Sam nodded and then said again, "Yeah, it's a difficult age. They want to be free, but they still need structure."

"How about you? Any kids?" she asked.

"No. No, I always wanted them, but life kinda got in the way."

She looked at him. It seemed to Sam that she was studying his face.

He was going to say something, but found himself looking back at her. Then he realized that he was staring so he tried to think of something to say.

"Is this... is this your husband's grave?" It felt like an idiotic thing to ask, but it came out.

"Yes." She turned around to look at it.

Sam looked at it too. Then he gasped.

It read "Keith Thompson".

"Oh my God," Sam said.

He stared at the stone marker and then he looked at Claire.

*   *   *

Ricardo looked at the clock. It was one a.m. He had been writing, in a trance, for almost six hours. He felt exhausted. He printed the story out and read it quickly. "How odd," he thought, "there's no sex in this story. It's just about love." He thought about a title, and then suddenly realized the pun buried deep in the story. He laughed out loud. He was always amazed at how horribly mischievous the muses were. "I left my heart in Sam Francisco. Jesus," he thought, "that's terrible. I'll just call it 'I Left My Heart.' I'll have to see if the publisher likes it." He turned off his computer and went back to bed.

Chapter 3: Winter Thoughts

It was now early December in Hamburg. A light snow had fallen overnight but was expected to melt by the afternoon. The light snow that had fallen on Ricardo's heart was not expected to melt quite so soon. He turned sixty-two last month.

He stood in his kitchen staring at the calendar on his refrigerator. Only a few more weeks until he would leave for his "vacation" in Panamá, said "vacation" being five weeks unpaid leave he had negotiated with the firm. He started negotiating unpaid leave a few years back, on some vague hope of eventually being able to cobble together a few months off every year, but then he discovered Panamá and started using all his paid and unpaid time to go there.

The memory of the wedding the previous August had long since evaporated from his mind. He never had rekindled a friendship with Jim, and had no idea how Jim and Susan were doing... and he didn't care. Work was just a place he went to each day, where he closed his door, processed papers, and tried to leave early each day so he could go home and write. He always found it ironic that the thing he hated most—sitting at a desk at work, drafting pleadings on his computer—was so like the thing he loved most—sitting at a desk at home, writing short stories on his computer. But that's how it is. Like being married and having a mistress. Both involved fucking, but one was obligatory and one was delightful.

Eve had also evaporated from Ricardo's life. Like many of his better affairs, it managed to last several months. But then there came a week where she avoided him and then, and when he asked her directly about it, she confessed she had let her husband move back in with her, and they were going to "try and make the marriage work". When she said that, Ricardo just nodded, wished her well, and walked away. There was nothing more to say. "Making the marriage work" was an expression that he never understood. It evoked no image for him, no picture, no idea of what one does to "make a marriage work". He wondered if it was like towing an old car into the shop and asking if they could make it run again. That was as close to an image as he could get. It simply made no sense to him. Something either worked or it didn't. She might as well have said she was going to try and grow a third arm. But he was sincere in wishing her well. He bore no malice. He would miss her, or more precisely, he would miss her body, those breasts, those nipples, that pussy, that ass. She had given him access to her body for almost four months, and let him do some very naughty things to her, and for that, he was thankful. He always felt thankful to women for the sexual favors they granted to him, even though he knew they were getting their needs met too, and that they had had sex before him and would have sex after him, and would climax again with their legs wrapped around someone else. He understood all that. But nonetheless, he was thankful.

But this morning, as the snow lay on the ground, he was not thinking of Eve. He was looking at the calendar and counting the days. He turned towards the coffee pot, refilled his cup, went over to the desk, sat down, and began to leaf through his folder labeled "Panamá trip". He had his plane reservations, his hotel reservations for the first two nights stay, his passport, and his map. All seemed in order. He would start this trip in Panamá City and work his way southwest along the Pacific coast towards Santiago and then towards the city of David. Hopefully he could return at some future point and check out the Caribbean side. After this next trip, he would be approaching sixty-three... which marked his target date for exiting his job and the United

States.

Something in Ricardo had changed in the past year. Perhaps it was losing Eve as a lover. She certainly had brought a certain twist to his lovemaking. Perhaps he was approaching some burnout point at work, when every probate case involved ungrateful grown children clawing for an undeserved share of their parents' estate, parents whom they had ignored in life. Perhaps it was Ricardo's own age, and the fact that he was approaching what he had defined as a crossroads... what other people defined as retirement. But perhaps the truth was that Ricardo's crossroad involved one last chance at doing something in his life that meant something to him. He has become obsessed with one thing: creating an environment where he could just write.

All of Ricardo's jobs throughout his career had involved writing in some fashion or other, but those jobs always involved technical or legal writing. But over the past few years, Ricardo had discovered that he had a certain passion, more like an addiction, for writing short stories. He wrote them under an assumed name, of course, because more often than not, they were sexually explicit, and Ricardo had a job to protect. He didn't write them to sell, but he would send them out to magazines, usually porn magazines or edgy arts journals, and occasionally he would sell one. It always brought him a certain excitement when a magazine issue would come out with one of his stories, but the excitement was always temporary, because the magazine disappeared the following month when the new issue came out. But when his *Messieurs* book was published, he was hooked. Maybe it was the rush of seeing his book in the bookstores. Maybe it was the reviews, or the smattering of fan mail that his publisher forwarded to him—he didn't know. But it might as well have been pure heroin. He was hooked into something. He would come home from work, eat a quick dinner, open a bottle of wine, and sit down to write. Sometimes the words came fast, and sometimes they didn't. Sometimes he could only produce one page of material in a night... but he didn't mind. He simply enjoyed the activity. He looked forward to it. He maintained a good relationship with his publisher, and had been working on another book of short stories entitled *One Hundred Brothels*. The book wasn't about brothels so much, although it did of course involve a lot of sex, but the publisher liked the title, and hoped to capitalize on the modest success that *Messieurs* had in the gay/poly/S&M demographics.

The problem, of course, was time. Working forty to fifty hours a week at a job he didn't care about drained not only his time but his energy. He had examined his savings, his projected Social Security benefits, his small pension benefits, and concluded that he simply could not retire before sixty-six and continue to live in the states. But... but if he moved somewhere where the cost of living was dramatically less, he might be able to pull it off. He had spent months researching Ecuador, Panamá, Costa Rica, Nicaragua, Guatemala, and Mexico, charting out the costs of living, the health care systems, the crime rates, the quality of life, and of course the availability of brothels and bathhouses. Finally, he settled on Panamá.

Ricardo looked at the calendar again, and recounted the days.

Chapter 4: La Chorrera, Panamá

"Está abierto?" asked Ricardo through the open window of the Restaurante de Los Cuñados.

"No, Señor," said the boy sweeping up inside the restaurant.

"A qué hora está abierto?"

"A las cuatro," said the boy.

Ricardo looked at his watch. It was three o'clock. He had an hour to wait until the restaurant opened.

"Gracias." he said.

Ricardo decided to walk to the park. It was only a few blocks away, and he, like the residents of La Chorrera, enjoyed sitting on the benches and watching other people go by.

La Chorrera was one of the larger cities in Panamá, about forty kilometers southwest of Panamá City. Ricardo had been there about two weeks, exploring the city, trying out the restaurants, taking in the culture and atmosphere, researching the prices of renting an apartment and trying to estimate the cost of living if he were to move there. He also had found time, of course, to check out the more submarine establishments that could speak to his personal needs.

The central park in La Chorrera was shaded by a few giant mango trees. Ricardo found a bench in the shade near the central fountain, sat down, made himself comfortable, and gazed around. There were always people in the park, but in this the hottest part of the afternoon, the native residents of La Chorrera knew better. Almost all of the strollers in the park were gringos from North America, pensionados, or tourists from other countries.

One could always differentiate the gringos. Unlike

the tourists from Europe, the North Americans were always overweight, sometimes not greatly so, but almost always with some extra poundage. The gringo men wore shorts, which the native Panameños never did. The younger gringos dressed all in khaki, as if they were going on safari, with huge cargo pants and backpacks. The older gringos wore colorful Hawaiian-style shirts or bright t-shirts. And they walked with their expensive cameras hanging down in front of their bodies, just in case there was a scenic picture to take, something to show the folks back home. The younger gringos carried their expensive smartphones in their hands, equally ready to take pictures, to post on Facebook or Instagram, also for the same purpose: to incite envy in their friends back home. The more savvy Europeans knew better. They dressed in neutral colors, and kept their cameras discretely tucked away in nondescript side-bags under their arms, for they knew the habits of the teenage petty-theft gangs, who would distract a gringo in a crowd with an "accidental" bumping, deftly cut the camera strap with a razor blade, and quickly disperse and disappear into the crowded mercado.

The long-time pensionados—those gringos who retired here years ago—were a little more difficult to pick out. Sometimes they were indistinguishable from the Panameños except for their white beards. Ricardo had noticed that the older Panameño men rarely grew beards. In addition, even the seasoned pensionados still maintained the US habit of wearing hats to ward off the brilliant sun. Ricardo thought this one difference was worth it, and he too wore a hat. But he had never seen a Panameño in a hat in any town or city in Panamá, although they were nearly universally worn in the rural farming communities.

He watched one obviously gringo tourist couple lumber arm in arm up the sidewalk. The man was wearing a t-shirt and shorts, exposing pale white legs which ended in dark socks and a pair of brown walking shoes. He had on a straw hat and sunglasses. The woman was hatless but was wearing one of those visors on her forehead, like the old-time gamblers. She also had big round sunglasses on. The man was wearing something around his neck, but it wasn't until they got closer that Ricardo could see what it was. It was one of those concealable passport holders that many tourists wisely kept their passport and wallet in. But it was supposed to be worn under the shirt, to prevent pick-pocketing. This fool was wearing it on the outside of his t-shirt. Ricardo just shook his head and looked away.

The gringos annoyed Ricardo because they represented the worst of the United States. They were flashy, loud, opinionated and—relative to most Panameños—rich. They came down by the thousands every January, to escape the wintry north, to lie in the sun on the sand like beached white whales, and to take endless photographs to foist upon their friends up north. They came with their money, their racist attitudes, and their demands. They got into arguments in restaurants when something wasn't to their expectations. They rented cars that were too large for the narrow roads and then honked at people to get out of the way. They threw their money around. Panameños, on the other hand, avoided arguments. Panameño culture was built on a type of laid-back collaboration, a kind of non-confrontation. Panameños would go out of their way to help someone. There had been many times when Ricardo was lost or was looking for a particular store or park or hotel and would ask strangers for directions. A Panameño wouldn't just give directions—he or she would say, "I'll show you" and walk him there, even if it was blocks out of their way. But gringos with their money and their entitlements were slowly destroying all that. They claimed they came for the unspoiled nature, but then demanded fancy resorts to stay in. Then of course, entrepreneurial foreign companies moved in and built the fancy resorts, driving the price of land up, attracting more tourists, which begot more resorts and upscale restaurants. Tourist areas had sprung up over the last ten years, on the islands and mainland beaches on both the Pacific and Atlantic sides, and the Panameño welcoming mood there was slowly changing. There was one old hotel near Playa San Carlos where Ricardo liked to stay, where the locals stayed, near the beach. The gringos either avoided it because it was a bit run-down, or they didn't know about it, because it didn't have a website and wasn't on TripAdvisor. But it was only twenty dollars a night and the rooms were large with big windows and simple furnishings. There was no restaurant, nor "continental breakfast", but each room had a small kitchenette. During the Panameño summers—January to May—the hot sun did heat the rooms up during the day, but there was a ceiling fan, and if you opened all the windows and cranked up the fan, it was tolerable enough. Besides, the beach was just a block away if you needed to cool down. Aside from an occasional young backpacker, however, Ricardo had never met any other Americans staying there. It was always just Panameño families with small children on an inexpensive vacation. But it was the first place where Ricardo had stayed three years ago when he first started visiting Panamá, and he still liked to stay there every year, for a few days at least. He would always try to fit it into his itinerary. But over the last two years, he had noticed a change. As more gringos discovered Playa San Carlos, the neighboring houses were being razed for fancy resorts with air conditioning and bathtubs and hot showers in every room. Panameño homes and local Panameño hotels didn't have bathtubs, or even hot water. They just had large shower rooms with what Ricardo called suicide showers: cold water showers with a small electric heater built into the showerhead, with electrical wires running from it into the wall socket. They didn't really heat the water, just took the chill out of it. But the gringo demand for hot showers, and hot water faucets in the sinks as well, was the first thing that impacted new buildings. All the new gated retirement communities for expats and retirees advertised hot water heaters and large Jacuzzi-like bathtubs. This amused the Panameños, because the daytime temperature year-round, even during the "winter" rainy season, was always warm, and even the coldest shower water was never really cold. If the locals wanted to soak in hot water, they would make the trek to one of several hot springs that existed, and spend the day soaking in extremely hot, naturally heated water. To put large hot water tanks in Panameño homes seemed like an unaffordable affectation to Panameños; but because of the

American dollar, the construction of new condos and resorts had adapted to American desires. And because of the profit to be made selling land to development companies to build the new condos and retirement communities for expats, the look and feel and culture of many of the island and beach towns had changed. Modest older homes that might have sold for $10,000 from one Panameño to another Panameño ten years ago, started selling to gringos for $60,000, then $80,000, then $100,000. Now they were being bought up, knocked down, and new homes quickly built to sell to new retirees for $200,000. Local restaurants that used to sell a dinner for four dollars to locals soon realized that Americans would pay fifteen dollars the same meal and raised their prices accordingly, pricing the locals out of local restaurants. There was a growing sense in the coastal areas that the dollars that gringos contributed to the local economy came with a rather hefty price tag.

Still, Ricardo thought, much of the country inland remained unspoiled. The inland towns, the dirt road cattle towns in the rural part of the country or the remote mountain villages, reachable only by a two-hour bus ride, these places were still largely undiscovered and uncontaminated by gringos. Young backpackers (and even old backpackers like Ricardo) were welcomed there. Meals at the local food stands were still cheap and good. People were still friendly.

A soft breeze started to blow through the park. Ricardo looked around. The midday shadows were beginning to lengthen toward late afternoon. A few shops on the edge of the park were starting to reopen after the afternoon siesta. Of course, Ricardo had to acknowledge that he was a gringo too, and he was there for the same reason that so many gringos came to Panamá, because it was cheap, because it was beautiful, and because he could, hopefully, retire here and live better than he could in the states. He had to live with this hypocrisy,, and he tried to make amends by always being courteous to Panameños, by speaking Spanish as much as he could, by never ever boasting about the United States, and by trying to blend in. Of course, blending in was Ricardo's lifelong skill, even in the states, where he had an equal number of hypocrisies to smooth over and try and live with.

He looked at his watch. It was almost four. He spent a few more minutes watching the people walk by, then got up and headed back to the restaurant.

Chapter 5: Los Cuñados

The Restaurante de Los Cuñados was owned by two brother-in-laws. Ricardo had met one of them, Miguel, at La Chorrera's bathhouse a few days earlier. After sex, they got to talking, and Miguel told him about his restaurant and invited him to come by that week. Ricardo had promised that he would.

As he walked back to the restaurant from the park, Ricardo thought about the past ten days. He had allotted two weeks to spend in La Chorrera, which he had mostly spent as he had intended: visiting small apartments that he found on Craigslist or through notices posted on the walls of the local mercados, checking them out, talking to potential landlords, explaining that it would be at least another nine months to a year before he could move here but that he wanted to see what was available. All of the Panameño landlords were gracious, showing him the apartments, talking about the bus lines, the best restaurants, etc. There were a few gringo landlords who seemed put out having to show an apartment to someone who wasn't going to rent right away. After the first week, if Ricardo discerned that the landlord was a gringo, he simply would not make an appointment to see the place—it just wasn't worth it.

Most of the apartments were basically just a room in a local Panameño family's house with its own entrance and bathroom and a small kitchenette composed of a microwave, a half-refrigerator, and a two-burner hotplate—what would be called a mother-in-law apartment in the states. These went for the equivalent of two to three hundred dollars a month. For the apartments that didn't have a kitchenette, the rent often included meals with the host family. Ricardo liked these places. He liked the host families and the idea of paying them directly. He also liked the idea of being able to practice his Spanish with locals. Plus, he thought that these places were safer than the large apartment buildings, although the apartment buildings were usually located near the universities, which meant they were nearer the bars. Those apartment buildings were built with university students in mind and were similar to American motel rooms, with a free-standing, albeit small, oven with a four-burner cooktop and a small refrigerator. The renters were generally foreign students, often Americans. Panameño students could not afford apartments. Even if they were married with children, Panameño students usually lived at home with their parents. Ricardo had looked at several of these motel-like apartments but didn't really like them. They went for between four hundred dollars to four-fifty a month depending on their location. At the high end of the scale were the small condos owned by gringos back in the states. The gringos either had bought them as vacation homes, or tried to retire to them but couldn't stand the slower pace of Panamá and had returned to the states, but in many cases, they let some management company rent them out for three-to-nine month periods. They had more of that American design, were usually in a gated community with a swimming pool, and the neighbors were all other gringos. While the comforts they offered were familiar, Ricardo hated them the most. Plus, they were the most expensive, going for between six hundred to nine hundred dollars a month.

In addition to looking at apartments and just walking around exploring the restaurants and sights of La Chorrera, Ricardo had spent some time assessing the potential of the city to satisfy his other interests. There was one gay bathhouse in La Chorrera and perhaps as many as thirty local brothels. The bathhouse was easy to find through the usual gay websites. One universal thing about gay communities, both in the states and in Panamá—they had embraced the internet decades earlier as the only way to communicate and share information. The brothels, however, were much more difficult to locate. Even though prostitution was legal in

Panamá, in terms of local brothels there was no advertising, no internet information, nor any way for a stranger to quickly locate them. It was mostly an under-the-table business, pretty much run for the pleasure of the local men rather than the tourists. The exception, of course, was the occasional large stereotypical brothel/casino that seemed to only exist for—and were only frequented by—gringos and tourists. Some of these casinos did advertise on the internet. These larger brothels were not numerous in Panamá, but they did exist—older hotels converted in order to accommodate gambling tables and a bar on the main floor, through which the girls constantly walked around, in a never-ending circle, chatting up customers, hoping someone would select them. Pretty much every casino Ricardo had ever visited in Panamá was a brothel. But the vast majority of brothels were local, small, almost invisible establishments. Ricardo was merely guessing when he estimated the number at thirty in La Chorrera. Most of these brothels consisted of two or three women sharing an apartment where they would take men after meeting them on the street or in bars. Other brothels simply were small hotels that would rent you a room for an hour or two, no questions asked, and charge an additional ten dollar "guest fee" for any woman you took to your room—women who conveniently parked themselves every night at the hotel bar. Prostitution was a common, but invisible, occupation in Panamá. Because of the Catholic culture, prostitution—like homosexuality or bisexuality—was just something you didn't acknowledge out loud. It would be considered improper, for example, for a tourist to ask a Panameño bartender where the local brothel was. At best, all a tourist could do was mention that he was all alone in the city, and maybe ask in a vague way where he might meet women. The bartender would invariably say he didn't know, but if the tourist was lucky, some woman would approach and sit down next to him in the next few minutes.

Ricardo had, however, developed a more successful strategy. If the neighborhood was safe to walk in at night (and the hotel owners would always tell him if it wasn't, because they did not want to lose a paying customer), he would wander about the city in the early hours of the evening, until he came upon a group of prostitutes talking together at some particular corner. They were easy to pick out because of how they dressed, and because no matter how engaged they were in conversation with each other, they would make eye contact with any man on the street. When he came upon such a group, he would greet them and explain politely that he was looking only to have dinner with some local woman, and if any one of them was hungry, he would buy them dinner, but dinner only, nothing more. Inevitably, one of the group would agree, and he would let her pick the restaurant, and he would indeed pay for her dinner, and again he would explain that he was only interested in dinner. But during the dinner, he would explain that he wanted to know where the brothels were, where the safest women were, in case, you know, at some future point, he might want to avail himself. He would sometimes go out on this mission several times a week when he first arrived in a new city, because he had to eat dinner anyway, and he always enjoyed the company, but also because after interviewing three or four prostitutes in a week, he could ascertain the common opinion about where the safest brothels were located. Then, at some point, usually during his second week in that city, he would visit that particular establishment. Ricardo always preferred brothels over streetwalkers, even as a young man in Spain, even as a middle-aged man in the states, because they were safer, cleaner, and more comfortable. Too many streetwalkers were controlled by pimps who'd just as soon mug a customer than provide a valuable service, whereas the brothels that catered to the locals depended on their local reputation for safety. Only once, years ago, had he picked up and fucked a streetwalker, but she was an American woman, working near the Radisson Hotel in Panamá City. Her name, he remembered, was Pam. She had approached him in the street outside of his hotel. She claimed she needed two hundred dollars for a return ticket to the states. Ricardo found that amount exorbitant for sex, but she was attractive. He bought her a drink in the hotel bar and they settled on one hundred dollars and went upstairs to Ricardo's room.

All in all, Ricardo found the experience agreeable.

Ricardo arrived at the door to Los Cuñados and went inside. Like most Panameño restaurants, it was small, with only five tables. The boy whom Ricardo had talked with an hour ago now had a white shirt on and showed him to a table, and then brought him water and a menu.

"Por favor, me gustaría una copa de vino tinto," Ricardo said.

"Sí, señor," said the boy, and hurried away to bring Ricardo a glass of red wine.

Ricardo perused the menu while he waited. Normally, Ricardo always ordered the casado, literally, the married man's meal, at whatever restaurant he was at, and Los Cuñados had the usual choices of chicken, fish, or pork casados. Ricardo always liked the fish casados—there would be fresh fish, lightly fried, with generous portions of rice, beans, plantain and a salad. It ran about six dollars in most places, although Ricardo noticed that the menu price here was seven dollars, but it was always a filling meal.

The boy returned with Ricardo's wine.

"Is there a daily special?" Ricardo asked him in Spanish.

"Si, señor," said the boy and described a meal of large shrimp sautéed in garlic and butter and served with rice and vegetables, for eight dollars. It sounded good, so Ricardo changed his mind and ordered the special instead. Then he explained that he was a friend of Miguel's and asked whether Miguel was there that night.

"No, señor, lo siento." The boy apologized and said Miguel was off today. Ricardo wondered if by chance Miguel was at the bathhouse.

"Okay, no hay problema." Ricardo explained that he would catch Miguel here some other time. The boy left to take Ricardo's order to the kitchen. Ricardo watched him walk away and wondered if Miguel ever took the lad to the bathhouse. Probably not. Panamá, like all Central American countries, was heavily Catholic, and most Latino gays kept themselves deep in the closet. Miguel's situation was typical.

He was expected to marry and raise a family, gay or not. So, he did. And like most Central American husbands, it was understood he would cheat on his wife. His cheating just happened to be with other men. His wife and family probably did not know, or did not want to know. And if it was implied, they would adamantly deny it, despite any proof.

Ricardo sipped his wine. It was tolerable. Panamá did not have a wine producing industry to speak of. It was a beer country. So, the restaurants imported inexpensive Chilean wine to serve to customers.

Other than the religious reasons, Miguel's situation was not that different from his own, Ricardo thought. Back in the states, Ricardo kept his forays into the gay world entirely to himself, the same way he kept his trips to the brothels in Canada entirely to himself. None of his straight co-workers had any idea. First of all, it was none of anyone's business. The human penchant for telling another person what one did sexually, or for daring to ask the other person what he or she did, was something that Ricardo never understood. He could never grasp the male bonding behavior of discussing sexual exploits, who one had banged etc., at the bar or around the water cooler. It always had seemed to Ricardo to be such a private matter. He wouldn't discuss cock rings, shaving pubes, or masturbation with some co-worker, so why on earth would he share whose genitals he had touched, who he fucked, or how the sex was? Secondly, he couldn't share his particular activities because no one would understand them. Hell, he didn't understand them himself half the time. Was he gay? He certainly enjoyed sex with men. Was he straight? He certainly loved women. Was he bi? It was a word he detested because it didn't explain anything. Ricardo just liked sex. With the right partner or partners, if there was attraction, it simply didn't matter if they were male or female. But if he was forced to pick one code-word to describe himself, he would have to resign himself to the bisexual label. It was just such a useless word. It was like saying that someone was American and stopping there without any inquiry as to age, religion, accent, state of origin, upbringing, education, political views, etc. It was just a way to label someone, to pigeon-hole them. But, like the word American, it did serve some purpose.

While his current home of Hamburg back in New York had a few gay bars, it was too small of a city to support an active gay culture. And besides, Ricardo had to protect his job. If he felt like sex with men, he would drive to Buffalo to the bathhouses there. And he always made sure that any vacation took him to cities where he had options.

Sometimes Ricardo wondered which he liked more: the men or the bathhouses. He almost had to admit that it was the bathhouses themselves. The bigger bathhouses in the states were all amazingly alike. The outside was nondescript, no signs, sometimes not even a street number, just a door. You had to have researched the web or gay newspapers to know the address. But no matter what city it was, once you found the bathhouse, the inside would unfold in the same way. You'd step inside, and there would be a dark corridor with a man behind a glass window. You'd tell him what you wanted, a locker or a standard room (which came with a video monitor showing porn) or a deluxe room (with a bigger bed and a larger monitor) or a specialty room (which might have a sling or gloryhole access to other rooms). You'd pay your money, sliding the bills under the glass partition. He would then slide a towel, a room key and a remote control for the video monitor back to you through the same glass opening, and then he would buzz you in through a locked door. Once inside, it would take a while for your eyes to adjust to the dim light. There would be stairs (either up or down) leading to a twisting hallway of rooms. You would search until you found your room, then unlock the door and step inside. Inside there was just room enough for a bed, the video monitor on the wall at the foot of the bed, angled so that you could watch it lying down on the bed, and several hooks on the wall for hanging your clothes. Usually, a couple of complementary condoms were placed by the bed, sometimes some packets of lube. Whenever Ricardo went to a new bathhouse and entered a room for the first time, he would peruse the porn channels to see if there were any videos featuring women. This was one of the indications

that made him sometimes question his self-definition as
bi or gay—he liked watching porn with women, preferably
a woman with two guys, but he always preferred a woman
in the video. The smaller bathhouses usually just had three
or four channels of just gay porn, but the larger bathhouses
would have twenty or thirty channels, mostly gay, but also
some with women, some lesbian, and some tranny porn. If
the porn was good, Ricardo would watch it for a bit before
getting undressed, just to get himself in the right state of
mind, which is to say, mindless. Then he would strip down,
grab his towel, and head off to the showers. One thing about
bathhouses: no matter what, they were "bath" houses. The
water was always hot, and there was always a steam room,
and sometimes a dry heat room. A bathhouse without good
showers and a good steam room simply could not stay in
business. Yes, many men came to the bathhouses for sex,
but they also came to stand underneath the hot water many
times, to soap themselves up, to celebrate their maleness, to
stretch out on the tile platforms of the steam room, to simply
be there naked and unashamed in their nakedness. Sex or no
sex, the bathhouses were a glorious invention, and Ricardo
loved them. He always wished that there could be co-ed
bathhouses, but he knew that would be impossible. Straight
men wouldn't know how to deal with the gay invitations,
the gay men wouldn't know how to deal with the women,
and the women wouldn't know how to deal with rejection.
With gay men, fending off unwanted attention was easy. If
someone approached Ricardo in the steam room and glided
a hand over his thigh, or even just looked like he might sit
down next to Ricardo, all it took was a slight shake of the
head to send that person away. It was a code of conduct.
All contact was consensual. Period. And there was nothing
personal about it. All men in bathhouses understood that.
But if women were there, it would be different. First or all,
men would instinctively feel like they had to talk to them.
There was no chit-chat in bathhouses, certainly not before
sex anyway. Secondly, heterosexual men wouldn't take the
subtle no for an answer from a woman. They would persist,
and that would break the cardinal rule of bathhouses.

Bathhouses were gentle and genteel places. No pressure, no noise, no talking. Just the sound of steam, and perhaps the sound of some young man sucking the fellow sitting next to you.

Ricardo was deep in reminiscing when the boy appeared with his food, a huge platter of steaming shrimp piled high over rice. How apropos, Ricardo thought, steam...

Chapter 6: La Chorrera Brothel

Ricardo spent four more days in La Chorrera before taking the bus to Penonome. He never did hook back up with Miguel in La Chorrera. He did manage, however, to visit a small casino/brothel there, one that he had heard about, and one that his research indicated was safe and reliable. Ricardo had taken a cab there. But when he arrived, he wasn't sure whether he was at the right place. There was a sign saying CASINO on the outside wall, but it was old and not lit up. He asked the cab driver to wait a minute while he stepped inside. He was, after all, in an unknown area of town, and even though it was the middle of the day, Ricardo did not want to be stranded there if the place was closed or if he had the wrong address. But once he looked inside, he knew it would be alright. He stepped outside, waved the cab driver away and stepped back inside. There were slot machines lining the wall and several blackjack tables in the main room, fairly well-attended by middle-aged men, mostly gringos judging by their girth. To the right there was a large bar, and a receptionist desk, where one could obtain a room for an hour or so. Many women were walking around, women with obviously enhanced breasts shown off in low-cut tight-fitting dresses. Ricardo went to the bar and sat down. Almost immediately a slender Panameña walked by and looked at him.

He greeted her. "Hola," he said.

"Hola," she replied, "speak English?"

"Of course," Ricardo replied. "Soy gringo, no?"

She laughed. "I'm working on my English."

"It sounds good. Are you working?" he asked, to see if she was available.

"Yes," she said, and sat down next to him.

"Buy me a drink?" she asked.

"Por supuesto," he said. "What'll it be?"

"Red Bull," she answered.

Ricardo signaled to the bartender and ordered her a Red Bull and a Coke for himself. Then they engaged in small talk. Her name was Leez, and she was nineteen. She had two kids at home and was working as a prostitute to support them. Ricardo had heard this story so often before—it always made him sad. Women with little education and no access to birth control were simply doomed to have children at an early age, and then, when their equally young paramours abandoned them, they were stuck in poverty, with few options to earn money. Prostitution was one of those ways. It was a timeless story. Leez excused herself for a moment so she could call home. One of her babies had a cold and she wanted to check with the woman who was caring for them while she was at work. While she was gone, Ricardo thought about this quandary as he drank his Coke. He knew all the conservative babble about prostitution being bad, and he didn't buy it for a minute. He saw it simply as a service, like the waitress bringing you food, or the masseuse alleviating your sore back. The fact that it was sexual didn't enter into the equation. However, *he was* opposed to pimping, the exploitation of anyone. And he had his opinions of capitalism and religion which he saw as the biggest pimps of all. By denying young women sex education, birth control and abortion, they guaranteed a certain percentage of prostitutes. Ricardo couldn't change that. Leez's situation was sad, but if she saved her money, hopefully she could raise her kids and provide for herself.

She returned to his side, and he was relieved to hear that her kid was doing better. Then the conversation turned to the issue of money. How much to go upstairs? First she asked for one hundred dollars, but then said she would take eighty. Ricardo wasn't going to haggle. He would pay the one hundred.

"Okay," he said, "let's do it."

They went to the receptionist desk. He rented a room for an hour, got a key and they went upstairs. The room was small but clean. She sat on the bed and asked if he minded if she smoked a cigarette first. He said he didn't mind. As she smoked, she began to undress, and Ricardo did too. Finally, they were both naked, sitting on the bed, with her smoking the rest of her cigarette. He rubbed her thigh. She was slender, with tiny breasts. She pulled the covers back and lay prone, still smoking. He lay beside her and ran his hands up and down her body. Strange, he thought, to be sixty-two and running his hands over a nineteen year old. A vision of Haley, the young prostitute who he was almost in love with once up in St. Catherines, Canada, crossed his mind. She was young too, maybe in her early twenties. But Leez was darker, hairier, with dark nipples. Ricardo leaned over and started kissing her nipple gently.

She watched him nibble at her small breast. He looked up, and she made a small apologetic shrug with her head and half-smile.

"Natural," she said, as if to apologize for her breasts.

"Hmmm?" he replied.

She explained that many of the prostitutes got breast enhancements but she couldn't afford it. She told him how the prostitutes with the biggest breasts always seemed to attract more men, especially gringos. She said that she hoped that when she had saved enough money, she would get her breasts enlarged so she could make more money."

"Oh," Ricardo said, "I like natural" and he started kissing her other nipple. She put the stub of her cigarette out in the ashtray and turned to face him. She pulled him closer with one hand, reached down to his cock with her other hand, and they got down to business.

Chapter 7: Back at the Hotel

Ricardo took a taxi from the casino back to the hotel where he was actually staying. On the ride back, he started thinking about Leez, about her dual life as a mother and a prostitute. He wondered what she thought about her work, whether she viewed it as a normal job or whether she ever felt demeaned. The set-up in most of the casinos allowed the prostitutes to pick their clients. Ricardo wondered if that made the work any easier. Whether she liked her job or not, she seemed real to Ricardo, natural and relaxed in his presence. Ricardo thought about jobs he had been forced to do and how he thought they had changed him. For some reason, he started thinking about some of the men he had met when he was in rehab, men who had everything yet seemed somehow not real, not genuine. He remembered some men who used rehab as just a way to avoid themselves. The problem wasn't them, they would say, it was the alcohol. A certain feeling began to come over him. By the time the cab got him back to the hotel, he couldn't wait to get up to his room and start writing. The following words flowed out of him...

Welcome to E.A.

"Well okay, I guess I'll go first this time. My name is Earl, and I'm an entrepreneuraholic. I started off the same way as the rest of you guys, you know, being the neighborhood geek kid who could fix any computer, and I quickly learned to monetize my skill. At the age of twelve, I

started selling prepaid advice where I'd help the adults buy computers, upgrade their systems, hook up their flat screens and just be on call for them for any problems they had—all for a monthly fee. But, like the rest of you, I learned the value of networking and franchising. And by age fourteen, I had a whole covey of younger kids working for me in bunches of neighborhoods, And they not only had to pay me for helping them solve their clients' problems, but they had to give me any discarded computers when they upgraded their clients. I would take all these computers and rebuild them, add some pirated software, and then sell them on Craigslist and eBay. Occasionally I would go through the hard drives. If there were any decent credit card numbers, well, I had some sources that I could sell those to...

"What? Oh yeah, thanks Bob...Sorry, this week we're supposed to talk about how we ended up here, the last project, the 'big heist' as Bob calls it. Well, it was a good one, I have to say. I still look back on it and marvel... Some of you may have heard about it when I got indicted. It made the papers... It was called the Wine Bank, and it worked kind of like a regular bank, except with wine... We started by going around to all the wine distributors in California and buying up all of their overstock, all the crap wine they couldn't unload, all the off-brands and imports. Those were our showpieces, you might say. Then we rented an air-conditioned warehouse on DeNovia Street and showcased those bottles in the front office area there, but with different labels of course. In the back office I had my computer set-up where I could print copies of more expensive labels, and we—and when I say 'we', I am of course referring to my former partner in the enterprise—Dave Bogle... oh sorry Bob, my former partner in the enterfail, Dave Bogle, who, as you know, absconded after he and I were indicted... Okay, where was I? Oh, yeah. So Dave and I would print these more expensive labels and slap them on the bottles. The hardest part was actually getting the old labels off the bottles. We used a special solvent for that... anyway, so the bottles that were on display appeared to be

good quality brands, not the utter trash wine that they really were. So, when the middle-class people came by, Dave could show them the type of wines that they could earn for free by cellaring their wine with us. When the rich people came by, we had a special room where Dave would show them the very, very nice wines that they could get for free by letting us cellar their wines.

"Of course, there's nothing for free. They all had to store their wine with us in order to get their free wine. And that's how the enterprise... oh sorry, the enterfail started. Let me see if I can explain it...

"I came up with the name 'Wine Bank' to give the impression that people could make deposits of wine in our cellar, and they would earn 'interest', which we called 'corks', for how many bottles they deposited. The more wine you cellared with us, the more 'corks' you earned. A customer would come in with their wine... well let's keep it simple ... say a customer came in with one bottle of a very nice wine. They would give us that bottle and we would immediately inscribe the label with that customer's client number in front of them so they could see us do it, but later we'd duplicate the label in the back room, slap it on a crappy bottle of wine and put their client number on that bottle so that if they came back and wanted their bottle of wine back, we could hand them back 'their' bottle with their number clearly handwritten on it. We got very good at always inscribing the labels in the exact same place. Most of them of course didn't want their wine back. That was the whole point. They wanted to upgrade to a better bottle. That's when they would get someone else's legitimate wine... Let me give you a better example. Say, for example, Claire GotBucks came in with her 2003 Flintload Special Reserve Cabernet, worth about ninety bucks. We'd mark it with her client number and handle it as if it were her firstborn child while she was in the shop. But we used a special ink that was easy to erase. As soon as she'd leave, we'd erase her number, duplicate the label, write her client number on the new label, stick that label on a bottle of cheap

cabernet, and put it on her shelf in the back. Then let's say a week later she's pursuing our online Wine Bank wine list, and she sees a 2001 Hurras Pinot Noir that she'd like to have, but it's worth $150. Well, let's say she's deposited 20 bottles with us this year so she's got enough corks to make a withdrawal and get that nice Hurras Pinot for free. Well, not exactly free, because she's paying two hundred dollars a year as a Bank member. And unbeknownst to her, she's given us her twenty bottles of good wine which she'll never see again. Now, that 2001 Hurras Pinot that she got was deposited by some other customer, and he'll never see that bottle again, although there was an identical bottle on that customer's shelf, well, at least a bottle of something with an identical label. So, Claire gets the Pinot for 'free' and she's happy, and so she's also happy to cellar more wine with us so that she can get more cork points. It was a great scam.

"What? The wines on the Bank's wine list? Oh, that's a good question. That's what the people were paying the two hundred dollars a year for... well, I mean, that's what they thought they were paying for. We told them that half of their fee was for cellaring costs but the other half went toward the careful buying of fine wines. Dave spun this tale about having all these great contacts with the best wine collectors and how we were so respected that they would give us huge discounts or even give us great wine for free. Dave was so good at schmoozing our customers—he was a real charmer. It was all horseshit, of course. But all these customers wanted so much to believe that that's the kind of benevolent wine connoisseur they would be if they had the money and the wine, that they needed to believe that such people existed. Anyway, Dave's pitch was that if they deposited their wines in our climate-controlled cellars for safekeeping, that they would get far more than two hundred dollars worth of fine wine back in a year, and that was the only true part. Many of them actually got six hundred dollars' worth of fine wines a year... but of course they lost six thousand dollars of their good wines in the process.

"Well, we were so successful, we started opening bank branches in Sonoma, Russian Valley, Alexander Valley, Sebastopol, St. Helena, and Yountville. Dave did all the front office customer contact stuff. I was the backroom guy. I created and maintained the software that kept track of all our customers and their wine, plus I had to keep the Bank's online wine list updated, plus figure out what to do with all the money that was coming in. Part of the reason we kept expanding was that we had so much money coming in we had to launder it somehow. We were just starting to plan branches in Washington State and Oregon...

"What, Bob? Our downfall? Well, I suppose you could say it was inevitable. From the classes here, I've learned that what we were running was basically a Ponzi scheme... but it probably could have gone on for years more if we hadn't started selling shares in the Bank. With all the branches that we had opened, we looked like a huge business. The expansion was Dave's idea, but the idea of selling shares was all mine—that a person could simply buy shares of the bank and get free wine without having to deposit wine. The share price was pretty steep, but they thought that they had collateral rights to our wine list, plus they got their share of free wine, and we kept telling them that we might take it public and they would make millions... Well, you know how it is from your own enterfails... once you get people excited and greedy at the same time, they'll believe anything and give you all the money they have. And that's what happened. We were making so much money... plus Dave and I had a lot of good wine that we drank for free. And people loved us. We got invited to all these parties where we ate and drank for free and signed up new customers. It was amazing.

"But... it didn't last. I always thought some of the real banks in town resented our using the word bank, I don't know... But one day we had the IRS and the SEC and the Attorney General's Office all show up at our door at once. It was ugly. We had sold so many shares and distributed so much wine that our warehouses were pretty empty. It didn't

take them long to figure out we didn't have near the inventory we claimed, except the original crap wine we had bought three years earlier. Dave tried to stall them by saying we had moved all the inventory to another location, and then he went on a buying spree and tried to stock another warehouse in one weekend with all this wine he had just bought. But they saw through that. There wasn't enough wine in all of California to match the inventory we were claiming on our books. I knew we were sunk, so I just got a lawyer and told him to work the best deal he could. And I have to say, given what I could have gotten, he did a pretty good job. After I got out of prison, I even gave him a very nice Cabernet that I had stashed away. Well, I guess that's about it. Any questions?

"Yes, Fred?... No, I'm still on probation, but I'll be off that next month.

"What happened to Dave? Well, after they caught him in Costa Rica and extradited him back, I had to testify against him of course—it was part of my plea deal. I didn't want to do it but it meant I only had to serve three months. Of course, Dave being thirty-seven and me being only nineteen helped too. The judge certainly believed that Dave was taking advantage of me. I guess I'll be about thirty when he gets out of prison. I'll probably have to change my name and move somewhere.

"Yes, John?... Well, originally it was my lawyer's suggestion, but after the first few months, I felt that this was the program for me. It helped me understand my addiction to the game of entrepreneurship, just how addictive the constant spinning and expansion of monetizing projects can be... that's why I've stayed on. I couldn't have survived prison if it hadn't had been for Bob and this program. I can't express my gratitude enough. This program has helped me to focus my life on something truly valuable—helping other people like me.

"My future plans? Well, I'm glad to say that Bob has accepted my offer to help him market this program to other state and federal prisons. I have certain computer and

marketing skills that I think will be very useful. There is such a need for programs like this all over the United States. We have such a powerful story to tell people and such a solid track record with this state's prison system that eventually I could see EA franchises in all fifty states. It has such a huge potential. We could even take it public.

"Any regrets? Well, I do miss the wine.

"Any more questions? No? Well Don, I guess it's your turn next. How did you end up here?"

Chapter 8: Penonome

The next morning Ricardo took the bus to the city of Penonome. He ended up spending a week there. Through a stroke of good luck, the Panameño owner of the first apartment he looked at asked him if he wanted to try it out for a week. He could stay there for seventy-five dollars for the week, to see if he'd like to rent it on a long-term basis should he move there. It was too good a deal to pass up. The apartment was what would be called a mother-in-law cottage back in the states—a small studio apartment built onto the Panameño's home but with its own separate entrance. It was basically one large room, with a simple bed, a table with two chairs, a small kitchenette and a bathroom. Outside there was a porch with a chair and a hammock sheltered from sun and rain by the overhanging tin roof. Because this entrance and porch was on the side of the main house, Ricardo could sit in the chair or lie in the hammock and see nothing but fields that rolled up towards the hills under blue skies. Very serene.

The owner's name was Armando. He and his wife lived quietly in the main house. Other than the first time they met, and when Ricardo said goodbye to him on his last day there, Ricardo never saw him or his wife.

The bed was a thin mattress set in a homemade wooden frame. There was no box spring. There was a bottom sheet but no top sheet. Two thin blankets lay on top. They were old and worn, but quite sufficient for the slightly cool evenings. Above the bed was a small window with a tattered curtain. Next to the bed was a small three-drawer dresser.

Across from the bed was the small wooden table with two mismatched chairs. Ricardo set his netbook computer up there. Using the pillow from the bed as a back pillow made the chairs comfortable enough for Ricardo to use. One of the main draws of this apartment was that it had Wi-Fi. Armando had explained that one of his sons had set it up for the house when he lived there so that Armando and his wife could watch TV, especially the soccer games. Internet connection was something that Ricardo required for his writing and his connections with people back in the states, especially his publisher.

From the table it was about three steps to the kitchen area. The kitchen was a model of simplicity. A half-size refrigerator was just big enough to hold about two days worth of food. A handmade shelf on the wall held a two-burner hotplate. Stacked on the shelf next to the hotplate was an iron frying pan and two pots. A cold-water sink sat under a large window with a draining rack that held two plates, some cups, and some old silverware. There was a table next to the sink for preparing food. That was it, except for the typical Panameño coffee filter by the sink, which consisted of a small wooden frame that held a white sock suspended from the top of the frame. The sock was held open by a wooden clip. One put ground coffee in the sock, placed a coffee cup in the space below the sock, and poured hot water into the sock. It was the equivalent of a reusable drip coffee system, one that was found in every Panameño home.

After paying Armando in advance, Ricardo went to the room, unpacked his clothes from his backpack, and arranged them in the dresser. He took stock of the kitchen and the time and decided he should go into town and buy some groceries.

Armando's house was located on the outskirts of Penonome on a dirt road. Armando had drawn him a map to the nearest feria (open-air market), which was about a mile away. Bus service was good in Panamá, but there was no bus service to Armando's house. While it was a pleasant walk on this summer day (January), Ricardo wondered how it would be during the rainy season. He knew from past visits that the rains can be torrential and turn dirt roads into mud rivers. Nonetheless, he was glad for this opportunity to partake of a trial run at simple living.

The market was bustling with afternoon shoppers when Ricardo arrived. Ricardo assumed that this was the last-minute rush to buy food for the evening meal before the market closed. There was a collective chatter of people talking, laughing, greeting each other and negotiating sales. A few of the stalls had small radios playing, all with different songs, and the conflicting music added more currents to the ocean of sound. And there were smells too, as some of the stalls offered freshly cooked meats, braising on sticks over small open fires built in large metal pails. Ricardo navigated from stall to stall eyeing the selection and the prices. He bought a small plastic cup of ceviche which he ate as he walked, worrying more about the cleanliness of the plastic fork they gave him than the raw fish he was eating. The pathway between the stalls was narrow and crowded, but friendly, as people squeezed by each other, being careful to step over the many extension cords that crisscrossed the ground. He appeared to be the only gringo there but no one treated him any different. The vendors all smiled, and were eager to chat, answer his questions and, of course, make a few coins selling him something.

He tossed his empty plastic cup and fork into a nearby trashcan and commenced buying. Whatever he bought, the vendors placed in used plastic bags for him to carry. He bought a small tin of cooking oil and a few bulbs of garlic from one stall, some bananas and plantain from another stall. He had grown as fond of fried plantain as the Panameños, who served it as a side dish with almost every meal. He stopped by a large fruit stall and bought some pejibayes, carambeloas, and one granadilla. A table on the outer circumference of the market had a few loaves of fresh bread left, and Ricardo bought one of those. Some radishes, an onion, two potatoes and a small bag of rice rounded out his purchases. His last stop was for fish. There were only two vendors with refrigerated cases, one with chicken and beef and one with fresh fish. Luckily, the fish vendor had ice. The vendor picked out the filleted sea bass that Ricardo pointed to, packed it in ice in a plastic bag and handed it over.

Chapter 9: Return to the States

After Penonome, Ricardo visited Santiago, Chotré and the David District and continued to talk to landlords, continued to check out local costs of living and to make a note of what diversions were available in each of the locales. However, at a certain point, his five-week "vacation" from work came to an end and he had to return to the states.

Flying back to the United States is always like entering an altered state of reality. For an American, the process of returning from anywhere back to the states is unreal, because step by step you are elevated from the third world to the first world. The signs start appearing in English only. You get the shorter line at immigration. The people in front of you and behind you in line are more and more English-speaking Americans, usually, if not always, complaining about something. No matter how intimidating the customs process is, you always pass through, and you are heralded into a privileged world. You are surrounded more and more (and finally totally) by fat white people. Then you arrive in the familiar airport in your home state, where everything is oddly familiar. You look to your left in the airport, and there's a McDonalds and a Burger King and a Wendy's, and you look to your right and there's a high priced clothing kiosk, a specialty electronics store, and a fancy book store, and it all seems so surreally normal. And if it feels too surreal, you tell yourself that you are tired, and you collect your bags, and find the shuttle bus home, or the shuttle bus to your parked car, or the taxi home or whatever. You are the worn-out American, home from the third world, and you tell yourself that you are worn out because of the flight, being cramped in economy class with no ability to move for eight or nine hours. You are exhausted, and the only thing you want to do is sleep. Sleep, sleep, and when you wake, you will be in your own bed, in your home, in your neighborhood, and there will be the sound of birds outside your window, or construction, or whatever. But it will feel familiar, and you will look at the alarm clock time, out of habit, and you will think, involuntarily, "I am home".

Ricardo came home. He had scheduled a few extra days of vacation time, in order to reacclimate himself to being back in the states. The first day, he stayed around his apartment, making notes about his trip, taking long naps, wondering what exactly he was going to do. One thing was certain: in two days, he would have to return to work.

Chapter 10: What Passes for Normal

Weeks pass. Ricardo is in a deep dreamless sleep. It is still dark outside, with just the hint of light on the cold horizon. At exactly 5:15 a.m., there is a small click, and the coffee pot comes on automatically. A small green LED light on the base of the coffee pot glows in the dark kitchen. Sometimes, in the dark, that small click is enough to penetrate Ricardo's sleep. But not this morning.

He prepared the coffee the night before, as is his custom. No matter how drunk he might be, he is never too drunk to prepare the coffee pot for the next morning. He uses the unbleached filters he buys at the local health food store. He pours in the Arabica coffee he buys at Costco. The Black and Decker coffee pot with the automatic brew function came from Target.

At exactly 5:20 a.m., the small alarm clock by the bed starts chirping. Ricardo reaches over and hits the snooze button. The coffee is still brewing. He can hear it hissing and dribbling into the coffee pot. He falls back to sleep. The alarm clock is a small folding travel alarm clock he got as a free gift when he opened up a checking account at the local bank five years ago. It is tuned into some satellite that automatically keeps the correct time, so that, for example, it automatically changes the hour when daylight savings comes or goes. Ricardo drifts back to sleep, aware that the alarm has gone off once.

At 5:25, the alarm beeps again, and again Ricardo reaches over and taps the snooze button. The coffee pot is in the final, and loudest, stage of brewing. There's the sound of steam as the last of the water left in the reservoir is vanquished. Ricardo knows that within the next minute, the coffee pot will be silent and the coffee will be ready, but he will still have four minutes left to sleep. But he accepts that he will have to get up at the next beeping of the clock.

And at 5:30 that beeping comes. Ricardo hits the snooze button again, but picks up the clock and checks the time, then presses a button on the back to turn the alarm off. He throws back the down comforter and sheets, climbs out of bed and walks naked into the cold kitchen. His coffee cup is waiting on a paper towel alongside the coffee pot, along with one plastic stirrer and a plastic square Ziploc container holding small packets of artificial sweetener. He pours the coffee, tears open two packets of sweetener and adds them, stirs the hot liquid, then places the stirrer and the torn packets on the paper towel and heads back to the bedroom.

The coffee cup was a gift from a former lover, a large simple white ceramic cup with a large H on it—the first initial of her name. Ricardo kept the cup in the back of the cupboard for months after she broke up with him, but the cup was a good size and weight. After about a year, when it no longer hurt him to see the cup, he started using it again.

Back in the bedroom he places the cup on the small set of bedside drawers and climbs back into the bed. The room is chilly, and he is glad that the down comforter is still warm as he pulls it over him. He bought the comforter a number of years ago at some fancy bedding store. It was expensive, almost two hundred dollars. But it is light, always warm, and seems to adjust to the varying temperatures of the seasons so that he can use it all year, save for the warmest summer months. He props the four pillows up behind him on the bed so he can half sit up in the bed, then he reaches over, takes the cup and begins to sip at the coffee.

Ricardo has lived in this particular apartment near downtown Hamburg for five years. It is a small apartment, but it suits him. There is just a living room area which flows into the kitchen, a small bedroom, and a bathroom. In the living room are the leather sofa which he bought new at a furniture store when he first moved to Hamburg, along with a leather chair he bought used about two years ago. Against the window is the desk where he writes. Next to the desk is a small bookcase, where books are stacked unevenly. There are too many books for the case, so some are piled on the floor.

The kitchen is a standard American rental apartment kitchen, furnished by the landlord, with a full-size stove, full-size refrigerator and a small microwave. The other gadgets on the counter, like the electric can opener, the toaster, and a small blender, are Ricardo's, items he has purchased along the way. The refrigerator is full of food, including smoked salmon from the local fishmonger, pre-roasted turkey breast from Costco, plastic bags of peppers and potatoes from the Safeway, a plastic bag of pre-washed salad, diet soft drinks, a bottle of white wine, and a few Hefeweizen beers from Trader Joe's. There is a cardboard quart container of egg whites with artificial color to make the liquid look like real egg, and there's a cardboard container of leftover Thai food from a dinner he had at a local restaurant a few nights back, a container that needs to be thrown out. The door shelves hold a half gallon of low-pulp orange juice, and jars of mayonnaise, mustard, pickles, a few small bottles of hot sauce and a large bottle of lemon juice. The freezer section contains frozen salmon filets, frozen vegetables and a loaf of organic whole-wheat pre-sliced bread in a plastic bag from the health food store.

Ricardo sips his coffee. Dawn is breaking outside. In the pale light that comes through the curtain, he can make out the various fixtures in the room, including another bookshelf and a large dresser. The open sliding door of the closet reveals a closet pole burdened by too many hangers holding too many clothes. Ricardo had been wanting for months to go through his clothes and get rid of the ones he no longer wears, but he keeps putting it off, not being able to decide whether to take them to Goodwill or to try and have some type of garage sale to get rid of not only the clothes but everything else that he cannot take with him to

Panamá. Ricardo continues to drink his coffee and ponder this dilemma. Maybe he could talk with Ethan. Ethan lives in a house with his wife and two children next door to Ricardo's apartment. Ethan's house is on the corner and has a small but nice, and visible, front yard. Maybe Ethan would be interested in having a garage sale on his front yard this spring. His yard has maximum visibility from two streets because of its position. Because he was supporting a family, Ethan is always looking for extra ways to make money. Ricardo's apartment building doesn't really have a good place to hold a garage sale. And Ricardo doesn't want to advertise on Craigslist and have strangers come to his apartment.

He starts making a mental list of how many things he would have to get rid of: the clothes, the furniture, the books, the two printers, the lamps, the small appliances, the bed... The list grows so large in his head so fast that he has to give his head a small shake to stop calculating the volume. He basically would have to get rid of everything, and take only what he could carry. There is no point in shipping anything down to Panamá—the cost of shipping is higher than the cost of buying the items new down there.

At exactly 5:50 a.m., his cell phone begins to play music. This is Ricardo's back-up alarm system. Ricardo places his nearly empty coffee cup on the small dresser by the bed, picks up the cell phone, turns off the alarm function, throws the comforter back and gets out of bed. He walks two steps, opens the bathroom door, steps inside and flicks on the light.

The bathroom is warm because Ricardo keeps a small oil-filled electric heater in there, one he bought at an Ace Hardware store. Ricardo does not like cold bathrooms, so he keeps this heater on low all night during the chilly months. It adds to his electric bill, but he thinks it is worth it. He sits down on the toilet, grabs a magazine from the magazine rack there, and begins his day.

A number of years ago, because of his age and his eating habits, his doctor recommended he drink some type of psyllium mixture every night, to keep him regular. Ricardo has changed his eating habits but still keeps the psyllium ritual. He buys the psyllium powder in bulk at Costco and mixes a heaping tablespoon of it every night into a glass of water and chugs it. Consequently, and habitually, every morning starts with a huge shit that seems to empty him out for the day.

Ricardo wonders if he can get psyllium down in Panamá. He wonders if he will need it.

After his toilet, he steps in front of the mirror and examines his face. Gone is the salt and pepper beard he had written about in *Messieurs*. His beard is completely gray. Not totally white but sufficiently gray to indicate a man in his sixties. The only possibility of being mistaken for a man of fifty is that the hair on the top of his head is only graying slightly. It has the beginning of that salt and pepper look that his beard had ten years ago.

He grabs his Conair electric beard trimmer, adjusts the length of the cutting blade and runs it over his beard, to trim all the hairs to the same length. Then he takes his Norelco electric shaver and goes over his cheekbones and above his mustache to remove the night's stubble. Then he takes his Wahl electric razor and carefully trims the outline of his mustache. He examines the results in the mirror. Once satisfied, he turns around to the shower and turns on the water.

The landlord in this particular apartment building had installed separate hot-water heaters for each apartment, and Ricardo is grateful that he has as much hot water as he wants. He lathers up and washes himself. Then he shampoos his hair. The soap he buys in twelve bar packages from Costco, and the shampoo comes from Safeway.

After showering, he dries off in the warm bathroom, hangs the towel up on the bar that holds the shower curtain and steps back into the bedroom, walking quickly over to the dresser drawer for underwear, then to the closet for shirt and slacks. Ricardo has all his work shirts laundered and pressed at a dry cleaner down the street. Even with his senior citizen discount, this still costs him two dollars a shirt. But to Ricardo it is worth it. He needs to look well-dressed for work; he doesn't like ironing; and the dry cleaners does an excellent job.

After dressing, he steps into the kitchen to make breakfast. He takes a paper towel and wipes off the counter where he had spilled a few drops of coffee earlier. He opens the refrigerator, takes out a carton of egg whites, a loaf of bread, some butter, and begins to cook breakfast.

Chapter 11: Memories

Ricardo hadn't been to the brothels in St. Catherine's in months. It was not from lack of desire but rather a lack of funds. But he had been to the gay bathhouses in Buffalo a number of times recently. The math was rather simple. A two-hour drive to St. Catherines and at least one-hundred fifty dollars at a brothel versus a twenty-minute drive and a maximum of twenty dollars for entrance into a bathhouse. He needed to save his money for his next trip to Panamá. Still, he missed a woman's touch. There was something about women that he could never get over, could never stop wanting. Maybe it was because they were so different from men—they smelled of perfume, and they liked to kiss, and their pussies were such mysteries. No matter how many times he made a woman come, he never really understood how it worked. Some would come simply if he licked their clit, while others claimed that they could only come if he inserted a finger or two in their vagina and found their G-spot. Others would only come by fucking. A very few would only come by fucking in the ass.

Ricardo didn't care by what method they came, but he cared deeply that they did come. Perhaps he was unlike other men in this regard, or maybe it was some special sensitivity that his gay forays had instilled in him. But to Ricardo, sex with a woman was all about the woman. It was about pleasing her, driving her wild, teasing her, making her break through all her inhibitions, until she screamed or moaned, and lost control. That was his personal definition of good sex. It didn't matter as much if he came or not, as long as he felt that the woman was utterly transported to some strange timeless place. If that meant he had to hold back, and eat them to one orgasm, take a break, then fuck them to a second orgasm, then take another break, eat and fuck them a third or fourth time, until they came again, and cried "enough" then that's what he would do. He felt, somehow, that this was his part of the deal. Women would finally consent to offer him their bodies, and his job was to make them glad they done that. He would try to work his orgasm into the final orgasm of the night if possible. One time when Eve had told him that she could barely walk the next day, her words had lifted his spirits higher than any orgasm of his could have done.

Still, Ricardo recognized that his ability to form lasting relationships with women was deeply flawed. He simply couldn't do it, had never been able to do it. He didn't know why that was and had finally given up hope of ever understanding it. When he was first going through rehab, he had talked with several therapists, to try and figure out why he was always alone. Some had theories about his childhood relationship with his mother or his father, or the fact that he had grown up in a foreign country, or the fact that his father was American and his mother was Spanish, or the fact that he was raised by his grandparents... The theories went on forever. Ricardo had finally stopped seeing any therapist and simply accepted it as his fate: he was going to be alone. Oddly enough, one palm reader he had gone to see a few years back in Antón, Panamá, had looked at his palms and said in the first few minutes of the session, "You will have many lovers, but no love... many lovers, no lasting union." She had pointed to all the small lines on the side of his palms and said again, "many lovers, no love." When Ricardo heard those words, he knew they were true. They felt true. He did not question them for a second. They were true and he knew it. And they took a burden off him. He stopped worrying about meeting that "someone special". He stopped agonizing whether he should join Match.com or any of the hundreds of other on-line dating services. He not only stopped trying to find that perfect one; he stopped trying to find *anyone*. If they came into his life, he was grateful to fuck them... But he stopped seeking out women, stopped trying to pick them up. He stopped hoping he would find a lasting relationship. When he was feeling cynical, he told himself that his timing for stopping was good, since the young women who appealed to him would no longer find him attractive at his age... and there was some truth to that as well. He noticed it everywhere, in parks, at work, in restaurants, or at bars. Women in their twenties and thirties never gave him a first look. It was as if he wasn't there. Yet, congruent to the psychic prediction, there were women. Sometimes young women. Women who would enter his life for short periods of time, wanting to be fucked intensely, and then leave. Eve was like that. And there were a few before Eve who were like that. But maybe the palm reader was referring to the prostitutes. Haley at the St. Catherines brothel was certainly like that. Ricardo wondered if he had small love lines on his hands because he frequented hookers, or whether he frequented hookers because he had small love lines on his hands.

Ultimately, it didn't matter. Ricardo knew his place in life. He was old. He would service women who came into his life. He would frequent brothels. He would frequent bathhouses. He kept in the shadows, under the rocks, under the radar, quiet, and alone.

Chapter 12: A Year

A year has passed since Jim and Susan's wedding. It was now August and the weather in Hamburg was hot. Ricardo was preparing for another vacation to Panamá. It would be "winter" in Panamá in September, meaning, the rainy season. Warm temperatures, but constant rain every day, all day. Ricardo had his plane tickets and his hotel reservations, and he had an appointment with a Panameño attorney to talk about obtaining "pensionado" status, the equivalent of a green card for gringos, allowing them to live there full-time.

Qualifying for pensionado status was not easy. The main obstacle was that a gringo had to have proof of money. Like everything else in life, money was always the answer. As Mack the Knife sang back in 1928: "When there's money in your pocket, things will generally turn out right." The requirement in Panamá was proof of a guaranteed minimum income of one thousand dollars a month for life before they would grant pensionado status. The only reason that Panamá, or any other Latin American country, wanted and tolerated gringos was because of the money they brought into the economy. Ricardo understood this. And while he could cobble together a variety of income sources for his retirement (a small pension, some savings and some investments, etc.) the gold standard for obtaining pensionado status by the Panamaño Migration Department, their definition of "guaranteed lifetime income", was Social Security benefits, paid directly to a Panameño bank account. Thus, in addition to his other income sources, Ricardo had applied for early Social Security benefits, despite the fact that he would receive less of a monthly benefit because of the early application. The benefits were set to start next January. That also marked the deadline for him to quit the law firm.

Obtaining pensionado status was important to Ricardo not only because it would allow him to live full-time in Panamá (the limitation for other visitors is three months) but because it would allow him access to their health care system, meaning, allow him to buy into their national health care program which, unlike the US system, is a one-insurer nationwide system with a fixed low premium and good health care. Some might call it socialized medicine, but Ricardo didn't care. It was a good system, and the health care services were excellent. And while he didn't have any particular health concerns now, he knew that as he aged, medical issues would develop.

As mentioned, it was August in Hamburg. Ricardo had been spending his weeks at work in a kind of mental haze, going through the motions, filing the appropriate probate forms, meeting with the probate personal representatives, going to court, and handling the distributions from the estates of the deceased. But his heart was not in any of it. He left work promptly at 5:00 each day. On good days, he went home and worked on his short stories. If the words were slow in coming, he would head over to the gym, and run on a treadmill to empty his mind. Either way, he was waiting until his vacation in September to get back to Panamá. Depending on the outcome of his upcoming meeting there with the Panameño lawyer, it was possible he might be able to retire there the following January. Of course, he hadn't mentioned any of this to his colleagues at work. They had, however, noticed that he was keeping to himself, and not talking as much as he used to. Some of them even asked him if everything was okay, in that concerned voice that people use when they're implying that everything is not okay. But Ricardo quickly assured them that all was fine, and explained that he'd just been extra-busy lately with some complicated probate cases. They accepted this explanation—and why wouldn't they? The law firm was a well-respected one in Hamburg, and no one who worked there would ever think of just up and leaving. The pay was decent, the work was, well… it was easy by law firm standards, and the partners were congenial. Even the attorneys, paralegals and secretaries who reached that magical retirement age of sixty-five tended to stay and work just a few more years to pad their retirement. A few years back, the two oldest partners announced they would wait until they were seventy to retire, on the excuse that waiting until seventy means that they would get the maximum monthly payout from Social Security. But Ricardo knew the truth: that people were always afraid to leave any type of security blanket. The law firm was a big comfortable security blanket with regular paychecks and good health insurance. Most everyone there had been there for fifteen or twenty years and it was family to them. And of course, no one ever wanted to think about death. But Ricardo thought about death. He thought about it a lot. He knew that life was much shorter than anyone expected—that at the very end, everyone's life was just a flash of lightning behind a cloud, just a brief illumination and then blackness. Waiting until one was seventy in order to reap the maximum Social Security payment seemed like insanity to Ricardo. Then what? Sit around the house?

Ricardo had only been at the law firm for eight years, but he had vested in their defined benefit retirement plan. Over the past year, Ricardo had constantly evaluated and re-evaluated his savings, his anticipated Social Security benefits, his investments, a small inheritance he had received from his grandfather, and his work retirement. He had analyzed it nineteen different ways, and had still come to the same conclusion: there was no way he could retire at sixty-three and live in the states. No matter how he calculated it, his possible monthly income after retirement would always be below the national poverty level. Plus, there was the uncertainly of health care coverage. Every new day brought a new Republican attack on the Affordable Care Act, and

Ricardo didn't want to count on something so affected by politics. But with Panamá's national health care plan, even his poverty level income would be sufficient for him to live down there, not luxuriously, but simply and comfortably. The more he looked at the math, the more he realized that he simply did not have a choice. If he ever wanted to write, he had to retire. But if he ever wanted to retire, he had to move to Panamá to survive. The bottom line was unequivocal. There was no other choice.

Chapter 13: Scarlet's

Ricardo took the pages out of the printer, took a sip of wine, and began to read "Scarlet's." It was his latest short story. The following words had flowed out from him onto the paper he now held in his hand...

It was not the kind of bar that Eddie wanted to be seen in, but nobody he knew would go there, anyway. "Scarlet's" was the dankest strip bar in town, dark and dirty, wooden floors that were never swept, sticky with spilled beer and God knows what else, pulsing red and blue lights on the stage but barely any lights anywhere else. There were a few tables right in front of the stage for the out-of-towners who thought the stage was where the only action was, but Eddie knew better. He always sat at one of the many tables that were in the many strange corners of the bar that had no purpose but to provide even darker places to sit and drink.

The girls were, on the whole, ugly. Hard faces, scarred with acne and years of drinking and drugging, stretch marks on tummies and tits, usually tattooed, often fat, often pregnant. Scarlet's was the end of the line for strippers, a place where the management never precluded anyone from dancing. Eddie knew some girls that danced up to the day their water broke and then returned to the stage a week after giving birth. A few of the more heavily-tattooed girls were owned by the bikers who worked as security for the bar. They were hard girls, too fucked up or too demented or too old to work the uptown strip joints. They were the bottom feeders. Eddie liked them. He liked them because they knew why they were there. They were there for the money, nothing else. No working their way through college, no aspiring porn queens, no illusions. They were all business. Hand jobs fifty dollars. Blow jobs one hundred fifty. They would each stumble around the back corners making small talk with customers, asking each guy to buy them a drink. If the customer agreed, the girl would sit down next to them or on their lap, run her hand over their crotch and ask if they were interested in going back to one of the more private rooms. Some regulars who haunted the darkest corners didn't even bother with the private rooms but would take a hand job right there at the table. Eddie preferred the private rooms.

The vice squad never came to Scarlet's. Occasionally some regular cops would walk through in uniform, if they were looking for a particular person. But as a rule, the cops let Scarlet's alone. The reason for this was that the I.R.S. owned Scarlet's. They had seized the building from some organized crime bigwig years ago for his unpaid back taxes, but they found they couldn't sell the building. It sat shuttered for years. Then the Outlaw Motorcycle Club approached the I.R.S. with a lucrative offer. Let the motorcycle club run Scarlet's for a high monthly rent and guarantee security. It was a win-win deal. The cops let Scarlet's alone because they knew who owned it. The bikers paid the I.R.S. the guaranteed monthly rent, and controlled security so that there were never any problems, and made a tidy profit off a cash-only business that included liquor, some discrete amount of drug dealing, and down-and-out hookers posing as dancers but turning as many tricks a night as they could. The bikers ran a tight business. Three or four of them sat in the corner all night long keeping an eye on things. They never had to say a word. Nobody messed with them. Business was good.

Eddie had been married for twenty-three years. He usually stopped at Scarlet's once a week for services his wife no longer cared to perform on him.

But on this particular night, something unusual happened. Eddie entered the club but had to pee before he got a drink. The toilet was in the back near one of the private rooms. It always stank. There was a toilet that was usually stopped up and a rusty urinal that looked like a cattle trough. Eddie stepped up to the trough, and while he was peeing, he noticed a small handwritten sign, scribbled in pencil on the wall in front of him, just at eye level. It said: "Kill your wife—no questions asked" followed by a phone number. Eddie thought this odd. It was not the usual drunk comment or dirty line that was usually on these walls. Eddie read it again, finished his business, zipped up and went back out to the bar. He ordered his usual drink and took it to one of the dark corners to find a table. No sooner had he sat down than Amber came by.

"How's it going, Eddie?"

"Pretty good, Amber. Just got here."

"Wifey let you out, did she?"

"Very funny, Amber."

"Want some company, hon?"

"You know I do, but not just yet. Come back in about five minutes."

"Okay, hon."

Amber lumbered off. She was a bit plump, but not quite over the hill and Eddie liked her blow jobs. He was glad she was working tonight, but first he had to think about that graffiti in the toilet.

Lately, Eddie had been thinking a lot about his wife. When he first met her, she was lively and exciting. They did things together. There was regular sex. Nothing spectacular, but regular. But after the first year of marriage, things had gotten stale. His job had become more demanding, but he was getting raises and moving up in the company. He was known in the company as a man who got things done. His wife, on the other hand, got nothing done. She failed to get several promotions and was stuck working in a dead-end part-time job for an accounting firm that she constantly complained about. She had developed rather unattractive jowls at the same time her hair was turning gray. She dressed dowdily. She looked middle-aged. Eddie did not like to admit it, but he was often embarrassed to be seen with her. He liked the attention of the young secretaries at work. They made him feel young and alive. One of them saw a picture of his wife on his desk in his office and asked if that was his mother. After that, he kept the picture in his desk drawer.

But the idea of killing her was not only preposterous, it was wrong. Eddie might have pushed the envelope on some of his business dealings, but he never did anything outright illegal. Yet, he had been wondering lately what exactly he was going to do about his wife. He had been wanting out of the marriage for several years. The two kids were grown and out of the house. He had even gone to see a lawyer last year, but when the lawyer showed him how much he would lose in the property division and how much would have to pay in alimony, Eddie decided not to get a divorce.

This past year things had gotten worse. She was on some kick about remodeling the house. Every week she would present him with new ideas about the kitchen or the bathrooms. "We need marble counter tops!" "The guest bathroom is too small." She even had an architect come in and give an estimate on plans for an entirely new back yard deck. "It's only $1500 for the plans and it will add that much to the resale value of the house," she insisted. Eddie did not want to sell the house. He secretly wondered if she wanted to improve the house with his money so that if she filed for divorce she would either get the house or get a larger share when the house was sold. After all, she worked in accounting.

His worst fear was his retirement. He had almost a million dollars in his company's 401k plan, and was hoping to take advantage of early retirement. His wife's company had no retirement plan, and she had never created one on her own despite his urgings. "Why should I?" she would always say, "I'm married to you." The lawyer had explained to Eddie that should he divorce her, she would be entitled to half of his retirement, even though he had worked for it, had fought his way up the company, and had worked the long hours for those promotions. In fact, the lawyer added, the judge could even give her more than half in lieu of any other property division. If that happened, there would be no early retirement. Eddie would have to work until at least 66 or even longer.

Eddie got up and went back to the toilet. He wanted to write down the number, just to ask some questions, he told himself. But when he walked in and looked at the wall, the message was gone. It had been erased.

Eddie went back to his table and took another swallow of his drink. Amber came up.

"Ready now, hon?"

"Yes, I am."

They walked back to one of the private rooms without talking.

*   *   *

The next week Eddie returned to Scarlet's. He was horny as usual, but he walked straight back to the toilet. The message was back on the wall. "Kill your wife—no questions asked" followed by what looked to be a different phone number. Eddie wrote it down on a piece of paper and left the toilet. He walked out of the club, across the parking lot to an old pay phone that was there. The club kept it there for drunk patrons who needed to call cabs. He stepped inside, put coins into the slot, and dialed the number.

A male voice answered, "Talk to me."

"I saw your sign at Scarlet's," Eddie said. "What's the deal?"

"You bring three thousand dollars tonight with a description of your wife, and an address where we can find her. That's it. We solve your problem. You don't know us. We don't know you."

"I don't have three thousand tonight..." Eddie started to say.

"Then no deal," and the line went dead.

Eddie thought about calling the number back, but the tone of the man's voice intimidated him. He hung up and walked slowly back into Scarlet's. He ordered a drink at the bar and found a table. Before he could sit down, an obviously pregnant stripper walked up to him."

"Hello sailor, want some company?"

87

"No, not right now," Eddie said and sat down.

He took a sip of his drink. How could this not work? he thought. I give someone cash, and an address. I never see them again. I live my life as normal. I don't know what will happen or when. Then something happens. I make sure I always have an alibi. Three thousand dollars is nothing to me. Worst case, nothing happens, and I put some graffiti on the wall about how it's a hoax. Worst case, I'm out chump change. Best case, I save half a million dollars and more.

A heavily tattooed woman staggered up to Eddie's table. "You look lonely" she said. Eddie looked at her eyes. She was obviously high. But she had big boobs.

"Want to go to a private room?" Eddie asked.

"You read my mind," was her reply.

Eddie took a gulp of his drink and got up.

*　*　*

The next week Eddie was back. He had three thousand in cash in his front pocket. He went to the bar and ordered a drink and sat down at a dark table. He could see Amber on stage dancing, holding her floppy tits out like offerings, one in each hand, to the men in the front row. A man got up and tucked a dollar in her G-string and Amber rubbed both tits into the man's eyes.

"I'm just going to talk with this guy," Eddie said to himself. "If the deal seems fishy, I'm out."

Eddie finished his drink, got up and walked to the bathroom. He noticed he was breathing hard.

The penciled note was up on the wall, "Kill your wife— no questions asked" followed by a phone number that was clearly different than the one Eddie had written down the week before. Eddie jotted it down on a 3X5 card and left the toilet. He walked outside to the payphone and dialed the number. His heart was pounding.

"Talk to me."

"I saw your ad on the wall at Scarlet's"

"Yeah?"

"Well, tell me more."

"You know the old junkyard on Route 2, past the Johnson place?"

Eddie knew where it was, the poorest section of town, a sprawling junkyard, a dumping ground that had existed before the city was incorporated.

"Yes, I know it."

"You bring three thousand dollars tonight with a description of your wife, and an address where we can find her. That's it. We solve your problem. You don't know us. We don't know you."

"Who... who are you?" Eddie stuttered.

"You don't know us. We don't know you. You have the money?"

"Yes."

"You have an address and a description of your wife?"

"Yes."

"You'd be better off with her dead?"

Eddie felt a sudden intake of air, an involuntary gasp.

"Yes," he said. "I would."

"Bring the money in thirty minutes or no deal. We don't know you, you don't know us."

The line went dead.

Eddie looked at his watch. It would take him at least thirty minutes to get to the old junkyard from Scarlet's, maybe longer. He ran to his car.

The road out of town was dark. It was an old two-lane highway with no street lights. Eddie drove past closed down gas stations, boarded up businesses, a couple of lowlife casinos and bars until he came to the old junkyard. "Le Dump" is what people called it in town. There was only one main gate into it, and it was open. Eddie drove in. The dirt road inside curved around heaps of old burned out cars, hills of broken glass, stacks of old washing machines, piles of housing parts. Eddie's headlights were the only light. He drove slowly until the road ended in front of a small trailer. A man was standing there. A big man. Eddie left his car running, left the lights on, and stepped outside of the car. He wasn't sure what to say, but the man spoke first.

"Did you bring the money?"

"Yes" Eddie said.

"Do you have a description of your wife?"

"Yes."

"Give it to me."

Eddie reached into his jacket pocket and pulled out a description he had typed at work that morning and printed out on the printer inside his office. He handed it to the man.

"Middle-aged white woman. Grey hair usually tied back in a bun. 5' 6", 190 lbs. Wears glasses. Has jowls. Usually wears a grey jacket. Does not wear high-heel shoes. Drives a black 2008 Ford Focus. Works at Grimaldi's Accounting Firm downtown part-time. Arrives at 1:00 pm each day, leaves at 5:00 pm. Gets her nails done each week on Saturday at Ruth's Nails on Winslow Street."

"The man studied it for a while, and while he did, Eddie studied him. He was at least six foot five, and weighed an easy three hundred pounds. He had the biker look that Eddie associated with the Outlaws: long hair pulled back in a pony tail, coarse beard, tattoos all over his arms.

The man handed the paper back to Eddie.

"Okay, I've memorized it. Make sure you destroy this paper."

"I will," Eddie said, "Can I ask how you will do it?"

"No," said the man. "You can't ask. It's better that you know nothing. Did you bring the money?"

"Yes."

"Give it to me."

Eddie hesitated. For a brief moment he wasn't sure he wanted to go through with this.

"How do I know I can trust you?" he asked.

"Listen buddy, we've done twenty five or so of these jobs for people just like you. Men who have gotten stuck in bad marriages, who can't get out because of money or children, or appearances. You'd be surprised how many Christians use our services. They can't get divorced because of the church, or because of the alimony laws... so we solve their problem for

them. You don't know us. We don't know you. It's perfect. Give me the money."

Eddie reached into his front pants pocket and handed the man the wad of bills. He watched while the man counted it out.

"Good," the man said. "It's all here. Do you want a drink?"

Eddie was surprised at this offer. "A drink?" he said.

"Sure," the man said. "Wait here."

The man went inside the trailer and returned with two glasses filled with an amber liquid.

"It's a sour mash whiskey, to celebrate the deal."

He handed a glass to Eddie.

"Thanks" said Eddie.

"Here's to honor," said the man and drained the glass.

"Okay" said Eddie and took a sip. It wasn't bad.

"Let me show you around the place" said the man. "You know a lot of people think that this is just a dump, but actually it's a very lucrative business."

"Really?" said Eddie.

"Yes," said the man. "Walk with me a minute and I'll show you."

Eddie glanced at his car still running.

"Hang on a second," he said.

He walked over to the car, turned off the engine, put the keys in this pocket and rejoined the man. They started walking down one path.

"For example, we recycle over five hundred tons of glass a year from this junkyard, all at a profit."

"Really?" said Eddie.

"And we bury all of our victims here."

"Excuse me?" said Eddie.

"Well, we have to put the bodies somewhere, and no one ever comes out to a junkyard except to get rid of stuff. Did you notice the pile of cars here? We dismantle all of the usable engine parts like alternators and generators and resell them. We have a big presence on eBay."

"Did you say bodies?" Eddie asked

"Uh huh, we got to put them somewhere. Now walk with me down this path. Do you see this pile of old refrigerators?"

"Yeah."

"Totally non-recyclable. Nobody wants them. They can manufacture compressors cheaper than we can salvage them. It's a totally non-profit area. So, we decided to improvise and now we use them as caskets."

"Excuse me?"

"Oh, by the way, I should have asked you earlier. Why do you want your wife dead?"

"Well, ah um, this is kinda hard to explain. I don't really want her dead, but I don't want to be married anymore, but if we got divorced, I would lose half my retirement and half the house..."

"You don't want her dead?" the man asked.

"Well, ah, the way the lawyer explained it to me, I can't afford to divorce her."

"But you just paid me three thousand to kill her."

"Well, I don't want to know..."

"You just paid me three thousand to kill your wife."

The man's tone had changed. Eddie looked at him. Eddie had dealt with such people in business negotiations and Eddie knew how to match an increase in bargaining."

"Yes, I did. That's exactly what I did."

"I see," said the man, who then pulled a large pistol from his jacket pocket and aimed it at Eddie's chest.

Eddie looked at the gun and then looked at the man and then looked at the gun.

The man pulled the trigger. Eddie didn't hear the explosion.

The man walked over to Eddie's body and retrieved his wallet and his car keys. Then he pulled Eddie's body over to one of the refrigerators and opened it. He yanked the wire shelves out of the refrigerator and stuffed Eddie's body into it and closed the door.

The man walked back to the trailer and stepped inside. After a few minutes he heard a familiar car sound coming up the road. He poured himself another drink. Then the door *opened, and Amber walked in.*

"I put him in that Amana on left side of the pile. I'll get the backhoe tomorrow and bury it. You have Pecos strip his car tomorrow. Here's his wallet and car keys."

"Good job, honey."

*   *   *

Ricardo put the pages down, went into the kitchen and filled his wine glass again. He liked the story. He felt that kind of glow inside that was more than just wine—it was the feeling that comes when somehow—and he never understood how—something he wrote felt right. He never knew where the stories came from, how they formed into words on the page, but there was not a better feeling in the world than when he read something he had just written and thought to himself, *"damn, that's good."*

Tomorrow he would figure out what magazines to send it to. But tonight, he just wanted to revel in the fact that he was part of some mysterious process called writing. It was the only time he felt truly at peace with the world.

Chapter 14: Marta

Ricardo considered Marta his only friend. He had met her almost twenty years ago, during his first attempt at rehab. Maybe it was meeting each other when they were both at desperate points in their lives that allowed them to forge a bond that otherwise might not have happened. It wasn't the hours spent in therapy group together—it was the dark nights when the panic would hit one or both of them, and they would find each other on the ward, huddle in a corner and just hold each other. When overwhelming disaster hits and two people can only hold each other and cry, something permanent connects their souls. It's as if a piece of each transplants into the other. They might not see each other for years afterwards, but when they meet again, that bond is just as strong as if no time has passed. He and Marta were never lovers, but they had an intimacy that comes from a certain type of love. Whenever one of them had personal turmoil, they could hear the other one's voice in their head, encouraging them to persevere.

After rehab, Marta returned to New York City, straightened out her life, started a new job and got married. Ricardo's life after that first rehab wasn't so smooth. During his return to rehab, Ricardo came to rely on Marta's letters of encouragement. He referred to her as his little lighthouse.

As the years went by, he and Marta always stayed in touch, by phone or letter, and they usually arrange to visit each other once or twice a year.

Marta knew about Ricardo's secrets, his writing, his sexual side. This particular evening, they were talking on the phone.

"You know Marta, the movies are full of stories of people who make it despite all the odds. It's a popular myth, a wonderful story. Everyone likes to root for the underdog. But you never hear about the ones who don't make it because of the odds, the ones who fade away, who go bankrupt because the dream they staked everything on didn't come through."

"Is that what you think will happen to you?"

"I don't know, but it's what I worry about. I know my step-by-step plan is solid, but it still doesn't stop the panic from hitting."

"Panic?"

"Yeah, panic. You know, like when you're making a major life change, like getting married or moving to another country, and you take that first step, like saying yes to the marriage proposal, or signing up for early Social Security. You know... the 'what-the-fuck-am-I-doing' panic."

"I *do* know. I've felt that way even in my best decisions. The actions you're taking now: are they reversible?"

"Well, at this point, I would say they are reversible. But not so much later on. As I get further down the line, I think the decision becomes irreversible. You know, once I give notice at work, and start receiving Social Security, once I'm down there. Then I think I could never reclaim the life I have now..."

"Hmmmm, what was it you once told me that Freud said? 'In small matters, trust your head, but in large matters, trust your heart.'"

Ricardo chuckled. "Yeah, I do remember that. But it doesn't make it less scary."

"Does it *feel* like the right thing to do?" Marta asked.

Ricardo paused, and took a deep breath.

"I don't know exactly how I feel. But whenever I think about the future, all I see is me in Panamá. I just don't want to fuck this up, you know. I've fucked up so many things in my life. But I was younger, and I could always bounce back. But this... this is different."

"Do you have anyone there you can talk to about it, someone to use as a sounding board?

Another long pause.

"No. Other than you, no. And maybe that's just another reason to make the move. You know, I've been here eight years, and I don't have a single friend."

"Do you think that will change in Panamá?"

"Yeah, yeah, somehow I do. People seem friendlier. I don't know. Maybe I'm friendlier to them. I have nothing to hide down there. Here, all I do is stay undercover."

"Yeah, well, you're in a job that requires a lot of self-muting, a lot of image maintaining..."

"Yeah."

"All I can say, Ricardo, is take it one step at a time, you know. While some of the steps might be irreversible, I don't think things will ever be irredeemable, you know what I mean? I mean, you're never going to end up homeless."

"I hope not."

Chapter 15: Kit and Phillipe

Sometimes things just happen. For no apparent reason, with no planning, and certainly without anybody deserving it, sometimes things just happened. And they happened to Ricardo too, perhaps like they do to everyone else.

Kit was a waitress in a small restaurant called Roots that Ricardo often ate at for lunch. She was about thirty, pretty and friendly, but because it was lunch, and he was usually absorbed in the cases he was working on that day, he never made much small talk with her, and besides he noticed that she wore a wedding ring, but nonetheless he was always polite and gracious, would ask her how she was doing, and he always tipped her well. (She later told him that it was the fact that he never hit on her that attracted her to him.) But at some point, they got to talking and when she learned he was a lawyer, she mentioned that she had a friend who had had some difficulty in the past and was trying to get some old convictions expunged off her record. Ricardo told her he didn't do that kind of law, but that he would look into the process. The following week, when he returned to the restaurant, he handed Kit a type of how-to guide for getting criminal convictions expunged, which he had borrowed from a criminal defense lawyer he knew. She looked at it seriously, thanked him, folded it up and stuck it in her purse. Ricardo didn't think much about it and ordered his meal.

The following Sunday, Ricardo happened to be walking around Hamburg when he ran into Kit. She was coming out of a flower shop carrying flowers.

When she saw him, she smiled and said, "Since we're outside of Roots I can give you a hug." And she did. Kit had nice large breasts and Ricardo certainly enjoyed this unexpected hug. They exchanged hellos and then she pointed to the flowers and explained, "I got these for the restaurant." She went on to say how every Sunday, this particular flower shop would give her the flowers that they hadn't sold the week before, the ones that were just about to go bad. She would take them back to the restaurant, re-cut them, arrange them in small displays at the table, and get a few more days of use out of them. They were free, and she thought they added to the ambiance of the restaurant.

"That's a generous thing for you to do for them," Ricardo says, indicating the restaurant.

Kit explained that she was not just a waitress there, but one of the shift managers, and got a percentage from the overall business. Since she was about to walk back to the restaurant to drop off the flowers, Ricardo offered to walk with her. She seemed to like that.

As they walked together, they talked. Ricardo noticed that she wasn't wearing her wedding ring, and asked her about that.

"Oh," she laughed. "I just wear that on the job, so the men won't hit on me. I'm not married."

Ricardo began to reassess his options. He gave her another look. She had a certain gypsy look, thick black curly hair, pulled back in a type of bun for work, but hair that Ricardo imagined would spring out in massive thick curls if it were unleashed from the hair ties. She had high cheekbones, almost a certain Russian look to her face, a look that would be fierce if she wasn't always smiling and laughing. Ricardo glanced quickly down her cleavage and wondered what the future might bring.

They continued to walk and talk. Ricardo told her his marital situation, twice divorced, no kids, etc. She asked him his age and he told her. Some men try to hide their age, but Ricardo didn't do this. Women found out sooner or later anyway, so there was no point in lying. However, he did make sure to omit any references to men, bathhouses, and any gay or bisexuality inclinations. No point in confusing her. They chatted more about this and that, and then she let it slip, in the way women do when they want you to know something important, that she didn't have a boyfriend and missed having someone to go out with. When they got to the restaurant, Ricardo started to say goodbye, and she gave him another big hug and thanked him for walking her. So he decided to ask her, and he did ask her, in as safe a way as he can, that if she wanted to go out for coffee or lunch sometime, he would certainly enjoy doing that, no pressure mind you, in the kind of words one uses to indicate that he is not going to hit on her. She said she would enjoy that and gave him her email and phone number.

As he walked away, he wondered, "What exactly just happened there? A woman of thirty just gave me her number."

But of course, he did call within a few days, and they did go out. And it was over lunch that more of Kit's story came out. She didn't have a friend who had a criminal conviction—*she* had criminal convictions. Right before her mother institutionalized her for thirty days, she got two felony theft convictions when she tried to shoplift baby cribs. She was living with her mother at the time, after having a miscarriage and breaking up with some guy. All this information just poured out of her. He tried to get a word in edgewise but couldn't. It was as if she'd been holding back telling someone for years. He tried to ask her if her public defender knew she had been institutionalized right after her arrests, but he didn't get an answer to that. In fact, all his questions went unanswered. So, he just listened and tried to take it all in. The judge had given her two suspended sentences to run concurrent, and she was now off of probation, and was finishing up paying off her fines. When she was released from the mental hospital, she didn't want to move back in with her mother because she believed (correctly Ricardo thought) that her mother was making her crazy, so she moved in with a gay friend named Phillipe. Phillipe worked at Jesse's, a gay bar down the street from Roots. But Phillipe's lease would be up in a few months and Kit was afraid she wouldn't be able to qualify for a place of her own because of her criminal convictions, which was why she wanted to get them expunged.

Ricardo listened in amazement. There is no end to how people fucked up their lives. Here was a beautiful woman, really just a girl, of 30, with two felony convictions, convictions that should never have happened if what she said was true—that she had lost her first baby to miscarriage and had gone off the deep end and was trying to steal baby cribs from two different stores and knew it was wrong and so she walked up to the cashier in each store and said, "I'm trying to steal this baby crib" and got arrested. She should never have been arrested and certainly never convicted. How a prosecutor or a judge would condone such convictions was beyond Ricardo, but that was why he never did criminal law. He knew how prosecutors just wanted scalps for their belt, no matter the human cost, and he knew how the judges were too overworked to pay any attention to the merits of any individual case.

But he was also suspicious of Kit's story, or rather, not her story as much as her ability to recount it. It made no sense to him, for example, looking at her, seeing this beautiful woman in front of him seemingly able to recount these events in a logical fashion, that when he asked her what county the convictions took place in, she didn't know. Nor did she know the year of the convictions. There was this huge disconnect between the image that he saw and the information that was being given to him.

Then she told him she had some papers back at her place, and if he would drive her there, she would show him the papers and they would answer his questions.

There were all kinds of red flags to this offer. Here was a woman with two felony convictions, who had been institutionalized, asking him to take her back to her apartment to answer questions that any other person would simply know, like what was the county in which she got convicted? But Ricardo looked at her full lips, her thick curly black hair, the bit of cleavage he could see, the rest that he could imagine, and of course...said yes.

He was relieved to see that her neighborhood wasn't that bad. At first he was afraid that she was taking him to some trailer park where he could be robbed, but actually, she lived in a rather upscale area. When they got to her apartment building, before they go in, she turned to him, kissed him lightly on the check and told him how much she appreciated him doing this. She then added that Phillipe might be home and for him not to mind if he was dressed in drag, which she explained, was how he usually dressed around the house.

Walking up one flight to the apartment, Ricardo wasn't sure what to think. The day so far had been so bizarre, why would Phillipe be any less so?

And Phillipe did not disappoint. Even though Kit had her own key, Phillipe answered the door and showed them both in. Yes, he was in full drag, but tastefully done. It was not the usual Dolly Parton over-the-top drag queen look. Rather, it was more the down-home Reba McEntire look: red wig, but not overdone, but with tight black dress, and high heels. Very passable, Ricardo thought. Ricardo extended his hand, "It's good to meet you," he said, "I'm Ricardo." Ricardo took this first move to find out if he was supposed to address Phillipe by another name.

"Oh, darling, I'm Phillipe, come right in, make yourself at home. I'm just doing a little cleaning up. Don't mind me."

Perfect little drag queen, Ricardo thought, and very attractive. Ricardo always felt comfortable with drag queens. He always felt he could talk openly, and even be a bit provocative with them.

Kit said it would take her a minute to find her papers, and she left the room. Ricardo took a seat on the sofa and waited. Phillipe seemed to be rearranging things just to stay in the same room.

"So, what do *you* do?" Phillipe finally said.

"What do I *do*?" Ricardo retorted, emphasizing the word "do" the same way that Phillipe had over-pronounced the word "you". "I don't do much, I'm a lawyer, and I do mostly probate work, but sometimes I do drag queens and women on the side." Ricardo smiled and arched one eyebrow.

Phillipe didn't miss a beat. "Only on the side? How limited. Have you tried face-to-face?"

Ricardo laughed. He liked Phillipe.

Kit walked in from the other room, carrying a shoebox overflowing with papers.

"Sorry they're such a mess," she said.

Ricardo thumbed through them. They *were* a mess, no organization at all. He looked at the front page of one Judgment and Sentence document where it had Kit's full name: Kitriana Pruitt. He realized somewhat embarrassingly that this was the first time he knew what her last name was. He also realized what Kit was short for.

"I tell you what," he said, "let me take these back to my office, go through them, talk to a friend of mine who does expungement cases, and I will call you. How does that sound? Or better yet, let's just have dinner next Saturday and I'll give you an update and give these back to you."

"Oh darling," Phillipe interjected, directing his comments to Kit, "sounds like you'll be getting some at last. Good for you girl. I'll make myself scarce on Saturday"

Ricardo laughed. Kit seemed oblivious. Ricardo took the box, and said his goodbyes. Kit walked him to the door and gave him a goodbye kiss on the cheek.

When Ricardo got back to his office, he called his attorney friend Mark Lettrip from whom he had originally borrowed the "how-to guide for expungements", and explained his situation. Ricardo did not want in any way to represent Kit, to be her lawyer, or to have any legal entanglements with her. If he represented her, the official conduct rules for attorneys would prohibit him from ever sleeping with her, and he wanted to keep that option open. But even if sex was not destined to happen, he still wanted to help her. So, he told Mark "Look, go over these files, I'll pay for your time. Tell me if you think she has a chance to get these convictions expunged. If she does, I'll make sure you get paid."

Mark agreed to call him in a few days.

True to his word, Mark called Ricardo back two days later and told him, "The first conviction is no problem. $500 and I can guarantee it'll be expunged. The second one is the problem. Technically she's not off probation until she finishes paying her fines on that, and she's got another $1000 to pay off. Then I'm pretty sure I can talk the judge into expunging it, especially with her mental health record. I would recommend doing them both at once. It's cheaper for her, and less confusing for the judge. Get her to pay off the $1000 and we're good to go."

"Thanks, Mark. Send me a bill for your time."

The following Saturday, Ricardo took Kit out to dinner and explained the situation. She was very pleased and said she could pay off the rest of her fines in two months.

They talked about many things that night, but Ricardo noticed that they did not talk about any of the details of her miscarriage, arrests, or commitment to the mental hospital. He let her lead the conversation, and besides, she was so pleased with the news he brought, and was chatting happily about this event or that event at work, that he did not want to spoil her good mood. He listened, smiled added a word here or there, but mostly just let her talk.

The impression he had of her when they had met outside of the flower shop stayed in his mind—that she had the kind of face that was like a tropical day: bright and sunny, just perfect weather, but that at any moment, dark thunderstorms could roll in. Ricardo hadn't seen that side of her, but he somehow intuited that it existed. He saw it in the slightly dark circles under her eyes, how her mouth had that slight twitch right before she smiled, and especially in how her eyes would every now and then have this micro-movement dart from left to right, as if at any moment she expected something to leap at her from the bushes. Ricardo realized that she was actually on guard, despite the gaiety of her laughter. Women who are always on guard are a problem, Ricardo thought. Eventually life proves them right, and then they feel justified unleashing their vengeance. Ricardo imagined that Kit could be very vengeful. And there was that one comment she had made earlier in the evening. Ricardo had asked her casually how she liked dating, and she had responded with something about having had some bad experiences with men, and when he said "Oh really?", she had casually responded, "Well, I just never have done well with men," which she said in a way as to change the subject, except that there was this slight emphasis on the word *"never"*.

That's the thing about "tells", as the poker players call them. People can't help themselves; they can't help revealing those tiny pinpoint scraps of information about themselves. It's subconscious. It was the way she said "never" that struck Ricardo—it came out so literally, as in *never ever*, as in the first relationship that all girls have—which is with their father. There was this flash of information, more like a vision really, that Ricardo got, that when Kit said she never had done well with men, she was really saying that the original relationship had not gone well. And in that quick flash of light there was the implication that the thing that had not gone well was sexual.

Of course, she said it in a laughing way. The casual observer would not have noticed any emphasis on any particular word, and a rational person would call Ricardo's flash of perception mere conjecture, a mere fantasy. But Ricardo had always trusted these perceptions, these keyholes of light into other people. Thus, he accepted without question that she had been sexually abused as a child, and he let her turn the conversation to other matters.

And thus he ended up, at the end of the dinner, at that point when a man has to decide, assuming the woman has given him the option of deciding, whether to steer events toward sex, as in the traditional "would you like to come to my place for a nightcap?" or whether to steer events towards a goodbye, as in "I have a busy day tomorrow; please allow me to pay for your cab fare home." In Ricardo's case, since he had picked Kit up from her apartment, his choices were limited to driving her to his apartment or taking her home.

Ricardo debated this in his head. Kit was beautiful, and he very much wanted to see her naked, to kiss those large breasts, to run his tongue around those lips, to undo those hair ties and let those massive curls explode, and he wanted to do more, to go down on her, where he hoped he would find more hair, lots more hair... Ricardo wanted to do all those things... But he also was very worried about what kind of person Kit would be after he did all those things. Everyone keeps up some pretenses before they make love, this is common knowledge, but some people change dramatically after they become intimate. They become demanding, needy, clinging, blaming, critical, hysterical, dependent, or simply crazy. And there were just too many red flags this evening; too many crazy red flags. As much as Ricardo wanted to have sex with Kit, he was simply too afraid of the person he would wake up with.

And then there was the problem with Phillipe. Ricardo was also attracted to Phillipe and, in different circumstances, would have already made a move to fuck him. He was cute as a boy and cute as a girl. Ricardo has a special attraction for drag queens, because as lovers they offered the best of both worlds—they were built like men but liked to fuck as women. It was a perfect combination. But here, with Kit living with Phillipe, there was an obvious problem. He couldn't hit on Phillipe without Kit being offended... and "offended" didn't really encompass the problem. Kit was a waitress at a restaurant that other lawyers patronized. Other lawyers that Ricardo worked with. If Ricardo hit on the gay male roommate of a waitress who might know other lawyers... well, that certainly would be diametrically opposed to Ricardo's long-standing practice of keeping his personal life totally separate from his work life.

Ricardo thought about all this and came to his conclusion reluctantly, just as he and Kit were finishing dessert. He then made the time-honored excuse of a busy day in the morning and offered to drive her home.

On the drive to her house, he picked up some clues that he had made the right decision. Kit was already talking about their next date, where they would go, whether she should cook him a meal at her apartment—the kind of statements that implied that they were already in a relationship. Ricardo steered the conversation around to her expungements, said he would introduce her to Mark, and estimated when Mark might file the expungement papers. That way, he figured, he could later use the "attorney excuse" (I can't fuck you because you're a client) even though he had taken great care to make sure she couldn't be classified as a client of his.

At the door to Kit's apartment, Ricardo stopped and stood in such a way as to indicate he was not going to follow her in, that he was going to say his goodbyes at the door. He thanked her graciously, told her what a great time he had, and said that he would see her soon at the restaurant (being careful not to say he would call to ask her out again). She also thanked him for a wonderful evening and leaned forward to give him a kiss. It was the kind of lean that he could answer with a full-on mouth kiss, even an opened mouth kiss, but he turned ever so slightly as to get a bit of her mouth and a bit of cheek. Slightly awkward but sufficiently ambiguous enough to suffice. After all, not everyone's aim is perfect.

He waved goodbye as she let herself into the apartment, then he got into his car and drove home, where he knew he had a bottle of wine waiting. He needed it tonight.

Chapter 16: At the Airport

Normally, Ricardo enjoyed traveling through airports as much as he enjoyed arriving at his final destination. He always thought that traveling to get somewhere should be a vacation in itself, what with all the movement, all the new people swirling around, all wearing different kinds of clothes, all the different languages and accents one overhears, and the simple joyful exercise of being able to sit in the waiting area by the gate and watch people without needing an excuse for looking. It was like people-watching at a foreign sidewalk café without having to put up with a waiter wanting to take your order. Normally, Ricardo enjoyed analyzing the clothes that people chose to wear for traveling. First he would start by looking at the shoes that people chose: the easy slip-offs for getting through airport security; the rugged hiking shoes with the short socks that indicated the serious outdoors person; the high heels worn by the young women who would sacrifice comfort for style; the variety of clogs, sandals or flip-flops emblematic of the laid-back travelers; the boots of the die-hard cowboy types; the casual moccasins of the khaki pants crowd; and the bright white tennis shoes of the very old men. Ricardo noticed how people rarely mixed and matched. The moccasins went with khaki pants; the hiking shoes with shorts or cargo-pocket safari pants; the boots with blue jeans, etc. It was like everyone was a flag from a different country, all flying their native colors.

But today Ricardo was tired. He was at the Dallas airport with a three-hour layover until his flight to Panamá. He was sitting in the waiting area by his gate, doing what people do in waiting area: waiting. He was tired from his early flight out of New York, but not sleepy. He had had too much coffee and was carrying too much left-over stress from work that he couldn't brush off.

The seats around him were filled with people, mostly young, but all of them on some type of device: laptops, netbooks, smartphones, iPads, iPhones, and tablets. Even the small children held small computerized gaming consoles, sitting quietly, totally absorbed while their parents surfed their own devices. Ricardo looked around some more. Every single person was on a device. No wait, there was one older lady in the corner reading a book, and one young soldier sleeping in his chair. But none of these people held any interest for Ricardo today. He turned his thoughts toward himself.

He had spent the last few months gathering all the documents necessary to apply for pensionado status. Each document had been issued by different official agencies. Each one was an original. Each one was notarized. Each one also had a state Apostille stamp indicating that the notary was authentic. He had his birth certificate, his letter of good standing from his bank, a recent bank statement, his criminal background check from the New York State Police, a letter from his investment firm, and the all-important award letter from the Social Security Administration guaranteeing him a definite social security payment for life, starting the following January. Just in case, he also had a letter from his doctor indicating his good health. He also had fifteen passport-quality photographs of himself, as required, ten from the front and five from the side. He had no idea why the Panamá Migration Office needed so many photographs, but his Panameño lawyer said they did, so he had them made.

As he sat there, he wondered for the millionth time if he was in his right mind, if he knew what he was doing, if he was making the right decision. He was embarking on a path that would forgo a good paying job, plus his well-regulated (perhaps *too* well-regulated) lifestyle: the familiar restaurants, the familiar bathhouses, the familiar brothels, his familiar ways of doing everything. And for the millionth time, a flurry of reasons why he had to do it flashed up in response to every doubt, without lessening the doubt, but at least addressing it. He closed his eyes and took a deep breath. He was exhausted from the constant second guessing he was doing. He opened his eyes and looked at his watch. Hopefully another hour and a half and they might start boarding.

He thought back to the past few weeks with Kit and Phillipe. Should he have taken Kit back to his house that night? Could he arrange to fuck Phillipe? What were the odds of getting them both in bed at the same time? Alas, as wonderful as that fantasy was (as that fantasy is to everyone who has it), he knew it was totally unattainable. If Ricardo's suspicions of Kit were right, she would inevitably want a magical father figure that no man could fulfill. As for drag queens, well, what they ever wanted was always a mystery. Ricardo wished he could fuck either or both of them. But he knew that it was not in the immediate future, meaning, it was a horrible idea. If at some future point, he could get away with one or the other and fuck them without consequences, he would do it. That's what it always came down to, he thought sadly. Consequences. If people could just fuck and walk away, it would be so much easier. But there are always these consequences, these "relationships" that form, like stalactites, weighing you down. That must be why he preferred brothels and bathhouses. There were no relationships, no friendships, not even any names. Ricardo was most comfortable there, in the land of total immediacy and no future.

He looked at his watch again: forty-five minutes until boarding.

He wished he had a drink.

Chapter 17: The Rainy Season

Panamá City was just as he remembered it, but wetter, much wetter. The mornings stayed sunny until noon when the sprinkles started, and then by one o'clock it would be a drizzle, and then by two o'clock there would be downbursts, and by evening there would be torrential downpours. It was best, therefore, to get one's business done in the morning, so that the afternoons and evenings could be spent inside the bars or cafes with the large iron windows open wide, watching the rain, which is exactly where Ricardo was this early afternoon. He was sitting by the window in the Café de los Sueños, drinking an Americano coffee (which he thought was ironic) watching the people scurry by under a sea of umbrellas on the sidewalk just a few feet away. Every so often the sky would boom with thunder. But the rain remained a constant, neither increasing nor decreasing, just continuing to come down in buckets.

He had spent each of the last four mornings meeting with lawyers, filling out forms, going to the US Embassy to obtain certain documents, going to a Panameño bank to open an account into which his Social Security would be directly deposited, going back to the Embassy, going to the Office of Migration, and going back to the bank. There were endless forms, some with odd questions (like, did he have all his natural teeth?) and with every form he had to attach a photograph of himself, and list the full names of his long-deceased parents. One form required him to be fingerprinted. It appeared that each different governmental agency he dealt with had a personal investment in making sure he was the person he said he was.

As it happened, today was his last appointment.

He signed some final forms in the lawyer's office, paid an additional fee, and was done with this day's business by ten o'clock. In terms of his pensionado application, there was nothing more to be done on this trip. The remaining time of this vacation would be spent on just that—vacation. The Office of Migration would send his lawyer a receipt in about a month indicating that his application had been filed. The lawyer would email a copy of that receipt to Ricardo. When he returned to Panamá in four months, he would show this receipt to the Migration window at the airport, and they would stamp his passport with a special stamp indicating that he could stay longer than the standard ninety-day visa. Six to eight months from that point, if the government approved his application, he would receive his official pensionado residency. Ricardo's plan was to retire from work in four months, put his few belongings into storage, and return to Panamá and search for a place to settle. Once he got his official pensionado residency, he would then return to the states to move what he could to Panamá and dispose of the rest.

After he had left the lawyer's office that morning, he had taken some time to sit in the park to watch the people who were also out enjoying the day. The benches in this park, as in most Panameño parks, were made out of poured concrete. Not exactly comfortable, but not bad. The sun was out, but a light breeze kept the heat down. The park was full of Panameños, because they all knew that the morning hours were the only time they could enjoy the park during the rainy season.

Because it was the off-season, there were blessedly few gringos, or any other tourists. Ricardo thought he probably stood out more because of this, but there was nothing he could do about that. There were only a few vendors working the crowd. But the few that were there did approach him, trying to sell various souvenirs or offering a shoe shine. He politely waved them off with a "no, gracias" and they left him alone.

An older woman with a child sat down on the bench near him. Ricardo assumed that the older woman was the girl's grandmother by the way she doted on the girl and sang her songs. Another woman, middle-aged, sat down next to the grandmother. After a short while the grandmother and child left, and the other woman moved a bit closer to Ricardo.

Ricardo looked at her. She had a pretty face, but her body was a bit heavy. He noticed she did not look away.

"I always like this park," he said in Spanish.

"Yes?" she responded. "Why?"

"It's just so peaceful (tranquilo)," he replied. "Whenever I come to Panamá, I always come here, to this park."

In actuality, Ricardo had never been to this particular park before. But he had decided almost automatically to adopt a neutral, friendly tone, as if he was simply chatting with a friend in the park.

"Yes," she said, "it's very beautiful. I can forget my troubles here."

There is something about Spanish small talk, Ricardo had always noticed, that was so much more self-disclosing than gringo small talk. Two gringos might meet in a bar in the states and talk for an hour. But at the end of that time neither one of them really knew anything more about the other than when they met. But in Latino cultures because there is so much emphasis on formalities in personal relationships, a lot more small talk is required, and people seemed to find ways to tell each other more about themselves in the small talk. In the next twenty minutes of chatting, Ricardo learned that Anna (which was her name) worked in the Hampton Hotel by the airport; that she was trying to learn English so she could get a better job in the tourism industry; that a lot of her friends had emigrated to the United States once they had learned English; that she lived in a small neighborhood (barrio) north of Panamá City; and that she rode the bus to work every day. And she learned from Ricardo that he was traveling alone; which hotel he was staying in; where he was from; and the fact that he was in Panamá to apply for pensionado residency.

Because she had asked him so quickly if he was staying in a hotel and if he was traveling alone, and because she kept referring to the problems she wanted to forget, Ricardo began to wonder if she might be angling to somehow ask him for money, or that she might offer to sleep with him for money. He did not assume this was her intention, but he merely played out that scenario in his mind in case the conversation should turn that way. She did have a nice face, with lips he wouldn't mind kissing, but she was thick around the middle, a bit older, and he could tell her breasts were saggy. Still, he considered his options. If such events were to come to pass, he could not take her back to the particular hotel he was staying in, because it was a small family-run hotel, and they simply would not let a guest bring a woman into his room who had not checked in with him. She had told Ricardo the neighborhood where she lived. While it would not have been a long car ride, maybe ten minutes, he didn't have a car and she obviously didn't. Thus, going to her place, whatever that might be, would involve at least a thirty- minute bus ride. Also, Ricardo didn't like the idea of being stuck somewhere in case he wanted to leave. He remembered one time, back in the states years ago, when he let some woman he had met in a bar drive him to her house, which turned out to be a trailer... in a run-down trailer park... on the edge of town. It housed her and her four kids. And when she and Ricardo arrived, the oldest kid, about twelve, said, "Who'dya bring home tonight, mama?" That had been a bad situation which Ricardo never wanted to repeat.

Those were the kind of things that passed through Ricardo's mind. In fact, they were the kind of things that pass through all men's minds when they talked to someone where sex might be a possibility. *Would I? Could I? How would it happen? What would it be like? Do I want to? What's the downside? Does the other person want to? What do I need to do or say to either make this happen or prevent it from happening?*

Anna and Ricardo continued to chat the way a mature couple might chat, sitting in a park on a sunny morning that was quickly turning into a cloudy day. Eventually, Ricardo decided that the effort involved in getting Anna's clothes off had too many obstacles today, but that he might be open to it in the future, if it were more convenient. So just before the first sprinkles began to fall, he said how much he had enjoyed talking to her, gave her his email address, and said in a friendly way that it is always good to make new friends in all parts of the world, and he hoped she would contact him, implying *after* he returned to the states. He considered this a win-win move. If she did seize the opportunity to contact him before he left Panamá, he would reassess his options, maybe ask her to dinner and get to know her more, maybe make sure the dinner was near a "love motel" where he could, if he wanted, rent a room by the hour. But if she contacted him after he had returned to the states, he would stay in contact, because, as he said, it's good to have friends, and he would be returning to Panamá soon and maybe the situation would be more favorable for sex later. Over the years he had learned never to miss an opportunity to set a good foundation for the possibility of sex down the road. Most women don't want to be hustled for sex, but they don't mind being open to sex if they feel the man is not hustling them. Ricardo thought of it as zen-cruising.

As he handed Anna the piece of paper with his email, the rain sprinkles began to increase. She put the paper in her purse and smiled when Ricardo said he hoped she would stay in touch but that he had to go before the downpour started.

He made it to the Sueños Café just seconds before the downpour hit. It was way too early to drink, so he ordered the Americano, took his seat by the window and waited, and watched, and contemplated.

Men, he had decided years ago, were all idiots when it came to relationships. No wonder so many women held them in such contempt. Men were simply incapable of handling a relationship because of the basic irresolvable conflict between their need to be mothered in a safe stable union and their need to fuck every woman they met. It was as if their emotional programming was directly opposed to their biological need. Ricardo recalled how, decades earlier, he had loved sleeping, spoon-style, with his first wife, pressed up against her back, his arms wrapped around her, because it placed his face and nose directly against the back of her head and her hair always smelled so sweet and reassuring to him. He looked forward to spooning with her every night. Yet, this was the same woman that he cheated on every chance he could, even sleeping with her best friend. Unlike most men, Ricardo never felt guilty or ashamed by his actions. He knew, even as a young man so long ago, that both sides of him were important—they were just irreconcilable. On the other hand, he wasn't proud of his actions either. In fact, he went out of his way to be discreet and undetected so as not to hurt the woman that he loved. He was simply trying to balance both needs. Most men, he had observed, tried to submerge the tomcat side of their personalities, and certainly that's what women and society demanded. But Ricardo found that practice to be destructive. Squelching the need to touch and kiss and fuck other people just made men bitter and passive-aggressive toward their wives. It was a no-win situation.

Eventually, most men came to a crossroads regarding this dilemma. Most stayed married. Maybe they had guilty affairs or not, but they seemed to shrink up as men. But some men (and Ricardo was one of these) took the other approach. They realized that they would never be able to fulfill most women's requirements for monogamy, so it was better not to lead women on about this. That was what most men did—they led women on subtly, even subconsciously, by implying that they might be good husband material, never mentioning their past affairs or their current desires. Most men did that for the time-tested reason that that's how they could get laid. And of course, since women are smarter than men, that's how most men also end up getting married. They get used to the good sex, and by the time a year has gone by, they've said so many things about being good husband material that they can't back out the caricature they've created, and the inevitable happens.

Thus, Ricardo had given up trying to be good marriage material. He had chosen a path that maximized his ability to have sex with different partners. Which is why he ended up frequenting the brothels of St. Catherines in Canada, along with the brothels, sex clubs, massage parlors, and gay bathhouses of every place he went.

He simply stopped viewing himself as able to be "in a relationship" with a woman. And the fact that he was getting his sexual needs met in St. Catherines took a lot of the pressure off him. He stopped going to bars, to parties and social events designated for single people. He stopped pursuing women the way that most men pursue women. But he remained open to women if they sought him out. That's how he met Eve. They had exchanged pleasantries when they ran into each other at work, but he never asked her out. But then one day, rather out of the blue, standing in the hallway that led to their separate offices, she asked him if he wanted to get together for a glass of wine sometime, and he said yes. She came over to his place that evening. After about half a glass of wine each, Ricardo simply leaned over and kissed her. She kissed him back. Then he took her hand and led her to the bedroom. She was there for sex. He was there for sex. There was no relationship-forming involved.

Although, sitting in the Panameño coffee-shop that afternoon, as the rain poured down, he had to admit that he felt sad when he thought about Eve. He had truly liked her, even loved her.

Ricardo thought about other women he had had sex with. He thought about the gay bathhouses. He knew he couldn't reconcile his liking sex with men with his love of sex with women. He preferred women, but sex with men was too exciting to pass up. There was no need to label it, no way to understand it, and certainly no point in explaining it. Ricardo was convinced that if his sexual activities were laid out for some self-appointed jury, he would be executed as a pervert or committed as a sex addict. But he was neither. At least, he did *not feel* he was. He always treated people decently, tried to be respectful, tried to be discreet, always practiced safe sex, and tipped the prostitutes well. He knew that it wasn't a life that anyone would admire. But it was the best he could do and remain human.

Ricardo thought about Kit and Phillipe and the sea of red flags that were waving around them. But he also realized that he had never explained his Panamá plans to Kit. Since he would be moving away from Hamburg in about four months, he wondered if he could have a brief affair with either Kit or Phillipe or both. She was, after all, beautiful, and Phillipe was, after all, a cute drag queen with a sense of humor. He weighed the ethical choices. He didn't want to hurt a woman who was already emotionally damaged. On the other hand, she was old enough to make her own decisions and he shouldn't act so patronizing. If she understood he was leaving in four months, maybe she would keep her expectations low. He decided to keep his mind and his options open concerning both Kit and Phillipe. He would explain to her clearly that he wasn't going to be staying in Hamburg, and simply see what developed from there.

The rain wasn't letting up, and Ricardo didn't want any more coffee. He took out his map—the one he had specially marked up—and examined his location. He was about equal distance from a massage parlor and a bathhouse. He debated which one to go to, and then signaled the waitress for his bill.

Chapter 18: Paradise

Everyone has a dream of paradise. It's part of our mythos, our human inheritance, our brain chemistry, our language, the very underpinnings of our communication. From the stories of the Garden of Eden, Altantis, Shambhala, Valhalla, Shangri-La, Mount Olympus, and the Elysian Fields, we learn to tolerate our present struggles, and to comfort others in their struggles with the promise that things can and will get better. It's the dream of a future time where life is perfect, the archetype of hope, that keeps us going.

And the dream takes many forms: hitting the jackpot in Vegas, winning the lottery, or retiring ("jubilación" in Spanish) and, of course, the biggest dream of paradise: finding true love. In the background of the dream, you can almost hear "Somewhere Over the Rainbow." But the one constant in all the visions of paradise is that it's always in the future. It always remains a dream.

Ricardo was no different. Single, debt-free, gainfully employed in a tolerable job, all the sex he wanted in the bathhouses of Buffalo or the brothels of St. Catherines—a freethinking person would look at Ricardo's life in Hamburg and think he was living the dream. Ricardo would disagree. For years he saw only the extended loneliness, the dreariness of his job, and the anxiety of being outed as a devotee of brothels and gay bathhouses. He spent enormous amounts of energy hiding his sexual excursions, picking the safest partners and practicing safe sex. He dragged himself to work and resented the eight to ten hours of time each day that he gave to his masters in order to obtain money to live. When he looked ahead at spending his remaining days in

Hamburg, he saw only a repetitive, mind-numbing life.

But in order to have a dream of paradise, you must first have a taste of paradise. And Ricardo often had this taste. It came over him like a trance when he wrote—it was a mood, a wave, a simultaneous focus and release, when he sat at his desk and just let words flow out of him. Sometimes he would look up and realize he had been sitting for several hours, typing words onto a computer screen, writing, rewriting, thinking, and rewriting again. When he would look up and see how late it was, he would realize that he had to stop writing and go to bed in order to make it to work in the morning. He resented that and would vow again to find more time to write.

But he also knew that time was time wherever one lives. Even retirees have their time chewed up with going to the grocery store, going to the doctor, going to the hardware store to find a washer to repair the sink that suddenly started to leak. Ricardo rationalized that he would have more time to write in Panamá as a pensionado than he would have in Hamburg as a retiree, but he didn't know that for sure. But he did think that there would be less distractions, that by living in a small Panameño town, there would simply be less to do. Thus, the time to write would, in essence, be forced on him. It was part of Ricardo's philosophy of life that people simply didn't have the willpower to change themselves. They only have enough power to alter their environment, to create the conditions that in turn create personal change. Try as he might in Hamburg, between the trips to the bars, the brothels, the bathhouses, the malls, the dry-cleaners, the barbers, the laundromats, the restaurants, the doctors, the liquor stores and all the other diversions that Hamburg and Buffalo offered, he could never manage to squeeze out more than a few hours of writing every other day. Just driving to the various places took enormous amounts of time.

Life's routines strangle us. They develop a power over our lives simply by the force of repetition, the way a river cuts an unalterable gorge out of rock. No one can change a routine once it is set. Legend has it that it was written on Plato's ring that "it is easier to create a new habit than to change an old one." Ricardo had always found this to be true.

And thus, Ricardo was trying to develop new habits. He had learned through his many visits to Panamá how to eliminate many expensive and time-consuming activities. With the warm Panamanian weather all year long, he needed only two days' worth of casual clothes when he traveled. Each night he would rinse out the clothes he wore that day in the sink and hang them up to dry. That eliminated trips to the laundromat and dry-cleaners. Furnished rooms in a Panameño house came with sheets and towels, and the Panameño family would change those weekly as part of the rent. Haircuts were four dollars. Restaurant meals averaged six to eight dollars. All he hoped he would need would be a furnished room with a kitchenette or with cooking privileges in the family kitchen. Then he could buy enough fresh food at the farmers market for about twenty dollars a week. He would restrict his search for rooms or apartments to the small Panameño towns where there had been no influx of expats to drive the rent prices up.

Sex was likewise both cheaper and less time-intensive in Panamá. In the typical small Panamanian town, there were no singles bars, no place where singles went to meet each other. Young people met of course, just like they do all over the world: in school or in church or just in the neighborhood. But there weren't places for someone of Ricardo's age and gringo-heritage to meet people other than the happenstance encounters in the parks, at the farmers markets, or in the neighborhood during the day. Small town Panameño bars were where couples or single men went to drink at night, but not single women. Therefore, for someone like Ricardo, the pursuit of sex was limited to the bathhouses or the brothels. Whereas the brothels in St. Catherines cost him almost two hundred dollars per visit, a trip to a local Panameño brothel topped out at forty to fifty dollars. Only the casinos that targeted their brothel business toward gringos charged a hundred dollars. Ricardo didn't care if whatever small town he eventually selected had its own brothel or not, so long as it was on a bus route near enough to a large city that had both brothels and a bathhouse.

The bottom line was that the pursuit of sex in Panamá was both direct and cheap, which would also free up time for writing. It wasn't that Ricardo was being Machiavellian about it. The facts simply were what they were. Ricardo was sixty-two. Sex was important to him. He wasn't going to give it up and shrivel up, like so many other men his age (and younger). Ricardo's only other pleasure was writing his short stories. He didn't think he was crazy for moving somewhere where he could maximize the only two things in life that gave him pleasure.

It's possible, of course, that Ricardo was making the biggest mistake of his life. It's possible that living in Panamá would turn out to be just as expensive, just as monotonous, and just as time-limited for writing as Hamburg. All Ricardo had to go on was an intuition that it would be better. When it comes to life's biggest decisions, that's all there ever is: just an intuition. The advice of friends won't help; all the books in the world won't help; even visits to the fortune teller won't help. There's just intuition.

Ricardo had another ten days left in Panamá on this trip before he returned to Hamburg. Then, he would have four months before his next flight back to Panamá. That flight might be the flight to paradise, or it might be the flight of Icarus. But he would not know which for a long time.

Chapter 19: The Parasille Hotel

Unlike most Panameño brothels, the Parasille Hotel and Casino in San José de David was owned by a well-known American hotel company. They would deny they were a brothel, of course, but the fact was, they owned and managed the hotel and casino, and the girls worked the casino with the hotel's permission. It was good for business. Any trouble with any of the girls and the hotel would banish them from the premises. It was rumored that the most attractive girls got rooms for free at the hotel so long as they worked the casino bar. Naturally, they were forbidden to take clients to their room. Their clients had to rent a room from the hotel and pay a "guest fee" for any prostitute they took to their room. It was a mutually beneficial financial relationship for the hotel and for the prostitutes.

Ricardo had a love-hate relationship with the Parasille Hotel. He liked that the hotel was safe and clean and that the casino was well run. But he didn't like the gringo prices at the hotel. Whereas he could stay in a small Panameño hotel or hostel for ten dollars a night, the Parasille charged one hundred fifty dollars. However, the North American tourists loved it there because all the hotel staff spoke English; there was free shuttle service to the airport; the hotel concierge would arrange sightseeing trips; and the room rate included a good buffet breakfast. It was just like being in the states, which is why the hotel did a thriving business. Even in the low-tourist rainy season they did okay, usually filling half of their rooms

However, it was precisely the presence of so many North Americans that Ricardo hated the most. They were all fat, carrying huge cameras and fanny packs, sitting in the hotel restaurant and bar, complaining about something. Gringos loved to complain. They would travel anywhere and find something to complain about. The weather was always too hot or too rainy or too windy; the food was too spicy or not spicy enough; the sightseeing tour was too long or too short. Nothing was ever perfect unless, of course, they were on the phone talking to someone back in the states, in which case, they were having a *wonderful* time, and everything was just *lovely*, all said to inspire envy and maintain status.

The prostitutes in the casino bar kept a low profile. They were under strict rules from the hotel management never to approach couples. In fact, Ricardo knew from experience that if he even sat near a couple in the bar, the prostitutes wouldn't approach him either (although, if a couple approached a prostitute, it was perfectly okay to do business—and many couples stayed at the hotel for just that reason). The prostitutes could dress sexy but not so sexy as to draw attention to themselves. They stood off against a side wall, huddled together, looking to the casual observer like cocktail waitresses who had just gotten off their shift at the bar. Only if a man sat alone at the bar could a prostitute approach him. House rules.

The prostitutes were also forbidden to go to the main lobby. Once they negotiated a deal with a client in the bar, the man had to rent a room, return to the bar and show the prostitute a key with the room number and a paid guest fee receipt. The man would then proceed to the room and the prostitute would show up about five minutes later. The name of the game at the hotel was plausible deniability. That, and money.

Someone had once told Ricardo that the reason the casino hotels liked prostitutes was because studies had shown that after sex with a prostitute men would return to the casino and gamble and not care how much they lost.

Despite all the reasons that Ricardo disliked the hotel, he would occasionally stay there. Especially if he had been traveling around Panamá for several days by bus and wanted a hot shower and the deep sleep that only an air-conditioned room could induce. The one drawback to the inexpensive Panameño hotels and hostels was that there was rarely AC. Instead, there was always a ceiling fan. That helped, but in the deep humidity of some Panameño nights, Ricardo would have trouble sleeping.

This particular late afternoon found Ricardo at the Parasille, sitting in the bar in the casino, having a cup of coffee. He sat in a corner far away from the few other customers in the bar. He had just arrived by bus from Santiago and was debating whether to stay at the Parasille and get one of the prostitutes, or whether to go to the Ralma, a Panameño hotel about a mile down the road that was near the Gran Calle. The Gran Calle was San José de David's best bathhouse. Ricardo considered his options. The Parasille room would be about one hundred seventy with tax. The prostitutes at the Parasille cost more, too. Usually between eighty and a hundred dollars for two hours, although at times they were worth it. The hotel only let the most attractive prostitutes work the casino bar. On the other hand, the Ralma would be about twenty-five for the night and the bathhouse would be another eight. But it really wasn't just a money issue. It was more a sex issue—did he want sex with a man or with a woman?

The urge for sex seemed to come from a different part of his body, depending on whether the urge was for a man or for a woman. If his thoughts turned toward men, then there was a distinct physical sensation—Ricardo thought of it as a humming—that seemed to originate from a place near the base of his cock, above his balls, inside his abdomen, slightly back, halfway toward his asshole. Humming was not quite the right word for it, but it was close. It was a vibration, a longing to be touched and grabbed down there. But if the urge was for a woman, then it was different. The physical sensation seemed to run all down the front of his body, from the top of his chest all the way to his balls—it was a longing to make full face-to-face naked physical contact with a female body.

When it came to sex, Ricardo could never predict which way he would feel, which sex he would prefer. He had often imagined that the ideal relationship for him would be as the third wheel to a male-female couple, where he could do either one or both. That would be the perfect long-term relationship for him. Assuming that he was capable of being in a long-term relationship which, unfortunately, experience had taught him he was not capable of.

As he sat there thinking, a woman walked up beside him as if she was intent on going somewhere else (which she was not) and she paused and spoke to Ricardo in English. "Are you waiting for someone?" Ricardo understood immediately that this was her way of asking if he was there with his wife or girlfriend.

"No, estoy viajando solo," he answered, indicating that he was traveling alone.

The woman switched to Spanish.

"Oh, you speak Spanish. Where did you learn it?"

"In Spain."

"Are you Spanish?"

"No, sorry, I'm a gringo, but I grew up in Spain."

She laughed. "Bueno, it's good to meet a gringo who speaks Spanish. I've been trying to learn English, but much of it baffles me. By the way, my name is Inez."

"Mucho gusto, Inez. My name is Ricardo."

"Mucho gusto, Ricardo. Are you here on business?"

"Not exactly. I'm here applying for pensionado status."

"Oh, you want to move here? It's funny. All the gringos want to move here and all the Panameños want to move to the US. I guess no one is ever happy where they are."

Such a true statement, Ricardo thought. He looked at Inez. She seemed to be in her late twenties, early thirties, attractive but not drop-dead gorgeous. She wore a simple cocktail dress that showed a little cleavage but not too much, just the type of outfit the hotel approved of. She had dark hair and a pretty smile, but somehow Ricardo didn't feel overwhelmingly attracted to her.

"How's business in the rainy season for you, Inez?"

She paused, giving him a look as if she was assessing him and his direct question. Then she answered,

"It's slow, one or two customers a night. Not like the dry season. Would you like to buy me a drink?"

"Of course."

Ricardo motioned to the bartender. Inez ordered a coke and Ricardo ordered another cup of coffee.

"What's business like here in the dry season, Inez?"

"Busy. Many gringos come here."

"I don't mean to pry, Inez, but I'm curious. A beautiful girl like you—the gringos must stand in line to talk to you."

She laughed at his obvious flattery.

"There is much competition in the dry season. Many girls work here. Many girls to choose from."

"I see. How long have you worked here?"

"About three years. Before that I worked a small casino in Colón, but the management there treated us mean."

"How so?"

"That casino wasn't a hotel like this place. Each girl had to rent a tiny room in the back of the casino where we took our clients. If we didn't make enough money to pay our rent each night, the casino boss would yell at us and sometimes hit us. Nobody liked working there. Some of the girls were not good people. They would steal money from clients and even from the other girls. I got robbed twice when I worked there."

"Oh dear... Do you like working here?"

She shrugged her shoulders, looked down for a minute, then said,

"It's better than most places. I am safe here, and I don't have to pay to work here, but the hotel still takes a percentage of what I make."

Ricardo hadn't known that the hotel actually profited directly from the prostitutes.

"How do they do that?"

"I pay forty percent of each client to the casino manager."

"How do they know how many clients you see?"

"Oh, the casino manager watches us like a hawk. He knows exactly how busy each girl is."

She gave an almost imperceptible movement with her head. Ricardo looked over towards the cashier area and saw a short fat man standing there, arms folded, his eyes scanning the casino bar. Ricardo had noticed him standing there when he first walked in but hadn't thought anything about it.

"Really, I had no idea they did that. Why don't you work somewhere else?"

"It's really no different anywhere else. Someone always wants to make money off a girl's body. Only the girls who open up their own shops really make money. But even they do it by charging the girls who work for them. In fact, some of the worst managers to work for are putas." She used the word "puta" for "whore" to indicate her contempt.

Ricardo felt depressed hearing all this. It was obvious from listening to Inez that this was the only type of work she had ever done.

"I'm sorry, Inez. That sounds rough."

Inez smiled. "Well, it's a living. I need to support myself and my children."

Ricardo always disliked it when prostitutes brought up the subject of their children. Most, if not all, of the Central American prostitutes he had ever met, being Catholic and poor, had one or two children, often before they were even twenty years old. He understood that many women want babies, that most women had babies, but to him, the image of babies fractured the image he liked to maintain in his mind of the young free-spirited sexy women who chose the sex trade because they liked sex and the money was good. He wanted to view his prostitutes the same way he viewed his gay partners—as sexual creatures freely choosing their lifestyles.

But now Inez had mentioned her children, and Ricardo felt impelled to ask their names and their ages. He nodded politely as she told him.

He glanced around the bar. A group of prostitutes was standing together in the corner, smoking cigarettes and looking bored. Across the bar two prostitutes were chatting up a pair of fat gray-haired gringos. The gringos were talking and laughing, and the girls were nodding their heads and smiling back, but to Ricardo their smiles seemed fake. Ricardo was fast losing interest in being with a prostitute tonight. He looked back at the other prostitutes standing in the corner. They were, like Inez, attractive, but they just didn't strike a chord in him.

Ricardo had been with so many prostitutes in his life, in Spain, in France, in Canada, and in Central America. Most of the time, it was a good-to-great experience, but sometimes, like tonight, he only felt sad, depressed, like the whole thing was a pointless exercise in thrusting and ejaculating. The problem was that he didn't know what else to do when he got horny and wanted human company. It was either the brothels or the bathhouses. His best times at the brothels had been when he actually cared about the prostitute. Haley in the St. Catherines brothel had been his favorite prostitute. He would always ask for her because she remembered his stories. She seemed to care for him, at least enough to take care of him sexually and also emotionally.

Sometimes he would meet a new prostitute and there would be that instantaneous click where, despite the business transaction, they shared a sense of humor or a common viewpoint. In those situations, Ricardo always had the impression that if they weren't engaged in the buying and selling of sex, they might actually be good friends.

But Ricardo was not clicking with Inez tonight. He liked her, but it was with a certain pity. Ricardo wondered if he would ever find another prostitute like Haley or another girlfriend like Eve.

He turned back to Inez.

"And how much do you charge?"

"A hundred."

Ricardo signaled the bartender for his tab. He took out his wallet and carefully palmed a hundred dollar bill he kept folded in the side pocket of his wallet for emergencies.

He paid the eight dollar bar tab and then said to Inez, "Listen, I've enjoyed talking to you. You seem like a nice girl." He reached out his hand to shake her hand. In his hand was the hundred dollar bill. "I'm not going to hire you tonight because I'm not in the mood for sex. But I want you to have at least one customer where you don't have to pay the casino manager. Don't look down. Just take what is in my hand and go to the bathroom to look at it. I don't want anyone to see."

She shook his hand and took the folded bill.

"Buenos tardes, Inez." he said. "Perhaps I will see you some other time when I'm in the mood."

"Buenos tardes, Ricardo. Gracias, muchas gracias. Vaya con Dios."

Ricardo walked out of the casino and smiled and nodded at the casino manager as he walked by him. The casino manager just looked away.

Outside, rain was falling. Ricardo hailed a cab and asked the driver to take him to the Ralma Hotel. He would check in there and then go to the bathhouse. No one took a commission off anyone there.

Chapter 20: Gran Calle

After checking into the Ralma, Ricardo headed down the block to the Gran Calle bathhouse. He had been there many times before, but always had trouble finding the door. Although it was the best-known bathhouse in San José de David, there was no sign, just a small number on the door. If you didn't know what number to look for, you'd walk right past it. Ricardo pushed open the iron door and walked up a few steps. A second door buzzed open as he approached, and he went in and walked up to the cashier. The entrance fee was nine dollars, up a dollar from the last time he had been there. He paid it and was buzzed through another door.

Panameño bathhouses were different from US bathhouses. In the Panamá gay world, there was much more emphasis on anonymity. Whereas a US bathhouse might have one darkroom section, a Panameño bathhouse was all one big darkroom, except for the pool area. That was another difference. Panameño bathhouses always had a small swimming pool and a large hot tub, both of which were well lit, but the sauna and all the hallways and all the rooms were in dark to semi-dark obscurity. All sex happened in the dark. Ricardo always chalked it up to the Latino Catholic guilt about gayness and sex. While gay diversity was tolerated in Central America as a concept, gay individuals still preferred their handjobs, blowjobs, and fucking in the dark.

In the US bathhouses, Ricardo could rent a room with a bed and a large monitor TV with ten to fifteen different channels of porn. But at the Gran Calle bathhouse, as with most Panameño bathhouses, you could only get a locker. There were plenty of rooms available, and they all had beds, but they were open for anyone to use. There was only a very dim light in each room, and a roll of toilet paper for wiping off any cum. Each room had a door you could close, but not lock.

As with most Panameño bathhouses, the Gran Calle provided a padlock and key for the locker, a towel, a small cotton sheet the size of a towel, and a pair of rubber sandals to wear. Ricardo went to his locker, stripped down, placed his clothes, valuables, and the towel inside the locker, secured the lock, wrapped the sheet around him, and headed off to the showers.

After showering, he went into the sauna. Unlike US bathhouses, where the saunas were just a large room, the Panameño saunas were part of the dark maze, except with steam. Ricardo felt his way along the wet tile walls, twisting and turning in the total darkness. Eventually, he found himself in a room where there were two other men. First he heard them, and then, as he inched his way towards the grunting, he felt them. The first man was facing him. Ricardo felt the man reach over and find Ricardo's cock. Ricardo reached out, touched the man's chest, ran his hand down past the man's nipples, and down to the man's cock. It was a tiny cock, but erect. Ricardo always felt sorry for men with tiny cocks. No matter what anyone said, size mattered. Still, Ricardo stroked it and the man stroked Ricardo's cock. Ricardo then reached around to feel the other man. Feeling down the second man's chest toward his pelvis, Ricardo realized that the second man was fucking the first man. Ricardo rubbed the second man's nipples and played with the first man's balls, but then left them to their fucking and felt his way out of that room, inching along the wall.

The next room had a little light, and Ricardo found a middle-aged man there, standing against a wall. Ricardo went up, reached up under the man's sheet and found his cock. This man had a normal size cock. The man reached down and rubbed Ricardo's cock. They stood there silently in the semi-darkness, masturbating each other while the steam hissed around them. Both Ricardo and the man were pretty hard. The man started kissing Ricardo's neck. Both of them hugged each other's back and ass with their free hand. Ricardo wondered if the man would cum on Ricardo's leg.

Ricardo hoped that he would.

Neither man came though. After a few minutes, Ricardo released his hug, and moved away in the darkness.

These types of brief sexual encounters went on for an hour or so between Ricardo and various other shadowy figures in the dark mazes or in the steam room. Whenever he got overheated by the steam, Ricardo would rinse off in one of the many showers in the bathhouse.

Finally, he went and sat in the large hot tub. There was no one in the pool or the hot tub. Everyone else was working the darkness. Ricardo sat alone in the hot tub, his naked body relaxing in the bubbling water.

The hot tub was situated under a skylight. Ricardo could hear the rain hitting the skylight. He shifted to a part of the hot tub ledge so that the water jet could hit the small of his back. As much as he was enjoying the bathhouse, he felt that same way he had felt at the Parasille—a feeling of wanting to be degenerate but not feeling sexy. It was a weird kind of horniness—if some dominate prostitute had approached him at the Parasille or some dominate man had grabbed him in the steam room, he probably would have submitted, but as it was, he just didn't feel like doing much more.

He consoled himself with the thought: "Well at least I've been to a brothel and a bathhouse in one afternoon. That's still pretty good, even if I didn't cum."

He climbed out of the hot tub, found his way back to the locker room, got dressed, left the bathhouse, and walked back to the hotel.

The hotel had a small bar, consisting of five barstools at the bar. Ricardo was the only one there. He sat down, ordered a drink, and reflected on the day and on his life.

He loved women and he loved men, which is to say, he loved women's bodies, and he loved men's bodies. Depending on the personalities involved, he loved some women and some men. Once the personality issues arose, the percentage of people he cared to spend time with dropped rapidly. Maybe that is what had killed it with Inez. Too much of her personality—her life—had entered the picture. All the information about her children and her getting beaten at the last job, and her having to pay a commission to the Parasille—it was too much information. He knew that if he had met her at his office or in a class somewhere, without any of the sex trade stuff, he probably wouldn't be interested in her. Heck, he wasn't that attracted to her when they met at the bar, but if she hadn't have told him so much about herself, he might have fucked her. It's odd how the most intimate of acts is ruined by actually knowing intimate information about the other person.

Ricardo wondered if this would be what his life would be like as a pensionado in Panamá: just brothels and bathhouses. Sex was certainly more available than in the states, and much cheaper, but that didn't make it any better. He thought back to how Eve would make love to him. Maybe it was because she was so carnal <u>and</u> he cared for her that made the sex so good. She would suck his cock, squeeze his balls, and run a finger up his ass. As he got closer to cumming, she would grasp his cock tight with her left hand, taking him deep into her mouth while squeezing and twisting his balls with her right hand. He loved how much she loved him cumming in her mouth. She never flinched. And he loved how she would take his last drop, raise her head to his, kiss him on the lips, pry open his mouth with her tongue, and force all of his cum back into his mouth, rolling it around his mouth with her tongue. *That* was good sex. Afterwards he could only lie there, arms extended, unable to move on the bed, while she laughed, got up to get a towel from the bathroom to wipe all the extra cum off his face and her face.

Ricardo wanted that kind of experience with every prostitute and every gay man he had sex with, but he never got that. He knew in his heart of hearts he never could have that deep of an experience with a stranger. But sexual relationships like Eve were hard to come by, and as he got older, almost impossible to come by, so he just assumed he would have to settle for prostitutes and bathhouses.

Actually, if he was totally honest with himself, he had to admit that one of his main fantasies about moving to

Panamá and living in some small town, besides writing, was that he would also meet some young Panameña woman who, for financial security, would become his girlfriend, someone he could see two to three times a week, someone he could teach Eve's tricks to, someone who would act like she loved him, as long as he paid her, and someone who he could act like he loved, as long as she didn't tell him too much about herself. Ricardo wondered if this was even possible.

The bartender brought Ricardo another drink without being asked. Ricardo wondered how many other pensionados the bartender had watched crash and burn in this bar. Ricardo didn't want to crash and burn. He just wanted time to write, have easy sex, and if possible, find some kind of love.

Chapter 21: Antón

Ricardo had only a few days left in his vacation. He sat in a small café in the town of Antón, drinking coffee. The day after tomorrow a bus would take him back to Panamá City, and the next day he would fly home. He took stock of what he had accomplished during his stay. He had met with lawyers, officially submitted his application for pensionado status, opened a bank account in a Panameño bank, and consulted with the US Embassy which had assured him they would start making his Social Security deposits directly into his Panameño account when the payments began in January. They also promised to give him an official letter in January addressed to the Panamanian Migration Department, stating how his Social Security payments were being made. That official letter was the last document Ricardo would need to file in order to receive his pensionado card. Once he received his card, he could join the country's health care program and have good health care for about sixty dollars a month.

He had also traveled around the country a lot on this trip, visiting Santiago, Chitré, Penonome, Colón, La Chorrera, and Antón. La Chorrera was still his favorite city. It was big enough to support many brothels and a decent bathhouse, but still had some smaller gringo-free neighborhoods where he could rent a furnished apartment for three hundred dollars a month. Plus, it was an easy bus ride to Panamá City where there were even more brothels, casinos, massage parlors, and bathhouses.

Ricardo planned to return to La Chorrera in January and make a choice of apartments. He had found a hostel that agreed to rent him a room for the month of January.

That should give him enough time to find an apartment. There were some negative moments too: times when he felt depressed; times when he doubted the rationality of his thinking; times when he worried about money; and of course, the constant sense of being alone. But all in all, considering all he had accomplished in the rainy season, it had been a successful trip.

Ricardo had sent an email to Kit, explaining that he was in Panamá for "business purposes" but would stop by the restaurant when he returned. He had gotten a response back from her, thanking him again for his help and saying how much she was looking forward to seeing him when he returned. He considered her email one of those double-edged swords: on one hand, it indicated her continual interest in him and thus, the possibility of sex with her. But on the other hand, it once again hinted how needy she was. But Ricardo had decided that he would see her again, explain his plans for moving, observe her reaction, and let things unfold. Who knows, it might be a perfect three-month affair. With two felony convictions, she couldn't get a passport, at least not until she had those convictions expunged, so that precluded her from following him to Panamá. And besides, if she was more interested in someone who was going to stick around and therefore didn't want a short affair with him, there was always the possibility of Phillipe. Ricardo liked to keep his options open.

Ricardo's thoughts once again turned to his aloneness, or rather, to the quality of being alone. Most people, Ricardo had observed, would do anything rather than experience their aloneness. And technology happily provided endless escapes: everyone seemed to have tiny buds stuck in their ears, all tuned to iTunes, or they were streaming videos on demand, or getting constant fun facts and news feeds from Facebook. If they left the house without their cell phone, they panicked and had to quickly drive home. It was all one huge electronic umbilical cord, creating the illusion of connectedness. Nobody wanted to feel their aloneness.

But Ricardo felt his. He had always felt it. It was not a

feeling of loneliness. Rather, it was a feeling of separateness, of being outside, detached from others.

He didn't think he was psychologically impaired. He could talk with other people; he could empathize; he could feel; he could love; but he also felt the limitation of these actions, the frontier of self that ended just short of where the other person began. All his life he felt like he was staying in a hotel room by himself while just across the hall there was a party going on, and he could hear the sounds of women laughing and men talking, and the clinking of ice in glasses. When he was younger, he felt so lonely that he wanted desperately to go across the hall and join the party, but as he grew older and gained experience with other people, he came to understand that there was no party. Everyone was in their own room by themselves listening to what they thought was a party happening just across the hall.

At some point years ago, Ricardo had come to accept his aloneness, his separateness from others, and by accepting his aloneness, he also came to accept his penchant for sex of any kind, hetero or homosexual, groups, bondage, whatever. He accepted his affinity for prostitutes, brothels, and bathhouses. He accepted the self that he was, a self who he knew most others would condemn, a self that did things that even he did not approve of. He would, for example, as he was walking down a street, look at women and silently decide which ones he would fuck. "I would fuck her, and her... but not her... not her... not her... her... yes her." It was a diversion which he knew stereotyped women according to their bodies and age. It was cruel and petty, but he accepted that he did this because it was true. He would fuck this one but not that one. He did judge on appearance despite how petty that was. He accepted his pettiness, his selfishness, his preoccupation with sex, his interest in things degenerate. It was who he was, and pretty much who he thought everyone was, if they would only admit it. But they wouldn't, and that only added to the separateness.

Ricardo signaled the waitress for a refill of his coffee. He took out his notebook and reread what he had written the night before. He was working on a concept for a short story based on the myth of Hephaestus, the Greek god who created the first woman (Pandora) as a gift for Epimetheus, the brother of Prometheus. Hephaestus, the myth goes, deliberated on whether to give women any male parts or not. Ricardo was trying to recreate the thought process that Hephaestus must have gone through in making that decision. Except that this short story was taking place inside the head of an eighteen year old boy who was contemplating a sex change operation in order to please his male lover who was bi. The eighteen year old was so in love with his boyfriend that, even though the eighteen year old wasn't trans, he wants to undergo surgery to become the perfect sex object of desire for his boyfriend—he wants to become both male and female. Ricardo had a lot of the development down, but he didn't have a final plot line yet. Does the boyfriend leave the eighteen year old after the surgery? Do the parents or the courts try to stop the surgery?

The waitress refilled Ricardo's coffee while he made more notes in his notebook. "Why do we so automatically try and change ourselves for our loved one?" he wrote. "Why do we feel we're never enough until we are loved more by the other than we love the other ourselves? Do we do what we do for the loved one because we love them or because we seek to enhance our own status in their eyes?"

The plot line where the male lover leaves the eighteen year old after the surgery made the most sense to Ricardo. It had an O. Henry quality about it, in a twisted way.

Ricardo sat in the café and wrote for the next two hours.

Chapter 22: The Palm Reader

The next day, Ricardo went to the fortune teller. The city of Antón was known for its fortune tellers, which would normally suggest a systemic tourist scam, except that some of the fortune tellers in Antón were actually quite good. Ricardo was at his favorite one, a palm reader named Alma. He put his coins on the table and held up his hands for her to see.

Alma studied his palms for a while.

"Wow," she said in Spanish, "big stuff that just happened again, and then another and another. Much emotional stuff too. How long has it been since I've seen you?"

"Maybe a year or so."

"Well, much change. No respite." She paused again, as if she was trying to think of how to say something.

"Um... can I ask you a question? Since you were last here, do you have any... any shame about something? Something like, you didn't use your skills when you needed to? It looks like something happened that was emotionally difficult, very emotionally difficult, and then somehow you have a little residual... hmm... the sense I see is shame."

"I don't know about that..." Ricardo said. He thought back over the past year, thought about his decision to move to Panamá. "Well, I am making plans to move here," he said.

"This isn't a travel thing. It's an emotional thing, an interaction... Was it with family, at work, with relatives? It looks like a failure of some kind, that somehow, somewhere, that you decided, 'I failed—I didn't do that well and now I have to make sure I don't fail again.' It's sort of like a shame, like you're keeping an eye on yourself, you're telling yourself... you're telling yourself, 'I'm watching you now'. But it's in response to not doing the right thing, to having failed at some point. You have this part going on now that says 'I can't make a mistake again' but it comes from this first part that says 'I made a mistake'. So it means that now as you take another step, and you look all around again and think 'Am I doing the right thing?' and then you do another action, and you think again 'Am I doing the right thing?' and it causes anxiousness, it causes mental whiplash, and it causes regret, because you think, 'Oh I could have done the right thing, but I didn't' That's what you have in your hand right now."

Later, while eating dinner in a small restaurant, Ricardo thought about what Alma said. He knew that when he was listening to her, when she was in front of him, what she said made sense. It felt right. But now, when he tried to analyze it, it seemed to slip through his fingers. What was the failure she referred to? Was it Eve? Was it the two failed marriages? His drinking? Was it quitting a career? Was it only being able to sell one or two short stories a year? Was it past or future? Was it his whole life?

Chapter 23: Air flight

The less said about returning to the states, the better. Ricardo always found the return flight back to the states to be an exhausting and humiliating experience. Airplanes were like cattle cars, and Customs was always a reminder of who's in charge.

As much as possible, Ricardo would try and put himself into a hypnotic state when he flew home, to sleep as much as possible, and if sleep wouldn't come, to create a dreamlike state where real life problem-solving was not allowed.

Ricardo would lean his seat back the allowed three inches and think of various things to induce this hypnotic state. He would think of women's breasts, especially the nipples, the variety of nipples, some light and small, some dark and long. He would think of nipples he had sucked, when he had sucked them, and whose they were. He would put names to each set of breasts and categorize which breasts he liked and why. Then he would do the same with women's pussies: remember them, analyze them, evaluate which ones he liked and why. He would pull up each memory as if from a fresh cold water well, and then savor it, reliving it, and enjoying it once more. For some reason he would always start with Maria, a lover from decades ago, whose pussy always tasted like avocados with its thick lips and sweet juice. He had never been with any other woman whose pussy tasted of avocado. In fact, he had noticed that many women's pussies tasted unique. After thinking about Maria, he would next remember Becky, whose pussy had these soft fleshy mounds on either side, mounds that when he rubbed his fingers up and down them as he licked her clit, well, it would drive her wild. Her taste was not particularly distinctive, but the sensitivity of both sides of her pussy was. Then there was Debra with her red coarse barbwire pubic hair. What he loved about her was that when he fucked her, she would breathlessly call his name over and over with each of his thrusts inside her. He truly had loved her, and the sex was good.

And that's how Ricardo would induce this hypnagogic state: by reliving memories of various sexual encounters. When he had exhausted the female memories, he would draw up the memories of men, the memories of bathhouses, the cocks, especially the big cocks, the cumming, especially the best cumming where long white ropes of cum shot out of his cock or another's cock.

And that's how Ricardo traveled by airplane, appearing to any other passenger as simply someone reclining in his seat with his eyes closed, content with the world.

The only thing different about this flight back to the states was that Ricardo was bothered by thoughts of Kit. She kept entering into his dream state, which was really not allowed because he had never fucked her. But he kept imagining what she would be like, how her breasts would be, whether she shaved her pussy or not. He hoped that she didn't because she had such thick wavy hair on her head, and he hoped she would be equally hairy down below. Ricardo had always preferred great masses of public hair. To him, the more pubic hair the woman had, the greater her femininity. Unfortunately, more and more, women shaved their pussies bald. To Ricardo, it made them appear like little girls, de-feminized. Maybe women thought that shaving their public hair made them more appealable to men, but when a man and a woman get to the point where they've taking off each other's clothes and are lying in bed, there is no more advertising necessary.

Maybe that's why he kept thinking about Kit—because he wanted to find out about her pussy, about how she kissed, about whether she used her tongue, and about whether she liked being eaten out. When it came to sex, curiosity and anticipation were irresistible forces.

Ricardo knew he would contact Kit when he got back to the states. He would first stop by the restaurant after the usual lunch crowd had gone, chat with her, and see if she was excited to see him. Then he would ask her out to dinner, and during dinner, at the appropriate time, tell her about his plans to move to Panamá. He would behave like a gentleman all during dinner but would make plans with her for a second date. That would give her time to digest his short-term availability. Then, if she was receptive during the second date, he would try and get her into bed.

However, he also had an escape plan. He would also question her gently about the "early bad experiences with men" that she had mentioned weeks ago. He needed to find out if his intuition about her being sexually molested as a child was true, or whether he was totally off base. If it was true, and if she was as emotionally damaged as such abuse usually, if not always, induces, then he would not try to bed her. A seduction in the face of such knowledge would only do more damage. Ricardo might be a sexual enthusiast, but he was not evil. He would not deliberately do damage. Besides, there was always Phillipe.

Ricardo shifted his position and continued to dream.

Chapter 24: Roots

Ricardo got back to Hamburg late Friday night. After taking the weekend to unpack and decompress, Ricardo returned to work the following Monday. Client folders were stacked on his desk, his computer was full of emails, and his secretary handed him a number of pleadings for his signature. Ricardo fell into the law office rhythm of constant work and billable hours as if he hadn't been gone at all.

At about 2:oo, he walked over to Roots, ostensibly for a late lunch, but in reality to see Kit. She looked great. However, the restaurant was unusually full, and she appeared to be the only waitress there, dashing from table to table. Ricardo found the only empty table and was about to sit down, when Kit saw him. She came quickly up to him and gave him a big hug.

"You're back!" she exclaimed.

"Yes, just got back a few days ago. How are you, Kit?"

"I'm great, just really swamped because Julie called in sick, so I have to cover the whole shift myself. How was your trip? Do you know what you want for lunch?"

"The trip was great, and I'll have the chicken caesar and iced tea."

"I want to hear all about it." she said, "One chicken caesar and one iced tea," and she dashed off.

A few minutes later when she reappeared with Ricardo's iced tea, he said, "I'll try and stop by when it's less crowded."

"Oh, please do, Ricardo, I'd love to hear all about your trip," and she was gone again.

Well, Ricardo thought, at least she was glad to see me. He decided he would try returning to the restaurant the following Thursday night, before the dinner crowd, and hope that he could catch her with time to chat. That way he could ask her if she wanted to get together at some point that weekend.

That evening, after work, Ricardo composed a long email to her, full of chatty info about his trip, and with just enough questions about how her to indicate he was still interested in her. At the end of the email, he decided to go ahead and ask her if she wanted to get together during the coming weekend. He ended the email with the vague but positive "just let me know".

However, he did not hear back from her. The following Thursday, he did go to Roots after work. The place was quiet. He grabbed a corner table. Kit was there, but she hadn't seen him yet. When she walked by his table, he said. "Hello Kit" at which point she turned, almost startled, and saw him.

"Oh, hello Ricardo. I didn't see you there. Here you go," and she handed him a menu from the stack she kept in the front pocket of her waitress apron.

"Did you get the email I sent you?" Ricardo asked.

"Yes, yes, I did," she answered. "I haven't had a chance to answer it yet, but I will."

She looked as if she was about to walk back to the kitchen.

"Ok, no hurry," Ricardo said. "How have you been?"

"Oh, I had to go to the doctor today."

Ricardo was a little taken back by this response.

"Oh, is everything ok?"

"Well, we'll see," and then she did turn and walk back to the kitchen.

Kit's mood and demeanor seemed totally different than Monday at lunch. She seemed distracted, almost confused. She returned with a glass of water and silverware for him.

After she took his dinner order, he asked her again. "I hope everything is alright," he said.

"Well, we'll know in a couple of months," she said, and left to place his order with the cook.

More people started arriving for dinner. Kit would

come out of the kitchen to attend to them but quickly return to the kitchen. She clearly did not want to visit with Ricardo, or with anyone.

Ricardo did not understand it, but he did what he always did in those situations: he simply let it alone. He would return to his routine, to his work, to his apartment, to his writing, and let time roll by. Maybe she was just having a bad day and would email him later that week. Maybe he would let several weeks go by before visiting Roots again. He would give the situation a little time and space. Ricardo knew how to float.

Chapter 25: The Cost of Invisibility

It was in the early in the morning on a Saturday, somewhere between three and four a.m. Ricardo had woken up to pee, and had just returned to bed. Just as he was falling back to sleep, a phrase started forming in his brain. "When Eddie finally cracked the secret of invisibility..." Ricardo knew Eddie was the character from his short story "Scarlet's" so he knew that this line about invisibility was some kind of a short story. He couldn't use the name Eddie again, so he reformed the sentence, "When Dr. Muret Von Hartz finally cracked the secret of invisibility, he couldn't believe it was so simple." Odd name, Muret, Ricardo thought. He wondered what he meant. He wondered if he should get up and start writing. It was so early, and the bed was so warm. However, he knew if he didn't write something down, it would be gone by morning.

He reached over to his night stand, turned on the light, and fumbled until he found his small notebook and a pen. He wrote down the sentence about Muret Von Hartz and the secret of invisibility, then put the notebook back, turned off the light and fell back to sleep.

The next morning, he got up around nine, made a pot of coffee, looked at the sentence he had written in his notebook, turned on his computer, and started writing. The following words flowed out of him...

When Dr. Muret Von Hartz finally cracked the secret of invisibility, he couldn't believe it was so simple. Complicated to achieve, but simple in theory. He had been working for years at Enadone Corporation, on a project to develop adaptable camouflage for military use. His team had been attempting to synthesize chromatophores from cuttlefish, to try and understand how cuttlefish were able to instantaneously change their skin to match any background. The concept that Enadone had pitched to the military—and that the military paid Enadone millions for—was that that it would be possible to create clothing that could always adapt ("self-camouflage" was the term Enadone used) to any surrounding. The idea was that every soldier would get the same uniform, but that the material on the uniform would always shift color and pattern to blend in with the background, whether it was desert sand brown, jungle dark green, or grassland green/grey patterns. The value to the military would be enormous, as would the profits for Enadone.

Muret was part of the team that had determined that the trick was in the electrical pulses that the cuttlefish nervous system sent to the chromatophores—a certain burst and voltage would create one color; a different burst and voltage would create another color; a third burst would alter the pattern. The pressure at work was intense, but the team had made significant progress and had even developed a prototype called Veneer, a cloth impregnated with synthetic chromatophores.

But Muret's real interest lay in a phenomenon of cuttlefish that so far no other researcher had noticed. Everyone could see how a cuttlefish could camouflage itself to blend into a reef, sand, seaweed, or blue water, and everyone had seen the cuttlefish go into a shocking fireworks display of color and light to confuse a predator, but Muret had noticed something else in his long hours of watching cuttlefish videos taken at sea. He noticed that some predators acted like they didn't even see the cuttlefish even when the cuttlefish was not camouflaging itself. He had seen film footage of sharks, seals, and dolphins—the natural predators of cuttlefish—swim right by a clearly visible cuttlefish when it was not camouflaged. Most people, Muret believed, simply assumed that the *predator wasn't hungry, but Muret had seen rare footage of that same predator going after other fish right after passing by the easy target of the cuttlefish. Without telling his colleagues what he was doing, he set up some experiments in the huge tank they kept in the lab, where he would put small hungry sharks in the tank with young cuttlefish. The tank had special electrical receptors throughout the tank and on all sides of the glass, to measure any electrical bursts, no matter how minute, that the cuttlefish would make. Most of the cuttlefish would employ their usual tactics: hiding, camouflage, ink, or dazzling lightshow followed by flight. Most of the time their efforts were initially successful, but within the small confines of the tank, eventually the predator would find them and eat them. However, Muret observed that the ones that escaped the predators in more than three different attacks developed a new strategy. It was as if the cuttlefish figured out that they couldn't keep using the same basic tactics in an enclosed tank. The next time Muret released the predators, these few survivors would not camouflage themselves. Rather, they would stay the same dark brown color but only move very slowly. The electrical receptors in the tank told Muret that whatever was going on indicated that the cuttlefish used an immense electrical burst when the predator first appeared. Muret concluded that some type of chromatophore was being switched on, but he couldn't figure out what the change was. The cuttlefish looked the same, in color and in pattern.*

He decided to switch predators to see if that made any difference with these surviving cuttlefish. Instead of young sharks, he used young dolphins. Again, he saw the same behavior: the cuttlefish would try the usual techniques of camouflage, but those cuttlefish that survived three or more attacks would switch to this new defense. And like the sharks, the dolphins would swim right past the cuttlefish as if they didn't see them. But what the tank electrical receptors were indicating was that the intense electrical burst that the surviving cuttlefish were using this time was slightly different.

Muret's breakthrough came when he then introduced

the young sharks back into the tank with the dolphins. The dolphins continued to ignore the cuttlefish, but the sharks went right to them and ate them. And these were the same sharks that the day before acted as if they couldn't see the cuttlefish. As the sharks engaged in a feeding frenzy, the electrical receptors in the tank indicated that some of the cuttlefish were switching back to the same electric burst signals they had used the day before with the sharks. That's when the dolphins started attacking the cuttlefish as well.

It took Muret a couple of days of thinking to come up with his theory of invisibility. He poured over the read-outs of the cuttlefish's electrical bursts when predators were introduced into the tank. He finally theorized that the cuttlefish, once they realized that their usual methods of camouflage wouldn't work in an enclosed tank, switched from simple camouflage to invisibility. Seeing an object depends half on the light that is reflected by the object but half on the receptors in the eyes of the animal viewing the object. The cuttlefish, Muret reasoned, must be altering their chromatophores to emit only a wavelength of light that the predator could not see, while absorbing any reflected light, in essence, making them invisible to the predator. But because that wavelength was different for sharks versus dolphins, the cuttlefish could only be invisible to one type of predator at a time. That was why, Muret realized, the sharks could eat what the dolphins couldn't see.

This change in wavelength had another curious feature: While a simple change in cuttlefish color required a low, but steady, electrical current throughout the cuttlefish's skin, the change to invisibility required a huge single burst of electrical energy, almost all of the available energy the cuttlefish had. But it was only a single burst, like an on-off switch, rather than a steady stream. That explained why the cuttlefish moved so slowly after turning invisible—it had used up all of its energy and was exhausted. And apparently, the effect on the chromatophores wore off after approximately three hours, because Muret noticed that if he did not removed the predators from the tank, that three hours later, the predators would suddenly start feeding on the cuttlefish.

Thus, Muret concluded, that cuttlefish had evolved, over eons, a last resort to predators: that when cornered by a predator with no escape, after all the usual camouflage tactics failed, the cuttlefish could, for certain predator species, alter its chromatophores to appear invisible to the predator. But this tactic came at a huge cost to the cuttlefish, because it wouldn't have any energy left to escape. It had to rely on being invisible to survive the threat. Because this last resort tactic was used so rarely in nature, no other researcher had figured it out.

At first, Muret thought about presenting his findings to his team and to his managers, but he ultimately decided not to. He had just recently come out on the losing end of the battle on the camouflage Veneer cloth project. The polyester material of Veneer was imbedded with the synthetic chromatophores, but it required a low electrical current to activate it. Everyone on the team agreed with using lithium batteries but couldn't agree on the delivery system for the electric current. It was clear that a conductor had to be woven throughout the cloth, but the political battle was over what type of conductor material. Muret was the only one arguing for a type of nano-silver thread called Silverment because of its superior conductivity. However; Silverment was expensive. The rest of the team was split between the less expensive copper and even cheaper aluminum. Muret preferred Silverment because he thought the nano-threads were similar in resistance to the cuttlefish nervous system and bore other similarities in molecular structure to the way the nerve patterns were structured in the cuttlefish. He could have compromised on copper because it had good conductivity, though not as good as Silverment. But he was adamantly opposed to aluminum threads because of their tendency to deform over time. Aluminum also forms resistant oxides at connection points, which can cause them to fail. He also feared that the electrical charges delivered through aluminum conductors would cause the chromatophores to deteriorate. He foresaw an unacceptable product failure rate, which he felt would put soldiers' lives in danger. He and his team-leader Michael Herrell and especially the division boss, Robert Ferris, had huge arguments about this. He remembered one big blow-up where Muret had accused them of premeditated negligence and warned them that if soldiers died, the blood would be on their hands. Muret had stormed out of that meeting. Nonetheless, the management team eventually went with aluminum thread because of the huge cost saving. The decision left Muret bitter about Enadone's true mission. Muret understood that the Veneer uniforms had to be inexpensive to manufacture, and he knew that aluminum treads would do well in prototypes and would do well in initial combat tests. But he thought it was unconscionable to sell the military a product that he knew would ultimately fail at the most critical time, in the middle of combat after six to eight months, when the soldier turned it on because he needed it most. He had come close to quitting the team over this dispute, but at that point he had just started his tests on invisibility and wanted to stay and continue them. So, he shut up and kept to himself, coming to work each day to work on the Veneer prototype, but staying after hours to work on his cuttlefish experiments.

During the early days of developing the Veneer cloth, when the team was still experimenting with different types of conductors, they had about twenty yards of Veneer woven with the Silverment threads. When management had abandoned Silverment, Muret had expropriated the Veneer cloth with Silverment from the supply area. He cut small pieces of material and sewed small bags with it. He then subjected the bags to a single burst of electric current that replicated the exact voltage and amplitude that the tank's electrical receptors had said the cuttlefish were using when sharks were in the tank. Then, Muret placed bait fish in the bags and placed the bags in the tank with hungry sharks. The sharks appeared confused, because even though they might be able to smell the bait fish, they swam right by it as if they couldn't see it. As Muret predicted, after about three hours, the sharks turned on the bags, tore them open and ate the fish.

It was then Muret knew he was on the verge of a fantastic discovery. He knew that theoretically he was right, but the problem was a mathematical one. If he could figure out the exact type of electric burst to give the Veneer cloth that would cause the chromatophores to emit only a light frequency that the human eye could not see, he could construct a uniform that would almost render a soldier invisible. Not quite invisible, but close. Muret understood that perception is more than just eyesight. The human brain is wired to detect differences, like light and shadow, or foreground and background, outline and interior, and especially movement of something against a still background. That was one of the reasons the cuttlefish's torpidity when it was invisible helped it to stay invisible. Predator brains, including human brains, fill in detail. Even if the predator can't see an object, as long as the background doesn't change rapidly because of a rapid foreground movement, the brain will see only background as it scans a scene. However, the first step was a daunting one. Muret had to figure out what exact pattern of electrical burst would render the Veneer invisible to the human eye. He had no cuttlefish patterns to duplicate—he would have to use trial and error.

Muret took all the Silverment cloth and all his notes home. For months, at home every night after work, Muret conducted experiments, meticulously writing down a systematic progression of different voltage/current/ amplitude combinations. He had a small workbench in his living room where a four-inch square piece of Silverment Veneer was spread out and tacked to the bench. It was hooked to a small generator that Muret had constructed from parts expropriated from work, a device where he could precisely alter each electrical variable, as he methodically worked through the millions of combinations. It wasn't until the fourth month *of experiments when it happened: a second after the electric burst hit the Veneer, the cloth simply disappeared. Muret blinked and looked again. Because he knew exactly where the cloth was on the bench because of the tacks, he could squint and force himself to see it, but if he turned away and casually looked over at the bench, he simply didn't see it. If he wasn't looking for it, his brain just filled in the background wood of the bench in what his eyes "saw". The cloth was, in essence, invisible.*

Muret called in sick the next day. He stayed home and thought about what his discovery meant. He could construct a head to toe uniform of Veneer and basically become invisible. What were the possibilities of such an invention? Clearly, there were military applications. He had already coined a name for his product: "Ninja". He envisioned an army of assassins, able to walk right past police and guards to do their dirty work. Obviously, it could be used for surveillance purposes too, a way to surreptitiously watch a crowd, or spy on political enemies. But Muret had grown tired of thinking only in terms of military applications, which always ultimately involved death. Were there any positive uses for this material? Could reporters use it to promote more transparency in government? To report on what really goes on behind closed door when politicians wheel and deal? Or to investigate polluters on land sites they couldn't normally get access to? Maybe the police could use it to investigate organized crime, mafia meetings, human trafficking, or drug cartels? Muret spent the day writing down ideas. Unfortunately, no matter the best intentions, every idea involved some type of spying or invasion, or some activity that would be considered a crime if the person was caught. The end of the day found Muret depressed. He had worked for so many months on this project but had never actually wondered what he would do if he actually invented it.

The next day Muret returned to work. There was a note on his desk, from Robert Ferris, the division chief, to come and see him immediately. Muret felt a knot in his stomach.

Had they noticed the missing Silverment? Was he in trouble?

He made his way over to the other building where Robert Ferris' office was. The secretary ushered him in. His team leader Michael Herrell was also there.

"Dr. Van Hartz," Robert Ferris said, "please come in and have a seat.

Muret sat down.

"Dr. Van Hartz, I'll come right to the point. Now that we have the Veneer prototype, we are going to be moving away from research and development and shifting into production and testing, and management has decided to reformulate our work teams. Dr. Herrell's work team is going to be split up and divided between Dr. Knowles production team and Dr. Mitchell's testing team. Dr. Herrell is being reassigned to the marketing division. Unfortunately, in this new alignment, we don't have a place for your unique set of skills."

Muret felt his mouth fall open and his face turn hot. He was being let go. He could hear Robert Ferris talking but the words became a buzz. He was going to lose his career; he had bills; he was forty-five years old, in a highly specialized area where there were few opportunities. He thought he was going to throw up.

Robert Ferris was droning on "...very much appreciate your valuable contribution to this project, and hope that our human resources department can offer you out-placement services and counseling if necessary..."

What was he going to do? He had worked for six years for Enadone before the new management team came aboard two years ago and sold this project to the military. It had been a rough two years, he knew, and he had many clashes with the new management team, especially Robert Ferris, but he always thought debate was part of the research culture, the slightly adversary nature between pure research and capitalism. He had done no planning about a new job. He'd have to start from scratch.

"...and I have instructed payroll to cut you a six month severance check today. Mr. Herrell will take you over there

now. For security reasons, we'll have someone go through your desk and return any personal items to you at your residence tomorrow. And again, we want to thank you for all of your contributions to this project."

Muret looked over to Michael Herrell. He had thought of Michael, not so much as a friend, but at least as a colleague, someone he could trust, even when they had disagreements, he thought of Michael as someone who had his back. But Michael mouth was tight, his lips bloodless, his face grim. Muret couldn't tell what Michael was thinking.

And with that, the discussion was over. Michael walked him over to Human Resources to sign some papers, then to payroll to pick up his severance pay, and then to his car. At the very end, Michael said, "Muret, I'm sorry. I know we had our differences, but I had nothing to do with this, believe me."

Muret didn't say anything. He just got into his car and drove home. It was only on the way home that he realized how lucky he had been to have removed all of the Silverment material and all his notes about his experiments months ago so that he could conduct his final experiments at home. There was nothing in his desk at work that could connect him to the missing Silverment and more importantly, nothing to suggest his work on invisibility.

Muret didn't leave his apartment over the next few days. He told himself he was a disciplined scientist and that he should take a disciplined scientific analysis of this job problem. He knew that he couldn't sue Enadone. Because of the nature of Enadone's work with the military, he and every other scientist who worked there, had signed strict agreements when they were hired. They were "at will" employees. They could be fired at any time for any reason. And slowly Muret began to realize that he could never market his Ninja product either. He had also signed "do not compete" agreements, saying that he couldn't use any of the ideas or projects or information he had gleaned from his work at Enadone at any future job. There was no way he could market a uniform imbedded with synthetic chromatophores—that *product belonged to Enadone. In order to market himself in the military hardware industry, he have to go back to the types of products he was working on before Enadone: compass gyroscopes for airplanes, sonar for submarines—products he hadn't worked on in eight years, products that he was sure other, younger, scientists, had advanced by light years since he last worked on them.*

The more Muret analyzed the problem, the more he realized that his joining Enadone and signing all those legal documents basically meant that he was frozen out of the military contract field. He was back into a corner, backed into a corner like the poor cuttlefish in the laboratory tank. Maybe he too would have to become invisible.

That thought stuck in his head. That night he began sewing a body suit. He took his time, because he didn't want to make mistakes and waste Veneer.

Two weeks later he stood in front of a full-length mirror and examined the result. This was no skin-tight superhero costume. In the first place, Muret's body was not a superhero body, but more importantly, because the body suit had to cover his whole body, he needed to leave enough cloth for airflow and for him to move. Veneer wasn't stretch material, so the body suit had to be baggy so that he could move. He looked like a deflated Michelin Man, with folds of material every foot or so. He had the tiniest slits open for his eyes. But he could move easily, breathe through the material easily, was comfortable, and most importantly, when he hooked up the battery and gave the suit a burst of energy, he was invisible. Or as invisible as one could be for the next three hours. He experimented with different types of light, and soon determined that twilight or early dawn was the best time to be invisible. At nighttime, the human brain shifts to other cues besides light to detect the presence of danger, and in very bright light, the ability of the brain to fill in that much background material from behind his invisible form was challenged. But in slightly low light, like dawn or early twilight, he could be invisible to the casual observer.

Muret would experiment by walking around his neighborhood at twilight or at dawn. There were always a few people about. He would stand in the middle of the street wave stop to cars coming down the street, being sure to jump out of the way in time because they never stopped. He would walk straight up to people on the sidewalk making strange gestures like Frankenstein. They acted like he wasn't there. He would take care never to get too close or to make any noise. After a week of experiments, he was ready for business.

His first order of business was Robert Ferris's house, which was located about a mile from where Muret lived. Muret calculated he could easily walk there and return home within his three-hour window. The first twilight he got there, he could tell that Robert was not home yet because the evening paper was still on the porch. Muret opened the mailbox and removed the bills, leaving the advertisements. There was a MasterCard bill, and what looked like a car payment bill. Muret slipped them into a Veneer bag that was attached to his waist and walked away. About a half mile away, he found a public trash can, and he removed the bills, tore them up, and threw them away and went home.

He did that each night for about a week. At first it gave him immense satisfaction to know that eventually Robert Ferris would be getting some nasty phone calls from creditors, but eventually, the thrill wore off. One night he timed his walk so that Robert Ferris would be arriving home about the same time that Muret would be arriving there. He watched him pull into the garage then simply walked into the garage behind him before Robert got out of his car and hit the button on the wall that closed the garage door and walked into the house. As soon as Robert Ferris was inside the house, Muret opened his car door and hit the button that opened the gas cap. Then he took a small bag of sand out of the Veneer bag and poured it into the gas tank, and then closed the gas cap. There was no side door out of the garage, so Muret simply hit the garage door opener on the wall and walked out as the garage door opened. He stood quietly outside and watched

Robert open the door to the garage, look at the open garage door, look around the garage, look outside the garage, shrug his shoulders, and hit the garage door close button on the wall. The garage door closed and Muret walked home.

Early the next morning, just for fun, Muret donned the body suit and stood outside Robert Ferris' house until the garage door open. He watched Robert Ferris drive away, until he got about four blocks down the road, where he came to a sudden stop and did not move. Muret watched him get out of his car and open the hood. Then Muret walked home again, happy.

Muret continued to visit the house of Robert Ferris every night for the next month and a half to check his mailbox and remove any bills. When Robert Ferris came home with a new car one night, Muret poured sand in its gas tank as well. However, one night he discovered that there was a new mailbox, one that locked and needed a key to open. Then he looked over at the garage and noticed two new motion sensors. "The man is learning." Muret thought. "When one is cornered, one adapts."

Muret stopped going by Robert Ferris's house for the next month. Muret had started to worry about money, and his worry about money had led him to a new project.

Muret had wondered if he could get easy money using the Ninja Veneer suit. He set up a small digital camera in his apartment and quickly discovered that the Ninja Veneer suit was detectable by camera. Not that the camera could pick up any more color or image than the human eye, but the camera did not fill in the background the way the human brain did. So, the camera image would show a picture of the room with a void where Muret stood, a silhouette of a figure, like a cardboard cutout. While the floppiness of the bodysuit made the silhouette oddly shaped, it was clearly a figure, albeit a ghostlike figure, of a person. Thus, Muret concluded he couldn't rob banks or ATMs or casinos, anywhere where there might be cameras. This problem also coincided with another limitation of the bodysuit: Muret did not trust it enough to *get close to someone. It is one thing for the human eye to scan a front yard in twilight for example, when a man in Ninja Veneer standing there in the distance would be invisible. But if that man moved closer, taking up larger and larger portions of the victim's view, then the victim's brain wouldn't have enough background information to fill in. The victim wouldn't "see" Muret, but he would see a formless thing of some type approaching him. These thoughts came to Muret because he was seriously considering how to kill Robert Ferris. At first, the thought was simply to wander about the rougher sections of town at night, maybe try and observe some drug dealers and once they had sold some drugs and were alone, clunk them over the head and take their money. He wasn't sure he could actually do such an aggressive act, but as an experiment, he tried it one time. He went downtown at twilight with a large monkey wrench in the Veneer bag, walked around the alleys until he saw a group of young men approach an older man on the street. They slipped back into the alley, and Muret watched one of the group hand the older man something, and then the man handed them something. Then the group left, but the older man stayed in the alley finishing his cigarette. Muret slipped up behind him and raised the monkey wrench. The man must have heard something because he started to turn around, but Muret's first blow caught in right above the ear. The man crumpled to his knees, and Muret's next blow sent him to the ground. Muret slipped the monkey wrench back into the Veneer bag and quickly went through the man's pockets. He found cash in several pockets and small celluloid bags of white powder in other pockets. Muret left the bags scattered about the man but took all the cash and quickly walked away. He was pretty certain that the man was still alive when he left because he was moaning. Two other men heard the moaning and came running down the alley to help, running right past Muret as he left the alley and walked down the street. Later that night he counted the cash. Twelve hundred dollars. Not bad for a day's work. And it answered the question of whether he was capable of assault.*

That was when the thought somehow morphed into killing Robert Ferris, if he could figure out a way to also take all of Robert's money at the same time. He hadn't figured out that part yet. But this dilemma did pose a new scientific concept to Muret. He started to wonder what other light frequencies the chromatophores were capable of emitting. He knew that they were emitting some type of light frequency that the human eye couldn't see, one that blocked any other light from emitting or reflecting from the chromatophore material. That's what made it invisible. Actually, it was that, plus the fact that the human eye was seeing the background material and the human brain was integrating the two to make him invisible. But, what if the chromatophores could be amped up, could pulsate ten or one hundred times the invisible light output, the way cuttlefish do when they put on their fireworks display to confuse predators? What if the chromatophore material could emit such an explosion of a certain light frequency to obliterate all the background material? So that he wouldn't be invisible, but for those few minutes, nothing would be visible? Then he could get as close to his victims as he wanted, because they would be, in essence, blind. Muret pondered this scientific problem for several days. He thought if he increased the chromatophore concentration in the material, and then increased the electrical burst, maybe he might be able to really take the Ninja Veneer bodysuit to a whole different level.

It was a few days later, while Muret was having coffee in his favorite sandwich shop, that Michael Herrell walked in. Michael saw Muret and quickly walked up to him and sat down at his table.

"I've left you several messages," Michael said.

"I've been busy," Muret replied.

"Well, I figured. I went by your house, and then I remembered you liked this place, so I came here. Listen Muret, I need to talk with you."

Muret looked at him and waited.

"We've run into a problem with the aluminum wiring."

Michael paused, looked down, and fidgeted. "Ok, I'll just tell you. It's a major problem. We showed the military the Veneer and they loved it. We priced it out for them, and they loved the cost too. Then Enadone signed a contract to deliver the first one hundred thousand uniforms. But now we're finding that the chromatophores are failing in the cloth."

"They're getting burned out by the current in the aluminum," Muret said dryly. "I told you that would happen."

"I know, I know. We ran tests. We had to order new Silverment because we must have thrown away all the old material. We ran side-by-side tests. The Veneer with Silverment endures, and the Veneer with aluminum fails. The current through the aluminum threads somehow degrades the chromatophores."

"Uh huh. Didn't I write a memo predicting that?"

"Yeah, and that's why I'm here. You remember James on the team? Well, he showed that memo to Harold Francks, Robert Ferris' boss. Evidently, Robert Ferris had kept that memo from circulating to the whole management team..."

"Yeah? And so?"

"So, they've fired Ferris."

"Really? And where is he now?"

"I don't know. Still around, but the point is, we need you back, Muret. But we can't use Silverment. It's too expensive. We need to find something that works and fits into the production budget we've sold the military."

"Can you just tell them that Silverment is the only thing that works, and that they're just going to have to pay more if they want a good product?"

"Well, we may have to, but the problem is, Muret, and as an engineer you would have to agree that we don't know if Silverment is the only material that works, because we stopped experimenting when we had the three choices of Silverment, copper, or aluminum. Maybe there's another conductor that's cheaper than Silverment that might work almost as well."

"Almost as well? Is that code for an acceptable loss of

military life?”

“A bad choice of words, Muret. Maybe there’s another material that works better.”

Muret thought about this for a moment. Michael started to say something, but Muret just held his hand up signaling him to be quiet.

“Just let me think for a minute, Michael.”

“Okay.”

Muret was an engineer. It was all he knew how to do. He missed science. He missed the adventure of discovery. He missed the laboratory. But most importantly, he needed the laboratory and the resources of Enadone to continue with his project. He wanted to figure out how to be totally invisible. He wasn’t done with Robert Ferris yet.

“Okay, Michael. Here’s the deal: you give me my own laboratory, with the big tank, all the supplies, cuttlefish and chemicals I need, and I’ll come back. Deal?”

“Deal.”

*   *   *

When Ricardo looked at the clock, it was 4:30 in the afternoon. He was still in his bathrobe. He had been writing for almost eight hours, with no sense of time. He printed out what he had written and read it. He made a few changes, printed it out again, and re-read it. “What an odd story,” he thought. “What a good story.” He never had any idea where these stories came from or what they meant. He looked around his little apartment, and thought, *I’m the luckiest man alive.*

He wondered what he should title the story. First he picked “The Veneer Man.” But then he settled on “The Cost of Invisibility.” He normally didn’t write science fiction, so he knew he would have to research what publications to send it to, but first he wanted to take a shower and get a very late breakfast.

Chapter 26: The Quality of Mercy

Weeks went by. Ricardo heard nothing from Kit. He simply assumed that she had read his email and had decided that she was not interested in a man who wasn't going to be sticking around the area. He just assumed that one day he would get a nice email from her commenting on his trip but not saying anything about getting together again, the usual polite way a woman has of declining an offer. And he would have accepted that response. However, he got nothing. No email and no texts. As time went on, it annoyed him. One day, he decided to go over to Roots for lunch. He wasn't going to let the fact that she wasn't interested in him stand in the way of a good meal.

But he didn't see her when he arrived. He picked a table and sat down. A new waitress brought him a menu.

"Where's Kit today? Is it her day off?" he asked.

"Kit? I don't think she works here anymore." the waitress replied.

This startled Ricardo. She had worked there a long time and had told him that she liked it there.

"Really?" said Ricardo, "When did that happen?"

"A couple of weeks ago, right after I started, I think. Do you want to hear about our specials?"

That night he sent Kit an email. "Is everything alright? I went to Roots and they told me you had quit or something. What happened?"

He waited two days but got no response. Finally, against his better judgment, he called her cell number. But Phillipe answered.

"This is Phillipe," came the melodic voice.

"Phillipe! Hello, this is Ricardo. Um, I don't know if

you remember me. I'm a friend of Kit's. I met you once a couple of months ago."

"Well, of course I remember you, Ricky-boy. You're the hombre that only does women on the side."

"Yeah. Well, is Kit there?" Ricardo asked.

"No darling, she's still over at Mercy Center in Buffalo."

"What? What happened?"

"Oh, I don't know, some kind of female problem."

"What do you mean? What happened? When did she go there?"

"Now don't get your panties all up in a wad, Ricky-boy. I don't know nothing 'bout nothing. She got sick and her mama came, and they took her to Mercy. That's all I know."

Ricardo's head was spinning. More than anything, he hated vague answers to specific questions.

"Look Phillipe. Tell me clearly. What do you mean she got sick?"

"Well, she just got sick, said she wasn't feeling well, went to see some doctor, but that didn't help. They ran some tests. But I don't know what for."

"How could you not know?" Ricardo exclaimed. "You're her *roommate*."

"Honey, if Kit don't want to tell someone something, you can't drag it out of her."

"Well, what's this about her mother? I thought she didn't talk to her mother."

"Oh, so you know about that. Yeah, her mother's a piece of work. Well, really more like a piece of shit. But she's not crazy like Kit says. Anyway, one day her mama shows up. I think Kit may have called her, I don't know. But her mama shows up with some guy, and Kit tells me they're taking her to Mercy."

"Did Kit want to go with them?"

"Yeah, I think so. She was pretty sick."

"What do you mean, sick?"

"Well, she was throwing up a lot. Couldn't keep anything down. At first, I just assumed she was pregnant again, because she always gets sick when she's preggers."

"W-what? Um Phillipe, how long have you known Kit?"

"About two years, since she moved in with me."

"And how many times has she been pregnant since you've known her?"

"Ah, three or four. The girl's fertile, Ricky-boy. Very fertile."

Phillipe was beginning to annoy Ricardo now.

"Phillipe, what did you mean when you said she was having female problems?"

"Well, that's what her mama said. That's all I know."

"Have you gone to see her?"

"Oh, heavens no, Ricky-boy. Phillipe definitely does not like hospitals."

"Do you know what room she's in?"

"Hmm...sorry, no."

"Do you have any other information?"

"Uh-uh. Nada. Say, Ricky-boy, why don't you come over here and we can commiserate together?"

"Yeah, no. Phillipe. I'm going to the hospital."

"Okay baby, ciao. Some other time."

That was the problem with drag queens, Ricardo thought as he grabbed his jacket from the closet. Totally fucking unreliable. He ran downstairs, got into his car and headed off to Mercy Center in Buffalo.

As he drove, he tried to calm himself down. Mercy was a good hospital. She'd be under a doctor's care there. There was no reason to panic.

But he couldn't help but worry. Kit was one of those damaged birds, born damaged, or damaged young, one of those who seem to inherit more than their share of bad luck. Maybe that's why he felt drawn to her, felt like protecting her, helping her, because she seemed so battered. And yet, he had to admit, he didn't really know anything about her. The box of court records was the only verifiable evidence he had about her, and it painted a picture of a petty criminal lost in the criminal justice system. There was nothing in those records that corroborated her story of miscarriage and psychiatric hospitals. Yet here was Phillipe saying she constantly got pregnant. If that didn't somehow confirm her story then it solidified Ricardo's growing opinion that she was mentally damaged. Yet here he was, driving to Buffalo to see her. It made no sense.

Ricardo got to Mercy Center at seven o'clock. He didn't know what time visiting hours were over, but he was hoping eight. The parking lot wasn't crowded, so maybe it was a quiet night at the hospital. Ricardo walked through the automatic doors and up to the information booth.

"I'm here to visit Kit Pruitt." he said.

"Do you know what room the patient is in?" The woman behind the glass asked.

"No, sorry, I don't. She might be listed under Kitriana Pruitt."

The woman looked at a computer screen that was turned so that Ricardo couldn't see it.

"Are you a relative?"

Ricardo felt a wave of suspicion come over him.

"No, I am not."

"I'm very sorry, sir. Under HIPPA rules, the only visitors that patients may have are the ones they've listed as visitors."

"Ma'am," Ricardo said slowly, "I'm her lawyer. I'm here to see her on legal business. It's very important. Just tell her I'm here and I'm sure she'll put me on the list."

"I'm sorry sir, under HIPPA rules, we cannot even confirm that the person you seek is even a patient here."

Ricardo tried to control his voice.

"Ma'am, I am very familiar with HIPPA rules, and they say no such thing. Now, I am Kit Pruitt's attorney and I need to see her."

"I'm sorry sir. If that person is here, there is no visitation."

"Are visiting hours still open?"

"Yes."

"Then can you tell me why I can't visit her?"

"As I said, sir, the only visitors that are allowed are visitors that are listed by the patients."

"So, she is here?"

"I didn't say that."

"Is there someone else I can talk with about this?"

"You can call our omsbudsperson Ms. Wilcox in the morning."

"How about your legal department? Do you have a legal department?"

"Yes, sir."

"Can you give me their name and number please?"

"Yes, sir."

"And write your name on the card as well, please." Ricardo added tersely.

"Yes, sir." And she pushed the card under the glass partition to him. He took the card and left.

He felt furious on the drive back. All he wanted to do was visit a sick friend. What was the fucking problem? In frustration, he dialed Kit's cell number again, hoping Phillipe would answer. He did.

"Hello, darling."

"Cut the darling crap, Phillipe. They wouldn't let me see her."

"Well, I could have told you that, darling. No one can see her except her mother."

"Why is that?"

"Well," Phillipe said in a dramatic tone, "I don't know. I just know that's the way it is. Her mother told me that she was the only visitor Kit was allowed."

"Well, why didn't you tell me that before I drove over here?"

"You didn't ask, darling. But now that you're on the way back, why don't you stop by and visit me?"

Ricardo started to say no, but then paused. He would be refusing out of anger. But it was anger directed at the hospital, at the situation, not at Phillipe. Clearly there was nothing more he could do about Kit tonight. Tomorrow he could call their legal department and see what headway he could make. If necessary, he could leave work to "visit a client" during the day tomorrow, if he could wrangle an agreement from the hospital's lawyer. After all, it was clear that Kit wasn't going to be at home this evening, and Phillipe had invited him twice to come over. He thought of that red wig Phillipe was wearing when they first met. He wondered if he could tie her up a bit while he fucked her, just so he could vent some of his frustration.

"Phillipe," he asked, "do you have any handcuffs?"

"Of course, darling."

"Ok, I'll come over."

"Oh, goody. I'm just in the mood."

Chapter 27: Unchain my Heart

Ricardo hated those early morning dreams that came in the last hour of sleep. They were always crazy conflicted dreams. In this one he was in a public restroom at the town library where a large talkative man was pressuring him to have sex in the bathroom stall. Ricardo didn't want to, but the man was very persuasive and was not taking no for an answer. He had cornered Ricardo in the stall and was demanding to suck Ricardo's cock. The man had dropped to his knees and was undoing Ricardo's belt while Ricardo struggled to prevent him by holding onto the belt buckle. Meanwhile, a woman outside of the locked bathroom was waiting angrily to get in and use the restroom. She was starting to pound on the door. Ricardo woke up tangled in sheets, feeling trapped, agitated and exhausted. He lifted his head to look at the alarm clock. 5:45 a.m. "Shit," he said aloud, and let his head drop back on the pillow. The sheets were damp with his perspiration. He kicked the blankets and sheets off him, but he always slept with the window open and the room was cold this winter night, so he quickly pulled the damp covers back over him. He shook his head as if to knock the images and feelings out. His shoulders ached. He propped up the pillows and half sat up in bed and pulled the covers up to his neck. In the kitchen, he could hear the coffee maker automatically come on, and start to brew coffee.

He had visited Phillipe three nights out of the last five. Even though Phillipe was a total submissive in bed, Ricardo still fucked him hard, almost brutally. All three evenings had unfolded the same. Phillipe would banter about, refilling Ricardo's wine glass while he tried on different outfits and modeled them for Ricardo. Finally, Ricardo would pick his favorite outfit, Phillipe would put it back on, and Ricardo would drag him to bed, kissing him hard, undoing just enough buttons to expose his ass. Ricardo would then hold Phillipe's head down to his crotch in a feigned force scene and "make" Phillipe suck him until he got hard. Then he'd put a condom on and use the jar of lube that Phillipe kept by the bed to lube his cock up, then turn Phillipe face down on the bed, pulling his ass up in the air with his arm, and enter him from behind, sometimes twisting Phillipe's balls hard or slapping his ass. The thrusts were violent and deep, until Ricardo came. Then Ricardo and Phillipe would collapse wordlessly on the bed, not cuddling, just lying as they fell. After about five minutes, Ricardo would get up and leave. Sometimes Phillipe would get hard while Ricardo fucked him; sometimes not. But Ricardo never helped him cum. He would just fuck him and leave.

It was not the kind of sex that Ricardo enjoyed. Yes, it was hot and daring, and had the kind of thrill that role-playing provides. Yet there was no connection, no love, no tenderness. It was just flesh. Yet, the next day, without fail, Phillipe would call or text, asking Ricardo to come by again that night. After the third night, Ricardo made some excuse about work and stayed home.

Sex was like that, Ricardo thought. Totally dependent on the chemistry between two people, not necessarily what each wanted or intended. It was as if the intention or the preferences of the individual did not matter, that when two people came together, a third force, a chemical force, a genetic sexual force took over and dictated the type of sex they would have. Dominants could become submissive or vice versa. You could be swept away by people you weren't even attracted to. Sex had nothing to do with attraction or commonality or logic. It was just blind sex.

He thought about Kit. He had had zero success with Mercy Hospital's ombudsperson or their legal department in getting in to see Kit. Evidently, she had signed some paper saying only her mother could visit her. Ricardo and everyone else were simply excluded. However, Kit's mother did call Phillipe occasionally to give an update. Evidently, they were going to move Kit out of the hospital soon, to transfer her somewhere else, but where was unclear. Ricardo hated that Phillipe couldn't be more specific. But since Phillipe was the only contact with Kit's mother, Ricardo didn't see the point in yelling at Phillipe to make him try and get more definite information out of Kit's mom.

At one point, Phillipe told Ricardo that it was doubtful Kit would be coming back. He said some movers came and picked up her belongings from Phillipe's apartment.

"When this happened before, her mom would usually let me store her stuff here," Phillipe told Ricardo. "She would say something like, 'keep it for Kit, so it'll all be here when she comes back'. This is the first time that mom has moved it all out."

"What do you mean, when this has happened before? How many times has this happened?" Ricardo asked.

"Oh, usually once, sometimes twice a year. She either gets pregnant and disappears for a short while, or she gets sick or wacky and disappears for a longer while."

"Wacky, how?"

"Oh Ricky-boy," Phillipe would goad him. "You know as well as I do, Kit is a world class loose bolt on the factory floor. She's got a screw loose. Can't be fixed."

"She seems fine to me, Phillipe."

Phillipe just laughed. "She's a sweet girl, Ricky-boy. But she's damaged."

That's all Phillipe would ever say about Kit. It infuriated Ricardo that Phillipe might be holding out on him, not telling him some history of Kit that would explain things. Maybe that was why Ricardo fucked him so hard, out of frustration, as if he could fuck the truth out of a tranny.

Ricardo decided that he needed to stop seeing Phillipe, and that he needed to stop thinking about Kit. She clearly had psychological problems and was going through what she was going through, wherever her mother had put her. There was nothing Ricardo could do that would change that. And Phillipe was no help. Although it was easy sex, it was not the kind of sex that Ricardo enjoyed, and Phillipe's constant vamping and quips were annoying. Ricardo would have to make up some work excuse to give to Phillipe. Besides, the move to Panamá was coming up in a few weeks and Ricardo had to focus on that.

Chapter 28: The Visit

But a week later Phillipe texted Ricardo, asking if he wanted to visit Kit. Ricardo called Phillipe immediately.

"What do you mean, visit her? Where is she?"

"Oh darling, her mama moved her to this nut farm on the outside of Buffalo. Posh place actually. Mama said I could visit her Sunday afternoon. I asked if I could bring a friend, and she said yes. So, I thought you might be interested."

Ricardo knew that Phillipe was just using Kit as an excuse to lure Ricardo back, but still, he wanted to see Kit.

"Ok, yes, I'd like to go. Give me the address and I'll meet you there."

Phillipe gave him the address. "It's called 'Restoration Spa'. Isn't that that silliest name?" Phillipe said. "Spa my ass, everything is locked down tight. Still, the garden is nice when the weather's good."

"You've been there before?"

"Oh, yes darling. The last time Kit went wacky, her mama put her there for a week. But this time I think it's different. Her mama says Kit's in pretty bad shape."

"How so?"

"Don't know, darling. Mama doesn't say much. And Kit's the same way. Like mama, like daughter."

"You've talked with her?"

"Uh huh. She called last night. We talked for a bit."

"Well, how did she sound?"

"Out of it."

*   *   *

On Sunday, Ricardo drove to the Restoration Spa.

Phillipe was right. It was a posh place. A guard at the gate gave him directions to the building where visitors checked in. Ricardo drove up the long driveway, found the building, parked and went inside.

The lobby felt like a hotel lobby. Various small couches and chairs grouped together so people could talk. Art on the walls. A reception desk with two nurses behind the counter. Ricardo walked up and gave them his name. They found his name on the list of approved visitors, checked it off, told him it would be a few minutes and asked him to wait over by the window on some vacant couches. Ricardo walked over, sat down, and surveyed the scene. Small groups, mostly in threes, were gathering in various corners. Judging by the age of the people, Ricardo guessed each group consisted of two parents and a patient. Most of the patients appeared to be women. Occasionally there was a pair, consisting of an older woman and a younger one, probably a daughter. The ones he guessed were patients were dressed in street clothes, sometimes very stylishly, sometimes just in jeans. Some of them appeared to be nervous. Others appeared to be stoned and sat quietly while the "parents" talked to them. Ricardo assumed that Kit's mom must be footing the bill for this place.

He watched a young man in a suit enter through the front door and walk to the receptionist. The man looked vaguely familiar, but Ricardo couldn't place him. He wore an expensive-looking European-cut suit and had blond hair slicked back in a 1930's hairstyle. The receptionist chatted with him and then pointed at Ricardo. The man started walking towards Ricardo, smiling.

"Hello, darling."

It took Ricardo a second to recover. It was Phillipe.

"Oh Phillipe, my God, I didn't recognize you."

"Oh, I go by Ronald here, darling. Call me Ronald if any of the nurses come over or if Kit's mama shows."

"Is that your real name?" Ricardo asked hesitantly.

"Well, let's just call it my birth name. Isn't it awful? But around here, one has to keep up appearances, you know."

One of the nurses from the reception desk walked up

to Ronald.

"Mr. Resnick, Mrs. Pruitt called and said she will not be joining you today. I'll go ahead and bring Kit downstairs."

Ricardo marveled at Phillipe's real name. Resnick. Ronald Resnick. He realized that he had never known Phillipe to have a last name, had never thought to ask him.

"Thank you very much, Carla. We'll wait here," Phillipe replied.

Ricardo stared at Phillipe. The voice Phillipe had just used to address the nurse wasn't Phillipe's voice at all. It was lower, spoken without inflection. A very straight-sounding male voice.

The nurse smiled and walked away.

"What was that, Phillipe?" Ricardo asked.

"What was what, darling?" Phillipe said, in the voice that Ricardo recognized.

"That voice?"

"Well, darling, as I said, one has to keep up appearances. You can bet that mama would never let me near Kit if I ever let Phillipe out. No, my little Ricky. We live in a very politically-charged world. It's not easy being the world's best-known closeted drag queen. One time, mama came by without calling first and met Phillipe. Lucky for me, she never figured it out. She thought I was just Kit's roommate who was Ronald's sister."

Ricardo just shook his head. How did he get mixed up with such a crazy group?

He looked up to see the nurse approaching them holding Kit by the arm. He gave a slight gasp. Phillipe saw him look and turned towards Kit. They both stood up.

Kit did not look like Kit. Ricardo would have said that she looked horrible, but someone that pretty never looks horrible. But she was pale, and there was no expression on her face. Her eyes were looking at Ricardo and Phillipe, but they didn't seem to be focusing. Her hair was pulled back into a simple pony tail, but the color was dull. She was wearing a simple blouse and dress, with no make-up and no jewelry.

"Here she is," said the nurse. "I'll leave you here for a while Kit, so you can have a nice visit with your two gentlemen friends. I'll be back to check on you later." The nurse then looked at Phillipe and smiled. "Would you all like some tea?" she asked.

"No, Carla, thank you so much. We're fine." Phillipe said, again using Ronald's voice.

The nurse walked away. Ricardo looked at Kit.

"Hello Kit. How are you?" Ricardo asked, and then instantly regretted using that automatic greeting.

"I'm fine, Ricardo. Thank you for coming. And thank you, Phillipe, for bringing him."

"Oh, darling, I didn't bring him. He drove himself. I couldn't have kept this boy away from you. Let's all sit down and have a little chat."

They sat down. Kit stared at her hands.

Ricardo couldn't contain himself. "Kit, what happened?"

She looked at him, then looked down again. "Oh, just a little chemical imbalance, the doctors say. They're making adjustments in my medicine, and they say I'll be fine again soon. Things like this happen every once in a while, you know. It's just a temporary setback. That's all."

"I tried to visit you at Mercy Hospital, but they wouldn't let me see you."

Kit gave a little laugh. "You wouldn't have wanted to see me then, Ricardo. I was not quite myself. I'm getting better, though. This is just a temporary setback."

Ricardo sat back and looked at her. Phillipe was right: Kit was damaged. And yet he felt the strangest compassion for her. He wanted to hold her, to stroke her hair, to tell her everything was going to be alright. He thought briefly about trying to take her out of this place, get her evaluated by a doctor he could trust, get her out of her mother's control. Thoughts started racing through his mind. What kind of medication was she on? Was it helping or was it just making her worse? Could he move her into his little apartment? What about taking her to Panamá? But she had those felonies, and no passport. And there wasn't time. Could he get a court order for an independent evaluation? No, he recognized that that was a crazy thought. He had no proof of any mistreatment, and the spa probably had a good reputation and a league of lawyers. This was just another damaged girl with a domineering mother. A wave of sadness overtook him.

He leaned forward and placed his hand on her hand. Her hands were cold and didn't react to his touch. Nor did her face change expression.

"Kit, I am so sorry. I feel so... so sad that you're here, that you're going through all this. Is there anything I can do?"

Kit looked at him. Her mouth twitched into a half-smile. "No, I'll be fine Ricardo. This is just a temporary setback. It's a chemical imbalance, but I'm getting better. After I get out of here, I'm going to move back in with mama for a bit to help her out. Then I'll be fine." Her voice trailed off. "It's just a temporary setback."

Ricardo looked at Phillipe. Phillipe seemed to be deciding what to say next.

"Kit, darling, I did move your stuff over to your mama's like you asked. But you know, there's always a place for you with me. You know that, don't you?"

"Yes, Phillipe. Thank you. I appreciate that. I hope to be better soon, so I can get back to Hamburg and back to my job. I hope Roots will take me back."

Phillipe quickly changed the subject. "You know, darling, I was thinking that, while you were gone, I might paint your room. Would you like that? A different color, something more cheery than that powder blue? Maybe something like flaming pink to match your roommate?"

Kit didn't laugh. "No, don't change the color. I like my little bedroom just the way it is. I like the blue color. It's restful."

"Okay, darling. I'll leave it exactly the way it is."

They talked for a while longer. Or, rather Ricardo and Phillipe talked at Kit, and Kit occasionally responded, but there was wasn't much content to her statements, and certainly no emotion. Everything she said was said in that same flat tone. Eventually, the nurse came and told Kit that it was time to leave and Kit stood up. Ricardo stood up too and tried to give Kit a hug, but Kit just stood there without responding.

"Goodbye Kit, I'll come and visit you again. I hope you'll feel better soon."

"Goodbye, Ricardo. I'm sure I will. This is just a temporary setback."

And the nurse took her away. Ricardo sat back down and let out a sigh. "Jesus, Phillipe, that was excruciating."

"Yes, darling, just another one of life's endless supply of catastrophes."

Ricardo looked at Phillipe, squinted his eyes, and pictured him with his red wig and makeup. The transformation was night and day.

A sudden thought came to Ricardo. On an impulse, he said, "Phillipe, let me talk to Ronald." There was the tiniest micro-movement in Phillipe's face.

"Yes, sir, what can I do for you?" came Ronald's voice.

"Ronald, what's wrong with Kit?"

"Well, sir, in the first place, she's an epileptic. She has grand mal seizures from time to time. She takes a lot of medication for that, but it doesn't always work. That's why she can't drive. They won't give her a license. In addition to the seizures, or maybe because of them, she's has a serious manic-depressive disorder. Had it all her life. When she's very manic, she takes a lot of risks, shoplifts, sleeps around using no protection, hence the frequent abortions. When she's just a little manic, she is happy and works hard and is a delight to be around. But when she's depressed, she often sees suicide as the only way out. She's tried it several times. That's why her mother is so over-protective. Kit's her only child. Mama even sends Phillipe a little money to keep an eye on Kit. It's a tragic situation all around, and to be honest, it's not getting better. Did you notice that she was wearing a long-sleeve blouse?"

Ricardo had noticed but didn't think anything of it.

"That was to cover up the bandages. She slashed herself in Phillipe's apartment. Pretty badly. That's why she stayed at Mercy Hospital, and that's why she's on suicide watch here."

"Why didn't you tell me all this before?"

"Ricardo, we just met. What Phillipe tells you is his business."

Phillipe stood up, gave Ricardo a little smile, and said in Phillipe's voice, "Well, darling, I've got to run. There's a drag show tonight and this girl has work to do to get ready. Give me a call sometime and I'll show you my round-the-world act. I think you'll like it."

And he was gone.

Ricardo sat back down. He didn't know who was crazier, Kit or Phillipe. Clearly, Kit suffered more. Or maybe, Ricardo thought, *I'm* the crazy one, because I'm mixed up with these two. He shook his head. How do some people find themselves in such horrible places in life? He just didn't understand it.

Several of the other groups in the lobby were saying goodbye to each other. Ricardo stood back up, walked over to the reception desk, took out one of his business cards, and handed it to Carla the nurse.

"I don't know what the protocol is for getting on the regular visitors' list, but I would like to be on Kit's visitor list if possible. I'm only in town for a few more weeks though. Then, I'll be out of the country."

"Thank you, sir. I'll see what I can do."

"Thank you."

Ricardo walked out to his car. He didn't really expect that his name would be added to the visitors' list. And he was right.

Chapter 29: Preparation

The next day, Ricardo called the office and told them he wasn't feeling well and was going to stay home. He felt fine, but he needed time to think, to think and to pack. He sat at his writing table, took out a legal pad, and started making a list of things he still needed to buy for this next trip to Panamá. Then he looked at a calendar and picked a day when he would submit his resignation at work, just enough time to let them reassign his cases and start the hiring process to replace him, but not enough time for them to regroup and try and make him stay. Then he sat and wondered if there was anything he wasn't thinking of that he should be thinking of; were there questions he wasn't asking? The thought crossed his mind. *You'd think a nice guy like me would have a better plan than this one.* It was an odd thought. He wrote it down on the legal pad, and while he was writing, he started visualizing a small cabin in winter. Then another image came to him, and then another, and then another. Then he realized that this wasn't about Panamá. He opened up his laptop and started typing. The following words flowed out of him...

That Is the Question

You'd think a nice chalet like this would have a better heating system than just one wood-burning stove, thought Duncan. But that's all there was. It sat there like a fat Buddha in the living room, a fat black Buddha, Duncan thought. Luckily, he found where the owner had stacked several cords of wood on the side of the chalet. This must have started off as a covered parking area, thought Duncan, as he looked past the stacks of wood to the boxes, lawn mowers, lawn furniture, rakes and ladders all stacked underneath the overhanging tin roof. A cold wind blew steady through the two steel beams that supported the overhang. Duncan grabbed two of the smaller logs and hurried back into the house. Now, where would they keep matches? he wondered. He rummaged through the kitchen drawers until he found an old box of wooden matches. Then he found some brown paper bags under the sink, which he tore up and crumpled into little balls and shoved under the two logs which he had placed in the stove. He checked the flue to make sure it was open, then lit the paper. It smoked, and then a tiny flame started. He lit another ball of paper with what remained of the match and then closed the door of the stove and watched the flames start to lick the wood through the dirty window of the door. The wood was dry, and it caught fire quickly. Duncan pulled off his gloves and held his hands up near the stove. He could just begin to feel some heat filtering out. Good, he thought, I won't freeze to death.

Duncan looked around the place. Tiny living room with a tiny food area with a sink and a countertop. No refrigerator. Just the stove to heat food up on. I wonder if there's any canned food in the cupboard? He thought. He got up and started opening the cabinet doors. Inside one he found several cans of beanie-weenies, and one can of chicken noodle soup. He had seen a can-opener in the drawer where he had found the matches, and he grabbed it and opened a can of beanie-weenies. He removed the top completely. There was no trashcan, so he left the can top on the counter and walked back to the wood burning stove and placed the can on top. Then he got a spoon from the drawer and sat down in a chair next to stove and slowly stirred the beanie-weenies while the fire crackled and began to heat the room. After a few minutes he lifted the spoon to his mouth. Still cold. This was going to take a while, he thought. He placed the spoon on a small table by the stove and sat back and waited.

How did I come to this? he thought. Where did I go wrong? He thought back to a few weeks ago, when he was teaching English Literature to the high school sophomores. It was such an easy gig. He had done it for three years in that crappy high school with all its meetings and protocols. But he put up with the bullshit because he liked teaching, especially Shakespeare, and he liked the students, well, he liked the eager students, the ones who wanted to learn.

His method of teaching was simple, and it structured all his time in the classroom so he really didn't have to do that much. He'd take a play and spend three quarters of the class having the students read it aloud, taking turns. Then they would discuss what they had read for the last fifteen minutes of class time. Then he would give the usual assignment to write a one page essay on what these passages meant. Duncan rarely read what they wrote, except for some of his favorite students, like Daphne or Caroline. The rest he would glance at, scan them for a misspelled word which he would circle as if he had read the whole paper carefully, and then assign a grade, usually a good grade so no student ever complained. With Daphne and Caroline, he would make a comment or two.

The fire was roaring now. Duncan went outside and grabbed two more sticks of wood, came back in and added them to the flame. He picked up the spoon and gave the beanie-weenies a stir. Steam was beginning to rise from the can. He felt hungry and gave the spoon a taste. Warm, but not hot. A few more minutes.

They were doing Hamlet just a few weeks ago, one of Duncan's favorite plays. Each student would read aloud for about five minutes, until Duncan said, "That's good," and asked the next student to start reading. His theory was that students wouldn't read anything they were assigned to as homework, so it was better to have them read it in class. That way, they could ask questions as they went along. He recalled that when they got to Hamlet's famous To Be or Not to Be soliloquy, it just so happened to be Daphne's turn to read.

"To be or not to be, that is the question," she started.

Duncan interrupted her, and asked the class, "Exactly

what does that mean? What does Hamlet mean when he says, 'to be or not to be?'"

Four students raised their hands. "Yes, William." Duncan said.

"Well, he's asking what he should do."

"What he should do about what?" Duncan asked.

"Well, about the whole situation, his dad's murder, his uncle, you know."

"Okay? Stephanie?"

"Isn't he asking whether he should go on living or not?"

"Say more," Duncan said.

"Hmm, well maybe it's like he's asking if he should kill himself, you know, to be, like to be alive."

"Okay. anyone else?"

"Well, is he asking who he should be?" volunteered a voice from the back of the class. Duncan looked. It was Emily, the shy girl he couldn't figure out.

"Say more."

"I don't know, it just feels like he's asking who he should be."

"That's good, Emily. That's the thing about Shakespeare. His work is open to interpretation. Maybe Hamlet is asking whether he should be a man, the man that his ghost father wants him to be, the man to avenge his father's death, or maybe he's asking whether he can go on at all. Okay, Daphne. Continue."

"To be or not to be, that is the question. Whether it is nobler in the mind..."

Duncan watched her read. She was leaning forward, concentrating on the words. From where he stood, he could look down her open blouse and see the rise of her breasts as they disappeared behind the line of her bra that was just barely visible. He loved those breasts. They were so perfect, so firm, the way they rose to her small nipples. He thought back to the night in his apartment when he first took off that bra and kissed those nipples.

"Excuse me, Mr. Petersen, what are fardels?" The voice of Eric Willis interrupted Duncan's reverie. "Where it says 'who would fardels bear' what are fardels?"

"Anyone?" Duncan asked, but no hand went up.

"A fardel is an old English word for burden, Eric. It literally refers to a pack, a bundle, like a backpack, something that weighs you down. So, in this line, like so many of Hamlet's lines, it's a metaphor for life, the burdens of life. Who would carry on under these burdens? is what he's asking. Okay Daphne. Finish this soliloquy."

"Who would fardels bear, to grunt and sweat under a weary life..."

Duncan gave the can of beanie-weenies another stir. The beans were bubbling now. He put a glove back on his left hand to pick the can up and began to eat. Who knew that beanie-weenies could taste so good?

"Soft you, now. The fair Ophelia. Nymph, in thy orisons be all my sins remembered."

"Thank you Daphne. Now, there are two things going on in this last line. First, Shakespeare needs to shift the focus. Hamlet has finished his soliloquy, and another scene needs to begin, so Shakespeare has Hamlet say, 'Soft you, now,' which means he's telling himself not to be so loud because someone's approaching, and then he clues the audience that it's Ophelia that's approaching, and that sets the stage for the next scene. But then Shakespeare throws this line in. 'Nymph, in thine eyes be all my sins remembered.' What's he talking about there? Anyone? Yes, Roger."

"Well, he's saying he's sorry."

"Sorry for what?" Duncan asked.

"Sorry for not paying attention to her?" Several of the boys in the class smirked.

"Okay, maybe. Anyone else?"

"Maybe he's sorry he cheated on her." It was Caroline.

"Okay. How did he cheat on her?"

"You know, by not being faithful."

Duncan looked at the clock. There were only five minutes left in the class. "Yes, faithful to the promises he made to her. That's a good point, Caroline. Or maybe he's talking somehow about his failure to act, his failure to measure up to his father's command to avenge his father's death, maybe he feels that failure when he looks into Ophelia's eyes. Or is he just wanting Ophelia to remember him? Okay, we just have a few minutes left of class. So tonight, I want to you to concentrate on just this one soliloquy—it's one of Shakespeare's most famous—and write one page on what you think it means."

Duncan scraped the last of the beans and franks from the bottom of the tin can. *I wish they had left a beer,* he thought. *Or a bottle of wine. I could really use a drink right now.* He got up and looked through all the cabinets again, but there was nothing of an alcoholic nature.

He sat back down. The fire was going good now. The room was toasty warm. It was amazing that such a small stove could heat up a room. He wondered if the heat rose up to what he imagined was a bedroom in the loft upstairs. He hoped there was a bed. He was beginning to feel tired.

He wondered who had turned him in. He thought it was probably Caroline. He should have let more time go by, let a summer pass at least, before paying attention to Daphne. But Daphne was so beautiful, with her short black hair and her pouty face. He just knew she would be such a good lover, and she was. She was a gymnast in bed, writhing and moaning. So much better than Caroline, who moaned but then cried and just wanted to be held.

Still, he had been careful. No texts, no emails, nothing to prove anything. His classes were very popular, and the students always gave him good marks in the surveys that the school did. He pointed that out several times to the discipline committee during that kangaroo court hearing they gave him. He would sue them, he would, as soon as he got on his feet and got a lawyer. He would sue them so fast.

Duncan felt very tired. The fire was dying down. The wood was consumed. He secured the stove's door. He put the empty beanie-weenie can on the counter. *Tomorrow I have to find where they put the trash,* he thought. *And I need to clean up the glass that I broke in the front door. I need to leave this place clean,* he thought. *It's the least I can do.*

He made his way up the stairs to the loft. And yes, there was a bed there, and the loft was heated nicely from the wood burning stove. Duncan lay down in his clothes, pulled the blanket over him and fell fast asleep.

He dreamed of chalkboards and student desks. He dreamed of meadows of grain moving softly in the breeze. He dreamed of actors donning costumes in the old Vic, getting ready to go on stage. He didn't hear anyone come into the chalet and make their way up to his bed.

But he awakened to the nudge of a nightstick. He opened his eyes and saw the dancing of red and blue lights across the ceiling of the room. It took him a minute to realize they were the reflections of lights from the police cars parked out in front.

"Are you Duncan Petersen?" said a voice.

"Yes."

"You have the right to remain silent..." began the voice.

And the thought crossed Duncan's mind, this is like being stuck in a bad play, a very bad play.

*   *   *

Ricardo looked at the clock. It was almost 5:00 p.m. So much for a day dedicated to packing. He printed the story out and read it twice. He never knew where these stories came from or why. He thought about Kit and Phillipe, but there didn't seem to be any connection to this story.

He stuck the story into a folder he was keeping for his publisher. He counted the stories in the folder. He was up to eighteen. He had sold a few of these to some magazines this year, but he always kept the republishing rights to them. If he could write a few more, this would be the book *One Hundred Brothels* he had been promising his publisher.

Ricardo realized he hadn't eaten lunch. That's how it always was when he wrote. He simply forgot about food or time. He would just type as fast as he could, stopping only to pee. Sometimes he would drink coffee, but never eat. But now he was famished. He went into the kitchen and started making himself a sandwich.

197

There's that old myth about humans just being the dreams of gods, he thought. Maybe the gods dream up our lives the same way we dream up stories. After all, he thought, my moving to Panamá does seem like something that would happen in a dream. It had that arbitrary dreamlike quality. He took the bread out of the toaster and spread mayonnaise on it, then took some slices of cheese from the refrigerator. Or are my stories like dreams? Some kind of code from the unconscious? And if so, he wondered, what am I trying to tell myself? He took a bite from the sandwich. It wasn't very tasty, but he was too hungry to care. He thought about opening a bottle of wine but decided to wait. He thought back to the last four or five stories he had written. He thought of Eddie in *Scarlet's*, the invisible Dr. Muret Von Hartz, and now this guy Duncan... all selfish men driven by sex or revenge... all three somehow limited by their lives... was this some version of himself? None of these men were admirable. Interesting men maybe, but not admirable.

But Ricardo knew there was no point in analyzing it. It was what it was. Stories came to him for some reason. And even when they were troubling stories, he had to write them down. It gave him some kind of relief he could not describe. It emptied him of something. It gave him some type of peace.

He thought again about Kit. She had her epileptic seizures, and he had these bursts of storytelling. Why were the gods so cruel to her and so kind to him? Her at the Restoration Spa... Phillipe playing Ronald or Ronald playing Phillipe... Ricardo going to Panamá. None of it made any sense, really. But it was what it was. It couldn't be changed. He thought of the French phrase *les jeux sont faits*. The game is fixed, or more accurately, the die is cast. He wondered if there was a Spanish idiom that meant the same thing.

Chapter 30: Impermanence

Two more weeks went by. Ricardo was at work. He had submitted his resignation, which came as a shock to everyone. There was a flurry of questions and concerns, many positive comments about his productivity and his value to the firm, and of course the inevitable subtle implication of betrayal for his decision to retire before he was sixty-five. But he countered with enough hints of "health issues that were not open for discussion," so that no one really tried to twist his arm too hard. There were no real health issues, of course. At least, Ricardo hoped not. He would no longer be able to afford them.

He had spent this day categorizing his files, creating a transfer log for each one that summarized the status of the case, the billable hours still pending payment, and the work that needed to be done on each. He had drafted letters to all his clients indicating that the quality of representation would remain the same even if a different attorney was handling their case.

He was at his desk when his cell phone rang.

"Hello?"

"Ricardo, this is Ronald."

It took Ricardo a microsecond to realize who he was talking to, and then, in another microsecond, he knew that this would not be a good call.

"Yes, Ronald?"

"Well, this isn't an easy call Ricardo. I know you cared about Kit, but... she's gone. She... she committed suicide last night."

Ricardo heard his own intake of air.

"What happened?"

"Evidently, she got a knife from the kitchen at the spa,

snuck it back to her room, cut her wrists. By the time they found her, she was gone."

Ronald's voice started to choke.

"She was supposed to leave the spa tomorrow and move in with her mother. Her mother said that if she improved, she might be able to come back to Hamburg and live with Phillipe."

Ricardo had nothing to say. He saw his hand reach for a pen and grab it like a stabbing knife.

Finally he said, "Ronald... I'm so sorry. I... I really liked her."

"I did too, Ricardo. I did too."

"Okay... well thanks for letting me know," and Ricardo hung up.

He watched his hand make stabbing motions at the desk, and then, tears began to well up in his eyes. Someone walked by his office, paused when they saw him, and quickly moved on. He got up, closed the door, sat back down, buried his head in his arms on the desk, and began to sob.

Chapter 31: God's Will

Why was every person's journey so different? What was it that brought us to this crossroads or that precipice? When Ricardo looked back at his life, he didn't believe the invisible hand of God guided his choices. He never heard the fates whisper in his ear. But he did know that every major life choice he'd made had a certain feeling to it, not a physical feeling, but an internal sense, something that took the decision out of his control. At each of his life's major crossroads, certainly both divorces, but even going back to his boyhood choice to leave Spain and come to America to live with his grandfather, or his decision to go to law school, his choice of women, or his choice of men, at every instance it was as if he walked up to the crossroads and stood there, staring first down one path and then the other, not knowing which way to go, and then, every time, the path would choose him. He never denied responsibility for his decisions, but he never felt that *he* had made them. It was always a feeling that the decision made him, not the other way around. His freedom of choice lay only in the ability to say no to something that felt wrong. But there was never any choice in saying yes to something that felt right. There is no freedom of choice, just a freedom of no. Yes, choices are made for you, Ricardo believed. The only thing one can do, he had determined years ago, was groom that feeling so that he could feel it when it happened, and let it do what it was going to do. He remembered a time in the late-seventies, before AIDS had been identified, when he met this famous beautiful man at a conference down in Florida. This beautiful man was a musician, and played piano at the bar, and sang in the most beautiful voice. And every night, Ricardo would go to the bar to listen to him.

All the other patrons loved his music too and said how lucky they were to have him perform there, because he had been sick recently, in and out of hospitals, and none of the doctors could figure why he kept getting sick. But he sang so beautifully. And one night the beautiful man came over to Ricardo's table and introduced himself and sat down, and he and the beautiful man talked. And Ricardo really liked the beautiful man, the beautiful man who was clearly gay, and the beautiful man invited Ricardo up to his hotel suite for sex and—for some reason that Ricardo did not understand at the time—Ricardo turned him down. Ricardo walked back to his hotel room alone, kicking himself for not having sex with the beautiful man. It was only a few years later, when Ricardo heard that the beautiful man had died, that it became clear that the man had had AIDS. And by saying no to the beautiful man, even though he didn't know why he was saying no, he had avoided what would have been the chance of getting a death sentence. That is the power of the tiny sense, Ricardo believed, that shadow of a feeling inside a person, that makes a person say no when he has no reason to say no, or makes someone say yes, when a more rational person would be over-analyzing the risks and benefits.

And so it was with Panamá. As a lawyer, Ricardo was well versed in analyzing risks and benefits, as were all his colleagues at work. Those few colleagues that he had mentioned Panamá to in vague terms were quick to point out the dangers: the crime rate, the tropical diseases, the foreign legal system, the lack of a safety net, etc. But there was nothing they said over which he hadn't already obsessed for months. He knew the crime statistics. He had received his Hepatitis A and B shots, along with tetanus, typhoid and yellow fever. He had two Panameño attorneys on retainer in case of legal problems. And he had applied for his pensionado status which, if granted, would give him automatic access to the Panameño health care system. So, to him it wasn't a decision that he was making—it was an irresistible calling he was following. The decision was making him.

Weeks passed since Ronald had called Ricardo.

Ronald later told him that Kit's mother had had her buried in some family cemetery somewhere. There was no service, or at least no service that either Ronald, Phillipe, or Ricardo were invited to. There was nothing to do but push it all down and move forward.

Ricardo's last day at work finally arrived. His cases had been distributed; his duties reassigned; his office was clean; he really had no reason to be at work, except that he was scheduled to be there. He sat at his large empty desk, just thinking. Just thinking.

How do people end up on the path that defines their life? He remembered a story he heard as a child in Spain about a servant who sees Death in the market and knows that Death is after him, so he flees to Samarra to hide from Death, and when the wealthy merchant who owned the servant confronts Death in the marketplace about losing a good servant, Death explains that he was just as surprised as the servant to see him in the market because he didn't have an appointment with the servant until the next day in Samarra. As a child, Ricardo marveled at the cruel twist of the story. As an adult, Ricardo shivered at the truth of the story. He just wanted to write. Panamá was just a means-whereby, hopefully not a Samarra for him. He was not some Under-the-Volcano burnt-out relic. He had a purpose in moving to Panamá. The bathhouses and the brothels were just necessary requirements, not the end goal. He just needed a place to write. He would move anywhere that had good brothels, bathhouses, good health care and a low cost of living. He just wanted to be able to live somewhere and write and get his basic health needs met. And his basic health needs included sex. If it wasn't for the need to have time to write, he would stay in Hamburg, which offered him all the sex he wanted, a well-paying job and health insurance... But the job sucked all the hours of the day from him... so he had no choice but to go.

He thought back to his own life. The two marriages, those two promises, the hopes, the two divorces, the recriminations, the moving, the various trips to rehab, law school, the brothels, Haley up in St. Catherines, the bathhouses, the dark steamy sex, the empty nights, the freedom, finding Eve, loving Eve, losing Eve, the trips to Panamá, the short stories, the thrill of seeing *Messieurs* in the bookstores, the utter monotony of probate cases, meeting Kit, losing Kit... it all blended into a story that he thought of as simply his life. To him, it was nothing remarkable. Maybe it had wider extremes than other people's lives. But Ricardo assumed that everyone else's life was filled with equal amounts of anguish, and with an equal inability to make sense out of them.

He looked at his watch. Two o'clock. He still had three more hours to sit at his desk to be available for anyone who wanted to drop by and wish him well. He just wanted to leave all this behind him, shed these memories the way that trees shed leaves in the fall, to let them all fall away, let them all be forgotten. Why couldn't he do that? Why couldn't he just let all these memories evaporate from him when he flew to Panamá? Did he have to carry the weight of Haley, Eve, Kit and Phillipe with him everywhere he went? Do we have to wear our memories like tattoos, he thought, wearing us down by the sheer weight of the ink? Snakes shed their skin. Why can't we? Why can't we just start again? Why can't we metamorphosize into butterflies?

These were the thoughts that went through Ricardo's head on that cold wintry afternoon in Hamburg, on his last day at work in the law firm, his last day as a employed resident of the United States, with a regular paycheck and good health insurance, and an established address and a reachable cell phone number. In just a few short days, he would be on a plane to Panamá. Maybe the plane would be his cocoon, the woven container in which he would begin to transform into some other creature.

Chapter 32: The Point of No Return

Ricardo was sitting at yet another airport gate area, waiting for the third and last leg of his trip to Panamá. The next plane would take him out of the United States. And while this flight did not mark his last time in the US, it was nonetheless indelibly marked, for it meant he had crossed the point of no return. While he did not know if he would live in Panamá for the rest of his life, he was clear that he would never return to the well-ordered probate lawyer life he had lived these past eight years.

The nervousness that he felt in the shuttle bus trip to the first airport in Buffalo had faded away, and had been replaced by a terrible sadness, a hollow feeling that he might not ever see certain people again. It went further than Kit. The loss of Kit, horrible as it was, was not of Ricardo's doing. Whether it was her genetics—those twisting DNA strands carrying depression genes that get tangled up with other destructive genes—or whether it was the Fates—twisting the strands of our lives and experience into equally self-destructive outcomes—Ricardo did not know, or care. All he knew was that he didn't play a hand in her choice to cut herself so deeply, too deeply this time for anyone to save her.

But Eve, and even Marta, they were different stories. Ricardo had loved them, needed them, for different reasons. And it was his doing that now moved him away from their presence. He thought of Marta, who had been the only lighthouse in his own dark days. Although he emailed her often and occasionally chatted with her by phone, he hadn't actually seen her in a year. And the fact that he would have email and Skype capability in Panamá didn't diminish the sense that he was moving away from her, that she would slip through his fingers as the plane carried him further and further away. And although he had seen Eve several times at the office building over the past year, albeit without much verbal contact, Ricardo still felt an irrational loss in leaving, as if her physical proximity, just knowing she was nearby, had provided him some comfort these past eighteen months. In his own way, he still loved her.

He couldn't seem to stop categorizing his other losses even though he knew it only made him sadder. He thought of Haley. He knew it had been years since he had seen her, but it startled him to realize that it had actually been seven years. He thought of that boyish body, those small breasts, and the image of her riding him cowgirl style. He wondered if she was a housewife in some Canadian suburb with squalling children now. Or even if she was still alive.

He gave his head a shake as if to scold the memory out of his brain. Then he looked around the waiting area. It was the usual collection of fat Americans grazing on airport sandwiches and chips while staring at iPads, tablets, netbooks, and Kindles. Here and there sat couples, thinner and darker, who were obviously returning home to Panamá. The older couples sat quietly, while the younger ones had joined the majority and also had their heads buried in electronic devices.

But the thoughts of Haley returned to his head. He thought of other prostitutes he had known, the many different brothels he had been to. Images of the steam rooms of the Buffalo bathhouses came up in his head as well. He would miss those, too. And while he knew there were plenty of bathhouses in Panamá, they weren't quite the same. He would miss the smooth shaved bodies of the North American male. And he would miss the soft lights of the Buffalo steam room which provided their own visual delight as other twosomes and threesome pursued their business. But then he remembered the bathhouses and the brothels of Spain and France and realized that this was not the first time he had left a country and a culture behind. This thought only made him sadder. Maybe it was in his nature, his DNA or the twisted strands of his own fate, to always be pulling away from those places and those people that he loved. He had always felt like an outsider, but here in this airport, on this day, in this country, he felt like the only person on earth, and these other fleshy forms circulating around him, sitting near him, moving in patterns all about... they were just phantoms, human-looking androids or aliens that he could not count on for anything, to whom he had nothing to offer, and whom could only offer him the feeling of flesh for brief stolen moments of time. They were form without substance, zombies, dead in thought, dead in action, simply moving because they had been set into motion. He was no longer an outsider to the world of humans—he was the only human left in a world of phantoms.

The loudspeaker over his head crackled on and started to compete with the other announcements from other loudspeakers up and down the long hallway. They were about to start the boarding process to his gate. Ricardo stood up and moved toward the line.

Chapter 33: Back in Panamá City

Panamá City was just as Ricardo remembered it from four months earlier, minus the torrential downpours. He arrived in the early evening, made his blurry way through Customs, past the crowded sidewalk outside of the airport full of pickpockets and gypsy cabdrivers trying to score a fare, and found a regulation taxi which took him to a standard North American-brand hotel. He had booked a room for two nights. The day after tomorrow he would catch the bus to La Chorrera. But tomorrow had had some business to take care of. Tomorrow was going to be a medicinal day. But all he wanted tonight was a hot shower and a good night's sleep in an air-conditioned room.

The shower was hot, the room was nicely air-conditioned, but the good night's sleep did not come. He dreamed badly again. Not that he had bad dreams, per se. He would have welcomed even bad dreams. But his mind refused to generate any images. His dreaming consisted only of long stretches of grey empty spaces, devoid of image or feeling, as if the hollowness he had felt for the last few days was being translated into visual emptiness. His dreaming was always like this when he felt this sad. There was only one cure to this type of sadness. The next morning, he would go to Maxine's.

There are brothels and there are brothels. Most try to affect a certain level of class, a certain elegance. Maxine's was just a whorehouse. A drive-thru burger joint in the midst of fine restaurants. Ricardo had been there a few times before. It was never his first choice. But in a pinch, it would do. You walked in, picked out a girl, paid the madam forty dollars, went to one of the closet-sized rooms that held only a small bed, did your fucking and left. Maxine's had just what Ricardo needed—no pretensions, no chit-chat, just a hot shot of immediate flesh and fucking.

The next morning, after a bland continental breakfast in the hotel coffee shop, Ricardo took a taxi over to Maxine's. It was located in a sketchy section of Panamá City, not the part of town a gringo should venture into on foot at night. Even during the day, Ricardo always took a cab there. It opened at nine in the morning, and Ricardo liked to be there right when they opened—it was simply a safer time of day to be in that neighborhood. He knew that there wouldn't be much of a selection at that time of day—only maybe two or three girls on duty—but that didn't matter. In brothels that used a line-up, the point was to pick the prettiest prostitute. But at Maxine's, physical beauty was not a requirement for working there. They would hire any girl—fat, ugly, old—it did not matter. There never really were any pretty ones to choose from. Pretty ones had plenty of other nicer places to work.

Ricardo paid the taxi driver and got out of the cab and walked into Maxine's. The madam was sitting at the same spot behind a desk by the front door as before. It was as if she hadn't moved from that spot in the last year. She looked up at him, nodded as if she might have remembered him, and said, "Which one?"

Ricardo looked over to the couch. Two girls were sitting there, each staring into their cell phones, either texting or playing a video game. Each wore a bikini top with a pair of short-shorts and cheap high-heel shoes. Each had a roll of fat hanging over the tops of their shorts. Neither one looked up at him. He picked the one with the smaller roll of fat.

"La una a la derecha," he said, indicating the one on the right.

"Rosey!" the madam called out. The girl on the right, startled, stood up and looked at Ricardo for the first time, and then nodded.

"Forty-five dollars," said the Madam to Ricardo. The price had gone up five dollars since a year ago. Ricardo paid her. Then he followed the girl to one of the small rooms. It held only a small mattress atop of a wood bed frame. A box of condoms was on the floor.

Once inside, the girl closed the door, and pointed to his pants, indicating that he should drop them. He did so and pulled down his underwear. She inspected his cock, lifted it up and looked underneath and, finding no lesions or discharge, grunted in approval and started taking off her bikini top and shorts. She wasn't wearing any underwear. Then she sat on the bed and waited for Ricardo to finish undressing. Ricardo got undressed, folded his clothes neatly and placed them in the corner of the room on the floor—as there was no chair or table—and sat down on the bed beside the girl. She was a dark-skinned Panameña, short, with long thick curly black hair that started low on her forehead. Her complexion, like most Panameñas, was creamy smooth. Her nipples were small and almost black in color. She didn't have any stretch marks on her belly. Ricardo wondered how she had avoided having babies so long, as she looked to be in her mid-twenties. Her pubic area was shaved, as was the custom among most prostitutes, to avoid crabs and lice. He ran his fingers up and down her forearm. It was covered with fine dark hair. Ricardo could only image how bushy her pubic hair would have been if she didn't shave. She reached over and began to work Ricardo's cock.

At first, he couldn't get hard.

"Acuéstese," Ricardo told her. She lay down. Ricardo started massaging her breasts with his left hand, letting his fingers gently ripple over those dark nipples, while he stroked himself with his right hand. Soon he started getting hard.

As soon as he was hard, she sat up, reached down to the floor and grabbed a condom from the box, opened it while Ricardo continued to stroke himself. She then pushed him down on the bed, unrolled the condom over his cock, wet her fingers with her mouth, and rubbed the spit into her pussy, and then squatted down over him, gliding his cock up into his pussy, and started riding him up and down.

Ricardo kept his eyes on those beautiful small pointed breasts, watching them bounce up and down as she rose and fell. He looked up at her face once, but she had a vacant expression and was staring into space. He quickly returned his gaze to her breasts.

Her pussy was very tight, confirming the lack of children. Ricardo's breathing started becoming more rapid. He reached up and grabbed her wrists and placed them on his shoulders so he could fantasize that she was holding him down and fucking him. She evidently was familiar with this role because she began to thrust more rapidly. She pulled her knees up so that she was now squatting on the balls of her feet so she could let the whole weight of her body fall on Ricardo with each downward thrust. The last thought that Ricardo had before he moaned and came was that she was very good. With his last ejaculation, he reached up and pulled her down on top of him and held her.

He could tell she didn't like being held, so he released her after a few seconds. He reached down and wrapped his fingers around the base of his cock, holding the bottom of the condom in place while she dismounted. She reached under the bed for a roll of paper towels. He pulled the condom off with a snap, wiped his cock with the paper towel she handed him, placed the condom in the paper towel and wadded it up. He then realized there was no wastebasket in the room. He looked at her with a quizzical expression, holding the wadded-up paper towel. She pointed under the bed. He bent down and peered under the wooden bed frame. There were twenty or more wadded-up paper towels under the bed. He tossed his in there among the rest, stood up and began to get dressed. Before he left the room, he reached into his pocket and found the twenty-dollar bill he had placed there earlier. He handed it to her.

"Gracias," she said, and opened the door.

Ricardo realized it was the first time he had heard her

speak.

He followed her out of the room. She walked over to the sofa, picked up her cell phone and returned to her texting or video game. The other girl was gone, probably in one of the other rooms.

Ricardo walked up to the madam and asked her to call a cab.

*   *   *

Back at the hotel, Ricardo placed a "Do Not Disturb" sign on the outside of his door and took another hot shower. He was beginning to feel better. He brewed some coffee in the tiny coffee pot in the bathroom, and drank a cup while he finished drying off.

While he was getting dressed, he looked at his watch. It was almost 10:30. It was too early for lunch, and he wasn't hungry. He started thinking about his morning, about Rosey's dark nipples, and about his strange addiction to sex. He didn't like the style of sex at Maxine's, but he needed it today. Sometimes he wondered if his need for sex was getting out of control. He was always careful, whether in the bathhouses or the brothels, but still, sex with strangers was inherently risky. Lately, he worried he was taking too many risks. As he thought about these things, a familiar feeling began to come over him. He pulled out his netbook computer, turned it on and began to type. Once again, he was carried away as the words flowed out of him...

What Happens Next

"What happens next?" Brian asked.

The girl didn't answer him. She just stood there, smoking a cigarette. Brian was strapped, spread-eagle, to two wooden posts. Leather straps held his wrists and ankles firm, although the strap around his neck was loose. He was naked except for his underwear. Earlier, when he was undressing and the girl told him to keep his underwear on, he had wished he had worn a fancier pair, something with color or a design, rather than basic white.

Brian could not remember when he first saw the "Introduction to Bondage" private lessons advertised on one of those Backpage websites. The ad claimed that everyone who tried it came back for more. He had done his due diligence, of course, checked out various reviews of the place. One thing about the internet: there's no shortage of people willing to review something. All of the reviews stressed how safe the place was. Pricey, but safe. So, Brian had called the number and made an appointment.

He showed up on time, paid the two hundred dollar cash-only fee to a woman at the front desk, who escorted him down a hall to a small room and told him to wait there. A few minutes later, Evette came in. At least, that's what Brian thought she said her name was. She made it very clear that she was going to do all the talking, that he was not to speak, that he could not ask any questions, that his job was to obey her, and that any disobedience would result in him being thrown out of the place. She told him to nod if he agreed to the terms. Brian nodded.

She told him to follow her, and he did. They walked down another hallway, with Evette in front. She was wearing tight leather shorts and a leather bustier with small chains hanging from various places. Her boots went right up to her knees. "They must be uncomfortably hot," Brian thought. Her skin was bare from her knees up to her ass. Brian admired how muscular her legs were. Her leather shorts ended right above the lower cheeks of her ass, and Brian watched her ass move up and down as she walked. "I'm enjoying this already," he thought. Evette's dark hair was tied back in a no-nonsense hair tie. Around her neck was some type of leather and metal device that Brian didn't understand. Other than that, she wore no jewelry.

They stepped into the room that held two wooden posts, situated in the middle of the room. They appeared to be bolted to the concrete floor. Various straps were attached to metal rings that lined the sides of the wood. A single plank of wood, about head-level, connected the two posts. Evette told him to undress. Brian obeyed, folding his pants and shirt and placing them on a nearby chair. But when he started to take off his underwear, she told him no, to leave them on, and to stand by the wooden posts. Then she quickly tied both his wrists to the upper portion and secured his ankles to the lower portion of the posts. When he was securely tied, she loosely fastened a leather strap around his neck and tied it to the wooden crossbeam between the posts. Then she stepped back as if to study him and lit a cigarette. She smoked slowly and looked him up and down. It seemed like a long wait to Brian. She was almost halfway done with the cigarette when he asked, "What happens next?"

Evette didn't answer him. She just continued smoking. When she was done with her cigarette, she dropped it on the floor and stepped on it. Then she turned to a small table to her left. Brian hadn't noticed the table before, nor the number of items on it. But now he did. And now he saw the small riding crop that was on the table. She grabbed it and swung it full force across his chest. The pain was sharp and hard. "Ow!," he screamed, "That hurt!"

"I told you, no talking!" she yelled back. "Now you will be punished."

She grabbed a small device from the table. It was a leather strap with a rubber ball in the middle. She forced the ball into Brian's mouth and then quickly tied the straps tightly around his neck. The ball kept his mouth propped open but made it impossible for him to talk or make any noise other than grunt. Plus, it tasted bad. Brian hadn't bargained for this. He began to panic. He started to protest but "uhhhhh uhhhhhh," was the only sound he could make. Saliva started to form at the corners of his mouth and drip down his chin and fall onto his chest. Brian looked down. The saliva slid down to the angry red welt that was forming on his upper chest where Evette had struck him. When the saliva hit the welt, it stung even more. When he got out of here, he was going to sue them. He would call the police. This was beyond adult entertainment—this was assault. He would close this place down.

Evette looked at him. "You're messy," she said, then she spat in his face. He winced. The spit hit him on his upper cheek and dripped down, mixing with his saliva. Brian was furious now. This was unsanitary.

"I'm going to punish you hard," she said and went back to the table. Brian now saw that the table held a number of devices. Evette selected a small cat o' nine tails from the table, stepped over to Brian and pushed the end of the whip in his face.

"See this whip? It's my favorite. See how there's a small knot tied at the end of every strand? They really hurt." Evette was smiling now, but it was not a friendly smile. It was menacing, gloating.

"Uhhhh nuhhhh nuh!"

"That's right, it's gonna hurt. But what I really like about this whip is this." She parted the leather strands and picked out a strand that had a tiny piece of wire tied into the knot. "You see this? If this one hits you, it cuts you."

"Uh uh, uh uh!" Brian shook his head no. He did not want this. This had crossed a line into something dangerous.

"Oh, I see that your neck harness is too loose," Evette said. She put the whip back on the table and went around behind him, untied the neck strap and then retired it tight so that Brian couldn't turn his head without the leather strap cutting into his neck.

"There, that's better," she said. Evette then returned to the table, picked up the whip and stepped back in front of Brian.

"I supposed you thought this was going to be all about sex," she said, and rubbed the butt end of the whip against the front of Brian's underwear, up along his balls and cock. "Well, it is all about pleasure, but the pleasure is going to be mine." With that, she flicked the cat end of the whip gently against Brian's chest. The ends of the whip spread out as they touched his skin.

"Uh-uh, uh-uh."

"No one can hear you here," she said, and with that she drew her arm back and struck Brian with the whip hard across his shoulders. It hurt bad. Brian looked down. A thin line of blood formed where the wire cut across his skin.

"Arrrgh arrgh nnaaah!" He struggled against the wrist straps.

"Yup, no one can hear you here, and I'm willing to guess that no one even knows you're here," she said as she struck him again.

"Arrrgh arrgh!"

"Yes, I could keep you here for days, and no one would ever look here, because you didn't tell anyone you were coming here, did you?"

She drew the whip back to her left this time, and hit Brian from the left side, raking the whip down across his side under his arm. Again, it drew blood.

Brian began screaming as best he could. This was insane. Someone needed to burst in and rescue him. Evette stood back and just smiled.

"Oh, you think that's bad?" she said. "When I'm done with you, you'll prefer this whip. Here's let me show you." She went over to the table and picked up a small metal stick and another small object. The metal had a wooden handle. Brian saw that the small object in Evette's other hand was a lighter. She flicked it on and began to heat the tip of the metal stick.

"This really hurts," she said.

The tip of the metal pole began to glow red. Brian couldn't control himself. All at once, he pissed in his underwear.

Evette saw it. "Oh dear, that won't do." She put the metal stick back on the table leaving the hot end extended over the edge. "We can't have you pissing and shitting here." She walked behind him and looked. "Well, at least you didn't shit. But we better make sure you don't."

She went back to the table, grabbed some items and turned towards Brian. "Why don't we just plug you up, so you don't shit?" In her left hand was a large black dildo. She squeezed some lubricant from a tube in her right hand onto the dildo and spread it on the top and all sides. She put the tube back on the table and, holding the dildo upright, walked around behind Brian and pulled down the back of his underwear. She squatted down and using the fingers of her right hand she separated his butt cheeks.

"Now where's that precious little asshole of yours? Oh, here it is."

Brian could feel the cold lubricant and the hard plastic of the dildo.

"Better relax, or this is going to hurt." With that, she began to push the dildo up into his ass. It did hurt. His sphincter tightened up involuntarily. She pushed harder. It hurt more. Brian was sure she was going to tear something. Finally, she forced the dildo past his sphincter muscles and up into his rectum. Brian felt like he was going to throw up. Fear gripped him. If he vomited with this ball in his throat, he would asphyxiate and die. He pushed the nausea down.

"Maybe just a little deeper," Evette said, and gave the dildo another shove. Brian could almost feel it in his stomach.

"Good," said Evette. "That'll keep any messes from happening." She stepped in front of Brian. There was lubricant on her fingers and she wiped them on Brian's face. "God, that almost made me horny," she laughed, and then she rubbed her crotch over her leather shorts. "But we still need to do some more work on you first."

"Nnnhnnhhhh nnnnnnhhhh."

"I told you, no talking." She picked up the whip again and snapped it across Robert's stomach. It burned.

"Ahhhhggg."

"More? You want more? Okay, we can do that. Maybe we should go a little lower." And she snapped the whip against his cock and balls. Pain wracked Brian's entire body. She struck him there again. This time harder. And again. And again. And again.

The last thing that Robert remembered, before he lost consciousness, was a scene from when he was about nine years old. Some of the older boys in the neighborhood had built a treehouse—a fort, they called it. Even though Brian was younger than the other boys, they let him join the club. Only boys were allowed up there. This annoyed the neighborhood *girls. One of the younger neighborhood girls kept pestering them to let her see the fort, and one day, when Brian was up there with the other boys, this girl was down below, calling up, asking to come up. The oldest boy told her okay, and she climbed up.*

As soon as she reached the top, the two oldest boys pulled her up through the trap door. One of them held her arms and the other one pulled her dress over her head. Then the oldest boy pulled down her underwear and they all looked. Brian looked too. The girl began to cry. One of the boys covered her mouth. Then one of the other boys reached in to finger the girl. The girl began to pee. The piss got on one of the boys hands, and he yelled, and then he punched the girl in the side. Brian felt very scared. He didn't know what was going to happen next.

When Brian regained consciousness, he was lying on a cot in another room. Evette was applying antibiotic cream to his welts.

"How was that?" she asked.

"It was good," Brian said. "I almost got to it this time. I was able to remember a lot more, especially more about what happened in the treehouse"

"I really don't like the wire bit."

"No, it seems to help. Let's keep it. By the way, the metal pole and the lighter was a nice touch. Keep that, too. That really scared me."

"Ok. Let that cream soak in a bit before you put your shirt on," she said.

"Ok. I'm just going to lie here and rest."

"See you next week?"

"I'll be here."

*   *   *

Ricardo looked up. He realized it was dark outside. He had lost track of time again. He looked at his watch. Six o'clock. He was famished. He picked up the phone and ordered room service. While he waited for his meal, he read and re-read the story, making small changes here and there. For once, finishing a story didn't leave him feeling satisfied. Normally, writing released something deep inside of him, so that afterwards he felt calm, depleted but happy. Writing was a lot like cumming. But this story was different. Again, it was another story about addiction, with another protagonist who wasn't exactly admirable, and who lacked self-awareness. It bothered him that his last few stories all were about men who had some type of personal blindness to their condition. But he still liked the story, even if it left him feeling unsettled. He was just saving it to the cloud program he used when his meal arrived. He hoped that after his dinner he would be able to sleep well and, more important, that he would be able to dream again.

Chapter 34: The Bus to La Chorrera

The next morning, Ricardo awoke feeling calm. He didn't remember any dreams, but he thought he did dream. After breakfast, he checked out of the hotel and walked the eight blocks to the bus station. There were a few tour agencies that operated private mini-bus services for gringos for an exorbitant fee, but Ricardo always preferred the local buses. Panameño bus stations were chaotic places, sometimes no more than a vacant lot with five or six buses arriving and departing at the same time, sending up huge clouds of dust. There were no posted schedules, no signs, and certainly no route numbers or maps. Gringos who spoke no Spanish simply found it impossible to navigate the sea of buses. It may have been that the chaos and confusion were intentional, in order to support the much-needed guides that worked for the hotels and tour services that escorted gringos to the bus stations and make sure they got on the right bus—all for a small fee, of course.

However, Ricardo's Spanish was good and he had taken these buses before, and after a ten-minute wait standing at a certain corner of the lot, the bus to La Chorrera arrived. Ricardo lined up with the other Panameños, paid his fee, and took a window seat a few rows back on the side of the bus away from the sun. He set his backpack on the floor between his legs and sat back for the 40-kilometer ride to La Chorrera. As he settled into his seat, he noticed for the first time the girl sitting in front of him.

She wasn't directly in front of him, as he was in the window seat and she was in the aisle seat, an angle which gave Ricardo a view of the back of her hair and right side of her face, and a small view of the top of her shoulder near her neck where her blouse ended as the skin curved down forward to her front. Her hair was black, of course, slightly wavy, and pulled back in a pony tail. It had been recently shampooed and was still damp. Ricardo could smell the scent of freshly-washed hair, intermingled with either a soap or light perfume. The impression that the fragrances left him with was that of freshness. As the bus lurched forward, Ricardo began to study this girl, or at least the part of her that he could see and sense.

She was obviously a Panameña, with that light, slightly olive, slightly café colored skin that he liked. The skin on the side of her face was smooth, with no blemishes. With her hair pulled back, he could see the typical soft wisps of female sideburns that appeared where her hairline ended and continued down in front of her ear almost to the lower part of her jaw. Ricardo never knew why he found hair on women so attractive, but he did. He leaned his body ever so slightly to the right to catch a glimpse of her nose. It was aquiline and her cheekbone was high. Her lips were full. He guesses that she was about twenty-five. She appeared to be gazing off into space, not thinking of anything. Although he could not see her body, he could tell that she was thin but not too thin. The tight-fitting blouse she was wearing implies she had some curves worth exhibiting.

Ricardo shifted his upper torso back, half-closed his eyes, and silently took in a deep breath, trying to capture more of her scent. It was a classic scent, but one he couldn't identify. It almost had the smell of a pine forest without the pine scent, something that opened the nostrils and implied a vast, silent forest. Yet there was a hint of something flora, a bit musky, just a hint, maybe a trace of rose or some other flower.

Ricardo exhaled, opened his eyes, and looked again at her neck, at the skin that flowed up from her collarbone to the firm line of her jaw. He wondered how wonderful it would feel to be kissing that neck, nibbling on that jawline, running his tongue over those soft downy dark sideburn wisps and then probing her ear with his tongue. He looked down at his hands and noticed the veins in them, how pronounced they are, like the hands of an old man.

He didn't know why he loved women so much. It's not like he had a history of successful love relationships with them. Either they had a personality that got in the way or *his* personality got in *their* way but either way, his past lovers, while frequent, never endured. He wondered if it was just the physical form of feminine beauty that he loved.

He glanced over to his left. Across the aisle an older woman, maybe thirty-five or forty, sat heavily on her seat. She was thick around the middle, and the fatty back of her arms jiggled as the bus rumbled forward. Although she could be half of Ricardo's age, he would not fuck her. It was sad but true. He considered how women fell into three distinct groups for him: women who were so attractive he would fuck them no matter how bitchy they were; women who were pleasant-enough looking that he would fuck them *if* their personalities were sweet and they seemed to like him and enjoy him; and women who did not physically appeal to him whom he would not fuck no matter how sweet, charming, interesting, or loving they were. He felt bad being so judgmentally chauvinistic, so cruel in his preferences, but he could not help it. It was how he felt. If a woman was beautiful and young, the world was hers... or at least Ricardo was hers.

He turned his gaze back to the woman in front of him and studied the details of her hair, how thick it was, how clean it looked, how the waves flowed together back and forth over her head, tighter and tighter down the back of her head as they merged into the white elastic band that held the pony-tail, and then exploded out the other side, fanning out down her shoulders and then behind the back of her seat. He looked at the tight light-blue blouse with a small bit of lace on the edges, the slight bulge of a collarbone that he could see, the shadow that her jaw made on her neck, her small ear with a simple earring consisting of a small purple amethyst stone in a silver setting. He marveled how he could feel so entranced by a complete stranger while at the same time knowing he would never know anything more about her, would never meet her, would never talk with her. He knew that some men had the gift of gab, and that they could—or at least claimed they could—strike up a conversation with any woman, using anything as a pretext to start chatting, then start saying witty things, all in an effort to elicit a laugh from the woman, a signal that she was relaxed and comfortable enough to laugh at some little joke. Ricardo had seen such scenes in countless movies. He had seen men in bars attempt such maneuvers, usually without success, but occasionally successful. But he couldn't do such things—it simply was not in his make-up. He wondered if that's why he wrote. Maybe that was how the brain worked— that people only had so much creativity, and some used it to chat up women, and some used it to paint or write. Maybe he was like the autistic kid who couldn't interact with others but could count cards in the casino or memorize train schedules. He didn't know. He certainly would not trade his writing for the ability to chat up a million women.

After about an hour, the bus arrived in La Chorrera. The girl sitting in front of him stood up. She was wearing tight blue jeans that hugged her ass—the preferred blue jean look among Panameña women. He admired her ass, especially the way the blue jean material curved up underneath and out of sight. He stood up. The heavier woman across the aisle to his left also stood up and stepped into the aisle between Ricardo and the girl. He followed them both out of the bus. They both turned to the left and walked up the hill. Ricardo's direction was to the right. He never did catch a glimpse of the young girl's face. He walked about twenty feet to an intersection and hailed a cab. The hostel where he's booked a room was off the beaten track, and Ricardo didn't feel like walking there. He got into the back seat and gave the cab driver directions.

The cab driver looked at him through the mirror above the windshield.

"You are American?" the driver said in English.

"Sí, soy gringo," Ricardo answered.

"Oh my God. Where you from?"

"'Estados Unidos."

"Oh my God. First time in Panamá?" the driver persisted in English.

"No, he estado aqui muchas veces antes," Ricardo answered, indicating he's been here many times before.

"Oh my God. You want woman? You want man?"

Ricardo decided he didn't like this driver. He was clearly pimping or hustling.

"No," Ricardo responded.

"Oh my God. I take you to nice hotel. I take you to nice brothel."

"No," Ricardo said, a bit louder.

"Oh my God. I get you young man. Good sex."

"Pare el taxi!" Ricardo shouted.

The driver immediately brought the taxi to a halt.

Ricardo threw a few dollars into the front seat of the cab and climbed out. The driver yelled something at him but Ricardo kept moving. It appeared that he would be walking the rest of the way to the hostel, after all. He was angry that the driver tried to hustle him, but as he walked along, he wondered if there was anything about him, besides his being a gringo, that elicited the hustle, especially wondering why the driver asked him twice if he wanted a man. Did this driver always pitch the same sex line to any older gringo man traveling alone? The man's English was quite poor, especially the incongruous "Oh my God" which preceded every question. Ricardo didn't know. He hoped he didn't look like a sex tourist. He didn't feel that he was a sex tourist. He didn't come to Panamá to have sex. He had sex wherever he went. He just happened to be in Panamá right now. Still, he was unnerved by the encounter.

After a number of blocks, Ricardo reached the hostel. The manager remembered him. The previous September he and Ricardo had agreed that Ricardo could stay for a month for seventy dollars a week. Ricardo had picked this hostel because it was one of the few that had some private rooms.

The manager showed him to the room that would be his for the next month. It was a tiny room, basically a small closet with a bed. But the door had a lock, the bathroom was down the hall and the hostel was safe.

Chapter 35: Wilson

Two weeks passed. Ricardo had looked at many apartments, and several habitaciones to rent in someone's home, but none fit exactly what he was looking for. In past visits, any safe place would do, but this selection of living space was something more permanent, a place that needed to work for months, possibly years. He wanted an apartment walking distance from the markets, bars, and bus stop, but not smack in the noisy center of the city. It had to be a place that was light and pleasant but also had to have enough privacy so that he could bring a guest home if he wanted, either male or female, for an undisturbed evening of intimacy. And most importantly, it had to have a writing desk and internet, and be quiet enough so that he could write. Several of the apartments came close but missed the mark for one reason or another. However, Ricardo was patient. He knew that the ideal place would turn up eventually. And in the meantime, seventy dollars a week was not bad for a safe bed to sleep in at the hostel.

This particular evening, Ricardo was having dinner at Los Cuñados. The same boy who had waited on him a year ago was still there and waited on him again. Ricardo saw Miguel talking to some women in the back of the restaurant. After a few minutes, Ricardo caught Miguel's eye, smiled and nodded to him. Miguel came over to his table with a friendly but quizzical look on his face. As an owner of a popular restaurant, Miguel couldn't remember every customer, and clearly he was trying to place Ricardo's face. Ricardo introduced himself and indicated in a low voice where they had met. Ricardo fully understood Miguel's need to keep his personal interests and activities private from the other restaurant personnel, who were probably family. So Ricardo behaved accordingly. To anyone watching, Ricardo was just a returning tourist saying hello to the owner of his favorite restaurant. Miguel and Ricardo chatted for a while, and Ricardo mentioned that he was looking for a place to live—which was actually Ricardo's true agenda in coming to Los Cuñados tonight—and Miguel said he would make some inquiries. Ricardo thanked him. Miguel excused himself to attend to other matters, and Ricardo returned to his meal. This evening Ricardo had pescado en salsa roja, a large fish filet sautéed in garlic and served in a spicy red sauce on a bed of rice with vegetables. It was very good, and Ricardo was hungry, and thus did not notice the man whom the waiter sat at the table next to Ricardo.

"I can tell by the way you like your dinner that you're an American," the man said.

Ricardo looked up, not sure how to respond to this ambiguous comment. The man seated at the adjoining table was what would be described as rotund—a heavy, beefy man, with balding red hair and a white goatee.

"My name is Wilson," says the man, unfazed by Ricardo's lack of response to his opening remark. His voice was loud and gregarious, the type of self-confident voice that people who like to talk about themselves have. He extended a beefy hand.

Ricardo didn't want to talk but couldn't be impolite. He shook the man's hand.

"Pleased to meet you, Wilson," he said. "My name is Ricardo."

"Yea-up, I can tell you're an American now," the man said, "by the sound of your voice. And I dare say, you're from New York, but not originally. No sir, not originally, but definitely recently."

Ricardo's was intrigued. "That's correct, Wilson. How did you know?"

"It's in the e's and the a's, New Yorkers add a slight u sound to the e's and they flatten their a's. But yours is faint, which indicates that you've lived there, hmmm, I would guess about ten years, just enough to pick up the sound but not enough to lock it in. Then there's your name: Ricardo. The way you pronounce it definitely says you were born abroad, and by the slight 'th' sound of your s's, I feel confident you were born or raised in Spain. And although you have an American bone structure to your face, there is a slight Spanish skin tone, very faint. Putting that all together, I would guess that your mother was Spanish and your father was American, but I admit, the guess about which parent was Spanish is based more on common marriage patterns than any observation."

"Wow! That's amazing, Wilson. Truly amazing. And what about the way I eat? You said something about that indicating I was American."

"Oh, that was a bit of an educated guess. Americans tend to hunker down over their food when they eat alone. They don't sit straight up—they guard it as if they're afraid someone might steal it."

"Wilson, I'm truly speechless."

"Yes, it's ironic that a linguist has that effect on people, isn't it?" With that, Wilson began to laugh, a booming laugh that caused people at some of the other tables to look his way. After he finished laughing, he said, "Well, Ricardo, I'm also dining alone tonight. Mind if I join you?"

Ricardo wasn't used to people being this forward. Of course, he had been spending most of his time with Panameños, who were by nature more reserved.

"Please do, Wilson. Mi mesa es su mesa."

Wilson moved his large hulk awkwardly over to Ricardo's table.

"My Spanish is pretty primitive, Ricardo, but I think you said 'my table is your table'. That's pretty funny."

The waiter, noticing the large man's movement, came over quickly, and asked in Spanish if everything was alright.

"What did he say?" asked Wilson to Ricardo.

"He just asked if everything was alright." Ricardo then addressed the waiter. "Está bien. Es mi nuevo amigo."

"I guess I'd better let you order for me, Ricardo. What's good here?"

"The fish is excellent tonight," Ricardo replied.

"Never touch it. Do they have any lamb or beef?"

"They do a very good picadillo here. It's a Panamanian dish with meat cut into little cubes and cooked with cubed potatoes and vegetables."

"Hmm...can they do a steak?"

"Well, I didn't see it on the menu tonight, but I will ask."

Ricardo caught Miguel's eye and waived him over and asked, as a favor, whether the kitchen could cook a steak for Wilson. Miguel said it would be no problem and asked how Wilson wanted it done.

Ricardo relayed the question and Wilson said, "Medium rare, please. And I'd like a Manhattan."

Ricardo translated and Miguel left to tell the cook and the bartender.

"Who was he?" Wilson asked after Miguel left.

"One of the owners."

"Well my, you do have connections. Yes, sir! You are a man to know."

Ricardo thought to himself that this man was certainly a character. This section of La Chorrera did not have many English-speaking restaurants, and Ricardo wondered why Wilson was in this part of town.

"Are you from the states, Wilson?" he asked.

"Well, yes and no. Born in North Carolina, but spent most of my youth in California. Living in Canada now. Montreal. Cold as shit there now. Glad to be here."

"Do you speak French?" Ricardo asked.

"Not a word, no sir. I know it's odd. Most linguists speak three or four tongues, but I only know English."

"So how did you get so good at deciphering where people are from?"

"Well, it's more of a hobby. I used to be an NLP trainer. Ever heard of that?

Ricardo had to think. "Hmm... neuro-linguistic programming, or something like that?" he asked.

Wilson beamed. "That's right! It was all the rage in the seventies and early eighties, but you don't hear much about it anymore. Yet, all the techniques are still valid. I use it every day. Noticed how I got you to order a meal for me that wasn't even on the menu?"

"You asked."

"No, it was more than that. You probably don't even remember, but I touched your arm ever so lightly when I said the word 'me' when I asked you to order for me—that was to ground you, to make you disposed to taking care of me... and you did! Thank you."

It was true. Ricardo had not even been aware that Wilson had touched him. Ricardo did not know what to think of this man.

"And now Ricardo, you're beginning to have doubts," Wilson said. "Notice how you turned your head ever so slightly to the right to look at me? It's a sideways look, suggesting you are thinking there's some angle to this conversation. Get it? Angle? Hoo whee, I love people." And with that Wilson started to laugh again.

Ricardo found himself smiling, in spite of himself. This fellow was certainly a character.

"So... back to my question, Wilson. How did you get so good at deciphering accents?"

"Well, as I said, I was an NLP trainer for many years, which certainly teaches you to observe people as to what they are doing in the here-and-now moment. But I was also interested in where they came from. Sometimes a person's body language can tell you that, like the way you hunkered over your meal. But a person's accent, how they speak the language, can tell you a lot more. So, I went back to school, took a hodgepodge of courses at different schools and basically taught myself. It's a great way to meet people. And sometimes get them to even pay for my meal." Wilson said with a smile.

"I'm not paying for your meal, Wilson." Ricardo replied.

"Ha," Wilson laughed. "The evening isn't done yet, Ricardo."

Just then the waiter brought Wilson's Manhattan. Wilson took a sip to taste it, swirled the liquid a bit in his mouth before swallowing, nodded in approval and took a huge gulp, emptying half the glass.

"Pretty damn good for Central America," he pronounced.

Ricardo couldn't decide whether Wilson was a harmless character, a bombastic gringo, or a psycho. He decided to change the subject.

"What do you do in Montreal, Wilson?"

"I work for Montevancia."

Well, Ricardo thought to himself, that explains why he was here in La Chorrera. Montevancia was a Canadian trading company that was heavily involved in shipping deals. Ricardo had just read an article about them in the paper that morning. They didn't do any shipping themselves but made money by buying and selling product on ships as they were in transit. Ricardo didn't understand the business exactly, but the newspaper article almost made it sound like Montevancia was in the distressed merchandise business, buying containers of product on huge cargo ships as they moved through certain ports, unloading the product and then loading it on other cargo ships to new locations. The article implied that lot of wheeling and dealing occurred in the business, not all of it on the up-and-up. But the only reason that the article had caught Ricardo's eye was that Montevancia had a large office in La Chorrera that employed about twenty-five locals, and there was a rumor that Montevancia was going to close that office. Even for a large city like La Chorrera, the loss of twenty-five jobs would hurt many families and many businesses. The article stated that Montevancia adamantly denied the rumors.

"Really? I just was reading about your company in the paper today."

Wilson laughed, "Yeah, I bet. Everyone's pretty stirred up."

"The article was something about rumors about closing the local office."

"Oh, yeah, that office is so history."

This off-handed remark startled Ricardo. The article quoted a Montevancia spokesperson saying the opposite.

"Oh," Ricardo said, I thought it was just a rumor."

"Well, it is a rumor, but it's a true rumor. I'm down here to give the employees the bad news. We're going to phase out that office over the next three months. We only set it up to establish business relations with enough local labor pools, shipping companies and gangs so that we could do business. Now that we have those contacts, we can run the whole operation from Canada with just one agent down here. Need a job, Ricardo?"

"Ah, no thanks, I'm retired."

"Ha, I bet you are. Down here to do some sport fishing, no doubt."

This was too much information too fast for Ricardo: Wilson's candid admissions, the reference to gangs, and the final reference to sport fishing, which was local slang for sex tourism.

"Ah... Wilson, a couple of questions... First, why are you telling me all this? It all seems rather explosive information to tell a complete stranger."

"Ha, no American's ever a stranger to me, Ricardo, no matter where they were born. Plus, it'll be in the paper tomorrow. Boy, the public relations dude had to do some serious backpedaling this afternoon with the press. Hoo whee!" Wilson started laughing again.

The waiter brought Wilson's steak. He stopped laughing, took his knife and cut a small piece, put it in his mouth, and tasted it as intently as he had swirled the first sip of his Manhattan. After a couple of chews, he swallowed, grunted approval and started carving another larger piece of meat. Ricardo watched with a mixture of amazement and disgust as Wilson attacked the steak, never putting either the fork or knife down, just cutting with the knife in his right hand, and moving pieces of steak to his mouth with the fork turned upside down in his left hand. It was the first time during the encounter that Wilson wasn't actively talking. Finally, about halfway through the steak, he put his knife down to drink some water.

"How's the steak, Wilson?" Ricardo asked.

"Pretty damn good, pretty damn good, if I do say so

myself. What's your second question?"

Ricardo had to think what his second question was.

"Oh, yes. What was that reference to gangs? You said something about setting up relations with gangs in order to run the business."

"You're a good listener, Ricardo. Ha. Okay, I'll tell you. Various criminal gangs, and I'm including the government in that category, run the shipping business down here. Well, not only down here, but all over the world. Transportation, the movement of goods from one place to another, has always been the most fertile soil for criminal enterprises. The Teamsters got nothing on the Panamanian gangs. They need to control shipping so they can move stolen merchandise, drugs, and launder money, plus run a smattering of legitimate businesses. But they still need a company like Montevancia to help them get rid of unwanted merchandise. We're like those birds that crawl around the inside of hippo's mouths, picking out bits of food, helping the hippo keep its teeth clean while helping themselves to a meal. The hippos keep their mouth open and let the birds do their work. The birds, for their part, are respectful and never, never shit in the hippo's mouth. Otherwise you'd have one flat bird." With that Wilson began to laugh again.

Ricardo spent the rest of the meal listening to Wilson tell one bizarre story after another, stories of various shipping deals, huge financial gains, huge financial losses, stories of shipping containers that were supposed to hold car headlamps that also held a couple of bodies shot through the head, stories of his travels all over the world, stories of swindles and double-crosses. By the end of the evening, Ricardo was worn out from listening. And, he had decided several things. First, he did not like Wilson. Wilson was the ugly American inflated ten times the size. Bigger than life, overbearing, gargantuan in appearance and expression. It wasn't just his huge body or the belligerent way in which he talked and laughed. It was the subtle racism that ran through many of his stories. Secondly, he decided he didn't want to reveal anything more about himself to Wilson. Wilson was definitely the kind of person who asks questions solely for the purpose of finding out information he can use against the person later. Thus, Ricardo avoided the usual back and forth one-upmanship that comprises more American male story-telling sessions. Instead, Ricardo simply let Wilson talk, and asked a few questions to fill any lulls between stories. At the end of the meal, Ricardo signaled to the waiter for his check, and said to Wilson, "Well, I thank you for a most entertaining evening, but I have to say goodnight now. I have a busy schedule tomorrow."

"Oh, really?" Wilson said. "What are you up to?"

"Oh, meetings with various people," Ricardo lied.

"Well, okay. I'm sure I'll see you around."

The waiter arrived with two checks, but Wilson grabbed them both.

"I know I implied that I would trick you into paying for my meal, Ricardo, but I was lying. I've got this. It's on the company tab anyway. Hoo whee!"

Ricardo started to protest but decided not to.

"Thank you, Wilson. I appreciate that."

Wilson started to laugh again.

Chapter 36: The Next Day

True to Wilson's word, the next day's paper had a front-page article about Montevancia's decision to reduce staff at the La Chorrera office, complete with promises from some vice president that this was only a temporary closure for "restructuring purposes" which Ricardo assumed was a complete lie. Sad, Ricardo thought. A job, any job, was so hard to come by here. It would be one thing to say up front that the job was only temporary. But Montevancia had led the city government and the employees on with stories about a job with a future.

But Ricardo soon forgot about Montevancia as he made his way through the day. This morning he had an appointment to look at another apartment, this one on the outskirts of La Chorrera. It was a bus ride away from downtown, which Ricardo didn't like. But the description in the flyer made it sound very nice, and the price was right. Like many apartments, this one was not advertised in the paper or on Craigslist. It was simply posted on a flyer at the local supermarket. A local apartment for locals, a way for the landlord to screen potential renters. But Ricardo had called the number the day before, introduced himself, and the owner agreed to show him the apartment.

The bus ride was a bit longer than Ricardo had anticipated, and the bus route passed through a sketchy part of town. Ricardo did not like that. He didn't want to be riding a bus home late at night after a bit of drinking and have to deal with potential muggers who might hop on the bus for a quick robbery. That was a definite drawback. Although, he could always take a cab if the hour was very late.

But he liked the apartment. The building was very

secure, and had a nice garden in the back with patio furniture. The living area was large and well-lit. He was tempted, but decided to think on it, and told the owner he would call him back in a day or so.

On the bus ride back from the apartment, his cell phone rang. It was Miguel. He had asked around, and a friend who lived near the restaurant had a house that had an attached apartment for rent. Miguel asked Ricardo if he wanted to see it that afternoon. Ricardo agreed and they picked a time to meet at the restaurant. Miguel would introduce him to his friend.

It went without saying that Miguel had an interest in having Ricardo rent an apartment near his restaurant. Ricardo understood that immediately. Heavily closeted Panameños like Miguel needed to establish a network of safe lovers because they couldn't be seen going to gay bars. If Ricardo rented an apartment near the restaurant, Miguel would have easy access to him before or after working hours without raising his wife's suspicions. But Ricardo thought Miguel was handsome, and their encounter at the bathhouse a year ago was quite engaging, so the benefit of renting a place near the restaurant flowed in both directions. Besides, Ricardo liked that particular neighborhood. It was quiet yet near the bus stop, the parks, stores and several bars and restaurants.

Ricardo met Miguel at two, as arranged, outside of Los Cuñados. They shook hands and exchanged pleasantries. Ricardo told him about the strange man who invited himself to his table last night, and Miguel commented that he wondered about that, but he had seen the man do the same thing twice before. Evidently, this was not Wilson's first trip to La Chorrera.

As they walked to Miguel's friend's apartment, Miguel asked about Ricardo's plans, and Ricardo shared his hope of obtaining pensionado status and living more or less permanently in Panamá. As Ricardo expected, this information met with Miguel's approval and they walked the rest of the way in silence. Ricardo could sense the wheels turning in Miguel's head.

Right before arriving at the apartment, Miguel explained that his friend who owns the house was married, but was also gay, or at least bi-sexual. However, his wife found out, was not happy with this situation, and had moved out, taking her mother with her. The mother was living in the small apartment attached to his friend's house, hence the available apartment. Miguel did not know if they would reconcile but suspected they would not. His friend had talked to a lawyer. One of the reasons he was renting out the apartment was because he needed money to pay for the divorce. However, Miguel emphasized, because the wife outed his friend to other people, Miguel would appreciate it if Ricardo did not mention to anyone how he learned of the apartment. Evidently, the friend, whose name was Eduardo, also understood not to come to Los Cuñados until the scandal died down. Ricardo considered this new twist and asked if Eduardo was good looking. Miguel assured Ricardo that he was but said that he was very shy and wouldn't disturb Ricardo unless Ricardo asked him over.

Perfect, Ricardo thought.

Miguel knocked on the door to the house and Eduardo answered. Eduardo was a slight fellow, dark skin with a crew cut. Even though Miguel had told Ricardo that Eduardo was thirty years old, he looked about eighteen. And the word shy would be an understatement. Eduardo could barely maintain eye contact with Ricardo and talked in a soft voice directly to Miguel.

The apartment was a bit small, but Ricardo liked it immediately. It was furnished with a bed, linens, a reading chair, a small but complete kitchen, Wi-Fi, and best of all a nice desk and chair for working. A large tree outside shaded the apartment from heat but the large windows let in plenty of light. There wasn't really a living room to speak of, but several folding chairs were leaning up against the wall in case more than one guest were to show up. Ricardo asked how much it is. Miguel tells him two hundred fifty a month with a one fifty deposit. Ricardo said yes immediately. He handed Eduardo cash and asked for a receipt. As Eduardo scurried off to find a pen and paper, Miguel thanked Ricardo for renting the apartment and asked him to keep an eye on Eduardo, explaining that being outed had been rough on his friend. "That will not be a problem," Ricardo assured Miguel. "Not a problem at all."

After Eduardo returned with writing supplies, Ricardo helped him draft up a simple lease and deposit receipt. Eduardo gave him a key, and Ricardo said he would return in the morning to move in. The three men chatted for a while, but then Miguel had to return to the restaurant, and Ricardo said he would walk back with him. As they walked back, Ricardo wondered if there might be some three-way scenes at the apartment in his future, with him, Miguel and Eduardo. He certainly hoped so.

After thanking Miguel and saying goodbye at the restaurant, Ricardo took a cab back to the hostel. Since his encounter with the offensive cab driver several weeks ago, he always looked at the driver before getting into any taxi, but he had not seen that particular driver since. At the hostel, he informed the owner that he would move out in the morning and went to his room to pack and then take a short nap.

Ricardo had picked up the custom of many Panameños of taking a short siesta in the mid-afternoon. Usually he slept about twenty minutes, a light sleep, just enough to refresh him for the late afternoon and early evening. But today was different. Maybe it was the excitement of finally finding an apartment, but he could not fall asleep at first, but eventually, he fell into a deep, deep sleep.

He was dreaming that he was in a dark café, where the only lights were candles on the wall. In the darkest corner sat a man, handsome, naked, and covered with scales, like a reptile. In the dream it seemed normal. Ricardo squinted to make out the scales in the dim light. They seemed to be large and green, with a touch of red at the tips. He looked at the man's head. It was bald, but his face was covered with tattoos, and his forehead was very bony. The man seemed to recognize him and waved him over. Ricardo didn't go. He stepped to his right. There was a large window overlooking a city far below. Ricardo had thought this café was at street level, but he realized it was thirty or so stories above the city. The tiny lights of the city glimmered and simmered through the distance and the darkness.

"It's beautiful, isn't it?" a voice to his right spoke.

Ricardo turned. The naked scaly man was now standing by his side. He was very muscular. Ricardo looked down to his cock. It was large and semi-erect, sticking out, almost in an angry demanding way.

"Yes, it is," Ricardo says.

A female voice came from his left. "It sparkles like a beautiful diamond necklace."

Ricardo looked to his left. There was a woman standing there, full-figured, naked from the waist up, large breasts with big brown nipples. She didn't have scales, but her skin seemed to emit a green glow.

"Yes," said the scaly man. "Like a beautiful necklace on the breast of a whore."

The scaly man and the woman both began to laugh, as if this was a shared joke.

Ricardo felt that he had to get out of there, but he felt like he couldn't leave. He didn't know his way around this city and he was afraid of getting lost.

Finally, he said, "I have to find my coat" and walked quickly towards the only door he saw. He heard the man and the woman laughing behind him. He pushed the door open and stepped through it.

He was outside, on a city sidewalk. It was bright in the midday sun. There was a lot of noise as traffic roared by. The light hurt his eyes. He wasn't on the thirtieth floor after all. He looked back inside the café, but it was totally different, like an empty dirty warehouse. He didn't know where to go.

Ricardo woke up suddenly. He was in his bed at the hostel. He looked at his watch. He had been sleeping for almost two hours. He felt horrible. There was a bad taste in his mouth. The dream felt ugly, dangerous. He had no idea what it meant and wanted to get the images out of his mind. He walked stiffly down the hall to the bathroom and splashed water on his face.

Back in the room, he decided that he should go out and get a bite to eat. It was early evening now, still light, but cooler. He grabbed a light jacket and headed down the block to a local bar that served food.

It was still early by Panameño dinner standards and the bar was almost empty. Ricardo sat at the bar and ordered a hamburguesa and papas and a glass of red wine. He still felt a bit disjointed and hoped some old fashioned US comfort food would help. The wine certainly helped. The food came quickly and Ricardo ordered a second glass of wine.

He was almost done with the burger when he heard an unfortunately familiar voice.

"I thought I'd find you here. I've been looking all over town for you."

It was Wilson. He plodded up to the bar and sat his huge bulk on the bar stool next to Ricardo.

"Looking for me? Really? Why?" Ricardo asked.

"Just kidding. I just happened to see you sitting here as I walked by." Wilson started to laugh. Then he says, "Hey, watch this." He waved the bartender over. "Un ceviche, por favor."

"Uh, Wilson," Ricardo said, "I think you mean to order a cerveza, unless you want some raw fish."

"Oh yeah, I wanted a beer," Wilson laughed.

Ricardo asked the bartender to bring Wilson a beer.

"So, what are you up to tonight, Ricardo?"

The question created a dilemma for Ricardo. He didn't want to tell him about the apartment. In fact, he didn't want to tell him anything. But the question hung in the air.

"Nothing much. I was feeling tired and I thought I'd grab a burger before going to bed."

"To bed? Ricardo, it's Friday night!" Wilson squinted his eyes and looked at Ricardo. "Unless you were out sport fishing today—maybe that's why you're tuckered out. Been riding some young native girl today, Ricardo?"

Ricardo felt himself tightening up with anger.

"No, Wilson. I have not."

Wilson started to laugh. "Well if you haven't been, you should be. Most beautiful women in the world. Every time Montevancia needs to send someone down here, I volunteer. Hell, I even vacation down here. Boy howdy, best pussy in the world."

"Wilson, I wish you wouldn't talk about Panameñas that way."

"Panama-what? Oh, you mean their women. Well, hell, prostitution is legal here. Perfectly legit. And the women here are different. They enjoy sex. Whenever I meet some young chickie down here who claims she isn't interested, I just say, 'I have one hundred dollars that says you are' and by crackie, they usually come around. Hoo whee! It's a beautiful country."

"Look, Wilson, it's a poor country. Prostitution is the only way some of these women can feed themselves."

Wilson gave a little laugh, just as the bartender brought his beer. Wilson took a huge gulp and said, "That may be, Ricardo my man. But look at me. I'm three hundred pounds. Think I can get laid in Canada? Hoo whee no! Down here, it's not a problem. Hell, some of them even take it as a challenge to figure out how to ride me. Besides, you shouldn't talk. You're down here by yourself and you're too smart to stay alone. I bet you've done your fair share of sport fishing. Ha!"

Ricardo had had enough. He signaled the bartender for his bill, but he had already calculated the amount in his head, and simply handed the bartender the money when he walked over with the bill.

"Wilson, I have to go. I have a busy day tomorrow. You enjoy the rest of your stay."

Wilson looked like he was about to respond, but Ricardo got up and walked out.

Chapter 37: The Ides of March

A month or more had passed. Panamá was now in the heat of its summer. The mornings were beautiful, but by afternoon it was hot and sticky humid. But the nights were cool and Ricardo slept in his new apartment with the windows open and a light blanket. Luckily for Ricardo, there was a fan above the bed for the occasional siesta, during which he slept nude. He had helped Eduardo install screens on the windows. Ricardo paid for the materials himself, for which Eduardo was grateful, but Ricardo had ulterior motives. While Dengue Fever, Chikungunya, Malaria, and Yellow Fever were very rare in La Chorrera, they are not unknown. Ricardo always carried a small mosquito net for any bed he slept in, and he used it until the screens were installed.

Eduardo had proven to be every bit as shy as Miguel had described. Ricardo knew that they going to have sex, but he was not sure how to proceed at first. But the day after the screens were installed, he knocked on Eduardo's door, and invited him over for a glass of wine, ostensibly to thank him for helping to install the screens. After the first glass of wine and some chit-chat, Ricardo moved over to the couch where Eduardo was sitting, smiled, and begins unbuttoning Eduardo's shirt without saying anything. Eduardo's eyes widened, but he did not protest. After the shirt was unbuttoned, Ricardo reached inside the shirt, began rubbing Eduardo's chest, and then he leaned over and began kissing Eduardo's neck. Eduardo's chest, like many Panameños, was smooth and hairless. His nipples were long and erect, which Ricardo liked. Eduardo leaned slightly forward into Ricardo as Ricardo was kissing his neck, but otherwise remained passive. Then Ricardo gently pulled Eduardo's face towards his and kissed him on the lips. Eduardo began to kiss him back, gently at first and then more eagerly.

Then Ricardo took Eduardo's hand and led him over into the bedroom area, sat him down on the bed, and gently pushed on his upper body until Eduardo was lying down. Ricardo then lay on top of him and began kissing him in earnest, rubbing his hands over Eduardo's pants and then over his crotch.

Initiating sex with strangers had, of course, a number of risks—aside from disease for which Ricardo always took precautions—the main one being, of course, disappointment. Between two men, the risk of disappointment usually centered on the size and shape of the other man's cock, and the performance of one's own cock. Panameño cocks, like most men from the Americas, could vary from small to quite large, and there was no way to predict from looking at the height or weight of the man. Shape and color likewise varied. Eduardo's cock was bit on the small side, but he was circumcised and the shape was straight. Eduardo obviously shaved what little public hair he had. As soon as Ricardo pulled Eduardo's pants and underwear off, Eduardo was erect. Ricardo reached over to the open drawer of his nightstand, removed a condom, unwrapped it and rolled it onto Eduardo's cock. He then began to suck it. Although Ricardo never enjoyed the taste of latex, he was, as mentioned, always careful. As he sucked, he played with Eduardo's balls with his left hand and reached up to Eduardo's chest with his right hand and squeezed Eduardo's nipples.

Eduardo began to moan. Ricardo didn't want him to cum too soon, so he stopped. He pulled another condom from the nightstand and unrolled it over his semi-erect cock, and then crawled up over Eduardo until he was over Eduardo's face, gently forcing his cock into Eduardo's mouth. Eduardo sucked on it greedily, as if he had been wanting cock for a very long time.

As soon as Ricardo was hard, he pulled out of Eduardo's mouth, reached into the nightstand again and grabbed a tube of lubricant, bent over and applied it to his cock, and then took a glob of it and reached up under Eduardo's balls, found his asshole, gently massaged it with the lubricated finger and then eased the finger up into Eduardo's ass.

Eduardo's eyes were shut tight. His mouth was open. Ricardo took another glob of lubricant and shoved it deeper into Eduardo's asshole. He wiped the extra lube from his fingers on the sheets on the side of the bed, lifted both of Eduardo's knees up to Eduardo's chest, and began to insert his cock slowly into Eduardo's asshole, in and out, gently, letting the lubricant on his cock ease the way. Eduardo's ass was tight, but soon Ricardo was all the way inside. Eduardo began to rock his head side to side and moan softly. Ricardo began fucking Eduardo, slowly at first, with long deep strokes, and then harder. After a few minutes, without either Ricardo or Eduardo touching Eduardo's cock, Eduardo came into the condom he was still wearing. A few minutes later, Ricardo came, moaned, and collapsed onto Eduardo.

Ricardo always felt that sex communication between men was fundamentally different than sex communication between a man and a woman. He always experienced sexual communication between men as immediate and operating on much more of a primal level. Ricardo knew the first time he saw Eduardo that if he rented the apartment, they were going to have sex, that Ricardo was going to be the dominant top, and that Eduardo was going to be the passive receptive bottom. It was in the first look. Words were not necessary.

But sex between a man and a woman was so controlled by social norms that it was almost impossible not to fall into one of the roles dictated by society. Between men, the unspoken sex communication happens at the first look. When two gay or bi men first make eye contact, if they're in the mood, the eye contact is all it takes to communicate that they are going to have sex. The only question is when.

But with women, the desire might be there, but the rituals must be played out, and no one can show their true hands until the walls are down, which might take many dates, then maybe, if both are uninhibited, maybe there might be sex...maybe.

Ricardo's experience with men was that there was not much sex discussion afterwards either. He and Eduardo never discussed that first afternoon of sex. Both simply went about their lives as if it had never happened. Eduardo never knocked on Ricardo's door, but if Ricardo wanted sex, he would simply go over to Eduardo's door, knock, and if Eduardo did not have visitors, Ricardo would beckon him to follow, and they would walk to Ricardo's small apartment and Ricardo would fuck him. Ricardo thought it was a good arrangement.

The rest of Ricardo's days involved settling into his new apartment, exploring the neighborhood, finding a barber, a laundromat, and a grocery store—and doing all the trips to various stores necessary to get all the little things that one always needs for a new living space: dish soap, toilet paper, salt and pepper, a spatula, garbage bags, etc.

Ricardo set up his writing desk near his front window. He got some good ideas for some short stories, and did some writing, but nothing usable was forthcoming, at least nothing that Ricardo would send out. But this is how it is sometimes for a writer. Ricardo knew he had to write when the words sprang forth, and that he simply had to wait when the well was dry. In the meantime, he had errands to run, exploring to do, and there was always the Eduardo option. Occasionally, Miguel managed to stop by. Ricardo hadn't quite yet managed to arrange a three-way, but he knew that it was only a matter of time. Ricardo had also located a few of the local brothels, but he hadn't had time to visit them yet.

Chapter 38: Wake-up Call

The beeping cell phone woke Ricardo from an afternoon siesta. It was Marta, calling on Skype from New York.

"Ricardo, how are you? We haven't talked in forever. I love your emails, but I miss talking to you my friend. Is this an okay time to talk?"

"It's a fine time, Marta. I miss you too. I'm doing well. Love my new apartment. Love living down here. Best decision I've made in a long time."

"And how's your love life, Ricardo?"

"Hmm, you know me. Nothing too excessive."

"And the drinking, Ricardo?"

Ricardo was always careful when talking about his drinking around Marta. Whereas Marta had come through rehab and stopped drinking, Ricardo had never really given it up.

"Under control. How about you?"

"Well... to be honest, I had a bit of a relapse recently."

"Uh oh. What happened?"

"I don't know. It kinda slipped up on me. For some reason, one afternoon last week, I was in a store, and I bought some vodka, I don't know why I did it, but... well, I got hammered. The next day, I realized what I had done, and I called my sponsor and he got me into a relapse group... It's been a week, so I'm hopeful it was just a slip-up."

"I'm sorry, Marta. This is the first one in a few years, no?

"Four years, to be exact, Ricardo. Four years gone down the toilet."

"They're not down the toilet, Marta. Those four years

will make it easier to do the next four and the next four after that. You can do it. I know you can. Is this the once-a-week relapse group, or the twice-weekly group?”

“Twice-weekly. My sponsor thought I needed that.”

“Ok... that’s okay. It’s better going twice a week. If it’s more than you need, you can change groups, but nobody ever died going to group twice a week. Stick with it. And you know, Marta, you can call me anytime.”

“I know, Ricardo... I was too embarrassed at first. I wanted to tell you but, I don’t know, I felt that I had let you down.”

“Marta, sweet dear, you know how much I love you. You had a relapse, that’s all. Stick with the group and the program. I know it’s hypocritical of me to be saying that, because I obviously don’t, but it works for you. Stick with it. How’s work?”

“It’s going okay. I called in sick the day after I relapsed, but everything there is fine. How’s the writing?”

“Eh, hit a bit of a dry spot these last few weeks. But that’s not unusual. Just waiting for the flow to start again. I just need one more story to finish this collection. My publisher calls me every other day. It’s nice to be wanted, I guess.”

“I envy you, my friend. You’re down there living the dream.”

“Ha... not exactly, Marta. You know it’s odd, but in the... well let’s just say, in the circles I move in, I make a lot of acquaintances... well, I’ll just say it... I have lots of lovers, people to share my bed with, but I don’t feel like I have any friends, any really true friends down here, people I can share my thoughts and true feelings with... It’s odd. I expected to make more friends.”

“Friends are important, Ricardo, but you know, really good friends are very hard to find. I mean, friends like us.”

“Yeah. I do miss you, Marta.”

“I miss you too, Ricardo.”

They chatted for about thirty or forty minutes more, reminiscing about the rough times and the good times they had had together. Chatting with Marta always felt so natural to Ricardo. She was the closest thing he had to a soulmate. After they said their goodbyes, he sat on his couch and let his thoughts wander. What was it about Marta that made him feel so good? Was it that she understood him? He wasn't sure she did, but she accepted him, never judged him. She could ask tough questions, but she was always supportive. Maybe he simply loved her—maybe it wasn't anything rational like "compatibility" or "mutual support". Maybe he simply loved her. If that was the case, he thought, then he really did not understand life. He wished she lived closer... but then it was he who had chosen to move so far away. He made that choice for good reasons, because he needed a place to write... and now damn it, he had hit a dry spell, and no stories were forthcoming.

Some writers claimed that writing was just a job, a vocation, a habit, a career. He had heard their explanations and stories in various seminars and workshops over the years—how a writer had to sit down every day and just write, even if he has nothing to say. But Ricardo had never believed that. To him, writing was a mystery. The words and the stories just came to him, and from where he did not know. Writing was a connection to something unknown, a world apart. Whenever that certain mood came over him, he had to stop what he was doing and just write what the voice inside him dictated. He never had any idea how a particular story would end. He would just write. His publisher asked him one time if he was interested in giving a talk at a writers' symposium, and he had to decline because he realized he would have absolutely nothing to say.

These thoughts and more swirled though Ricardo's head as he sat on his couch. He looked at his watch. Five p.m. Because Panamá was so close to the equator, the sun set every day at approximately 5:45 all year. He had less than an hour of daylight left. The parks would be cooling off now. Ricardo decided to take a walk. He left his apartment but decided not to go the Parque Central, the main park, but to a smaller one about eight blocks further. He wasn't feeling particularly sexual this late afternoon, but thinking about writing had gotten him thinking about sex. He had always been aware that sex seemed to act as a catalyst for his writing, that there was something about cumming that cleaned out all rationality from his mind and body and allowed the stories to spring forth. Maybe, he thought, if he had sex tonight, he'd be able to write tomorrow. And while he was not in the mood for sex, he knew that there were a group of prostitutes that hung around this particular park in the evening. He thought that maybe just watching them might spark the creative juices.

He got to the park and took a seat on one of the concrete benches. The sun was still a bit bright for prostitutes to come out. These particular women worked for a small brothel down the street but they trawled the park for customers and then took them back to their brothel. But like those creatures of the desert that avoided the sun and scurried about only under rocks, these particular women never appeared until the sun started to set. And about fifteen minutes later, right on schedule, a group of four women emerged from a building down the block and sauntered up into the park. They were dressed in the typical Panameña prostitute outfit: a short tight black dress, hardly a dress really, more like a wrap that ended right below their butt cheeks, a tight blouse with a small shawl to keep off the evening chill, and the requisite high heels. It's not the outfit so much that signaled their profession, but the fact that they stood together in a corner of the park, not huddled too tightly, but slightly apart from each other while they talked, and at the same time, scanned the sidewalks in all directions for customers. After a few minutes, they moved as a group to another part of the park, and then after about five minutes, to another part, slightly closer to Ricardo.

A few police cars drove by but paid them no mind,

since prostitution was legal. One of the prostitutes waved at one of the policemen, who waved back. Probably a customer. Ricardo watched as a young man approached the group. He started talking to one of the women. The other three immediately backed away from the conversation to give the couple a chance to talk privately. After a minute of discussion, the couple left together and headed back to the brothel.

The remaining three women chatted a while more and then moved to a spot even closer to Ricardo.

Ricardo could tell that the young man had selected the prettiest of the prostitutes, meaning the least-fat one. Of the three remaining women, two were overweight, with bloated stomachs hanging over the tops of their tight skirts. The remaining woman was thinner but looked obviously pregnant. Ricardo did not feel attracted to any of the three but was enjoying watching them. He knew from previous visits to this park that the women would remain there so long as there were at least two women left in the group. If one of the prostitutes left the group with a client, she would return to the group as soon as she had finished her job. But if business was good, and only two women remained, and another customer approached and selected one, then both women would walk back to the brothel, and the prostitute who didn't have a customer would wait until one of her coworkers was free to venture back to the park with her. None of the women would work the park alone—there always had to be at least two of them together. Ricardo assumed that was for safety, although he had always felt safe in this park.

The three women started to walk towards Ricardo. Since each of their previous positions had been at intersecting walkways in the park, Ricardo assumed they would walk past him to take a position at an intersecting walkway about twenty-five feet away from him. But as they passed him, the pregnant one slowed down and looked at him.

"Enjoying the evening, señor?" she asked him in Spanish.

"Yes, I am, señorita," Ricardo responded in Spanish

and smiled.

The pregnant one stopped. The other two women continued on to the intersecting walkway and waited for her.

"Are you waiting for someone?" she asked.

"No, I'm just relaxing."

"Are you looking for company?"

"No, señorita, no thank you, I'm fine."

She eyed him carefully, and then said, "But I saw how you watched us. I think you are looking for company."

"Not tonight, señorita. Perhaps some other time."

"Am I not pretty enough?"

This question caught him off-guard. He looked at her face, as if for the first time. She was "mixta," part Panameño and part indigenous. She had those thick lips and broad nose that appeared on ancient Aztec carvings. Actually, as Ricardo gazed at her face, he thought she looked like a warrior, handsome in a fierce way.

"Actually señorita, you are quite beautiful."

"Is it because I am pregnant?" She paused. "Have you ever made love to a pregnant woman?"

"No, señorita, I have not."

"You want to try?"

Ricardo admires her directness. She was being matter of fact, not pushy.

"Thank you, señorita, but not tonight."

She laughed. "Next time, I'll be even bigger."

Ricardo had to laugh, too. "That's true, señorita."

Then she got serious. "What difference would it make to you, señor—whether a puta is pregnant or fat or old? You are a man, no? When you want sex, you will copulate with any woman, no?" Again, her tone was matter of fact. But Ricardo thought that his first impression of her face was correct— *she was* a fierce warrior.

"I think it makes a difference, señorita."

"Really, you have copulated with women you don't know, am I right?"

"I have."

"When a man wants to copulate, he is like a bull. Any cow will do."

Then she began to laugh and added, "Next time, when you copulate with me, I will be a fat cow." She laughed again and walked off to join her fellow sex workers.

The sun had set. The three women moved to yet another spot in the park. As it got darker, solitary men appeared and started to approach the women and talk. Ricardo got up to walk back to his apartment. He felt ill.

Chapter 39: Is She Here?

Another two weeks passed. Ricardo had not been able to write anything. Nothing had come to him, and time had slowed to a crawl. He had been sitting in front of his computer all day, drinking coffee, making false starts and then deleting them. It was late in the evening. He was feeling anxious, wired up, crazed, demented. He went and knocked on Eduardo's door, but there was no answer. He went back to his apartment, paced the floor of his apartment but then decided he had to get out. The nearest bathhouse was far and would require a bus ride. Ricardo left his apartment and walked to that small park. He had never been there this late in the evening before. Many young men were standing in small groups. Ricardo tried to walk as if he had a purpose, as if he had somewhere to go. And while he did have a purpose, he really didn't. He looked around the park, but all he saw were men. He walked down the street to the brothel and knocked on the door. An older woman opened the door.

"The pregnant one," Ricardo asked in Spanish. "Is she here?"

The woman took a long look at him, then nodded, and beckoned him to enter. There was no waiting room, just a long hallway with doors. This is why the women had to go to the park.

"Wait here," the woman said, and disappeared.

Ricardo stood there for what seemed like a long time. Five minutes, maybe ten. He began to sweat. "What am I doing here?" he thought. "I should just leave. I'll give it twenty more seconds, then I'm going." He began to count to himself. "1, 2, 3, 4, 5..." When he hit eighteen, he heard a door open. A man hurried past him, head lowered, and out the door. Ricardo turned and looked down the hallway. The pregnant prostitute was walking towards him. She did look even more pregnant than before. She said, "I knew you'd be back." Then she gives a little laugh and said, "Come on, then." Ricardo followed her down the hall.

*　　　*　　　*

Later that night, back at his apartment, he opened a bottle of wine and turned on his computer. Ricardo kept a most secret journal on his computer, one that was double-password protected. It was the only place where he let himself write his innermost thoughts and fears, in a type of automatic writing kind of way. He used it as a cathartic, a purgative method, a way to exorcise and debride certain horrible thoughts that came upon him at times. He only wrote in it when he felt at the end of his rope. He would write in it, but never dared to go back and read what he had written. He poured a glass of wine and began to type, almost in a trance.

Do I really have any control over my desires? Or is the best I can do is to channel them under the cover of night? Have I changed at all? Can I change? Am I any different now than when I was a teenager jerking off in the locked bathroom, or when I was thirty-five and buying 'happy ending' massages at that massage parlor, or when I was forty-five and hiring escorts off Craigslist when my wife was out of town? Is this the best I can do? Is all my writing just a bullshit way to rationalize my situation, to excuse my bestial acts? Was that hooker right—that when a man is horny, he'll fuck anything? I have to admit, it's true for me. I'll fuck almost anyone. Maybe that's why I love the darkness of the steam rooms so much. I don't even see the face of the guy I'm fucking. I don't need to even rationalize that I'm fucking a complete stranger. In the darkness, it's not even a person—it's just a body with a big cock. And maybe that's why it's never mattered to me whether it's a man or a woman, cock or pussy, it's all the same—all I want is the touch of flesh, but especially the touch of flesh that wants to touch me as well. Isn't that really the great lie about prostitution? The great illusion—it's not about the sex but the pretending. I want them to want me—I pay them to act like they want me—and so they put on an act of wanting me... because there's no greater turn-off than a bored hooker. Where does this all end? Is this it? The rest of my life bouncing between brothels and bath houses? I left Marta behind, I left Eve behind... I know, I know, there was no possibility with either one of them to marry them or live with them. But there was some connection. There was some feeling. Am I no better than that asshole Wilson? I don't want to be Wilson. I don't want to be a sex tourist. I just want to write.

Ricardo started to cry, just a little. He poured himself another glass of wine, and then began to type again.

I know somehow the sex and the writing are connected. One drains me and the other fills me... I don't think sex with prostitutes or strangers is a sin, but I do recognize it's base. It's just carnality... but what else can I do? I have to have it... Maybe I am like Wilson in that regard. I don't want to think that, but maybe I am. He's fat and gross and obnoxious but, just like he said, it's the only way he can get laid. If he was only quiet about it, somehow, I don't know, somehow it would be okay. It's just so offensive to hear him talk about it, about using hookers like a piece of Kleenex for his cum. But, I'm in the same boat. I'm too passive, or too old, or too selfish, or too something to get laid any other way.

Ricardo took another sip of wine and thought about Wilson. "I don't have to approve of Wilson...but if I cannot forgive Wilson, then I cannot forgive myself. Maybe forgive is the wrong word. Maybe it's just acceptance." But then he thought some more. "Will that mean I will never change? Never be any different? I don't think sex is wrong, yet I never want to be recognized entering the bath house or the brothel. I don't want anyone to know my business. But maybe that's how it is... maybe that's just me dealing with society's judgments and not my own view of sex."

He thought of Marta, how she was always so steadfast, so much of a lighthouse to him. He depended on her. Even when he didn't talk with her for months, he always carried an image of her in his mind, an image of her smiling and listening to him, supporting him, loving him, guiding him no matter what. He started typing again.

I know I'm incomplete. I see that in myself. I see that in my writing. All my characters are incomplete... they're incomplete versions of me. Maybe that's why I write—to try and find a way, slowly, to try and get a handle on the incompleteness, on the hopelessness of being human. Maybe life is all one big relapse-prevention group where we take turns acknowledging our failures so we can get through one more day. I don't know. I don't know. All I know is that I need to be able to write again. Maybe I'm as gross as Wilson, but I can make it through if I could just write again.

Ricardo looked at the clock. Almost three in the morning. He turned his computer off, finished the wine, put the empty bottle in the trash and went to bed.

Chapter 40: The Wedding

The next day, sometime around noon, Ricardo woke up. He had a slight hangover. He made coffee, and ate a pastry left over from a purchase several days earlier. He turned on his computer and perused his emails. Nothing much except another message from his publisher saying that he still needed one more story to make the book complete.

He thought about the previous evening. He didn't remember what he wrote in his journal. He knew he was feeling horrible when he wrote whatever he wrote, but he didn't want to go back and read it. But this morning, despite the hangover, he felt okay.

He thought about the pregnant woman from last night. Her belly was large and firm. Her breasts were full and heavy. The areolas around her nipples were large and dark. He had to enter her from behind, doggy style. The lips around her pussy were large, but her pussy was remarkably tight and wet. And for once, she was a prostitute who didn't shave her public hair. But what Ricardo liked best was her knowing attitude, her laugh, her directness. After he had gotten hard, she simply bent over the bed, her ass towards him, and said, laughingly, "Fuck me this way." And Ricardo did.

He tried to separate the sex from how torn up he felt afterwards. The sex was good. His emotions were distraught. He wonders if, for once, he should go back and read what he wrote in his journal.

But for the moment, this moment, for some reason, maybe the effect of something, or maybe just a random reason, this man named Ricardo, in this Panameño apartment, felt okay. He remembered thinking the night before that all the men in his short stories were incomplete, and that he was incomplete. Maybe that's what he should write about. Maybe instead of trying to write a "story" to make his publisher happy, he should simply start to write about an incomplete man, someone like himself, a man with incomplete understanding of everything, a man who may never understand anything. He warmed to the idea. He went to his computer and opened up a new page. He stared at it for a minute. He thought of the pregnant woman. The sex was good, but it was just good sex. It wasn't love. He thought of Eve. He missed her. He missed the sex with her, but more, he missed loving her. And even more than that, in fact, most of all, he missed being loved by her. He began to type and the words began to flow out of him...

<u>Summer Wedding</u>

Ricardo was at a wedding. Generally he liked weddings, as long as they weren't his own. But this one was outside, under the hot August sun. He was sweating, standing there beside Eve. He knew the groom, and the bride was a friend of Eve's. Like most weddings, it started late. The minister was droning on.

Dear friends, on behalf of Jim Pategante and Susan Seligman, I welcome you all here today for this marriage ceremony. We are here today, on this beautiful sunny day, to encourage and celebrate the covenant that these two people, Jim and Susan, are going to make, and we are here to share in the joy that Susan and Jim experience as they pledge their love and commitment to each other.

Yeah, Ricardo thought, I bet Jim is just all atingle with joy right now, just flush with happiness... yes, flush is the right word, as he flushes his single life down the toilet. I bet he just wants to get through the ceremony without fucking it up.

We rejoice in the manner God has led them to each other and brought them to the place where they now stand.

Oh God, Ricardo thought, he's going to do a religious wedding. Jesus fucking Christ. It's bad enough we have to stand here outside because these idiots thought it would be romantic to be married underneath the large pine tree at this park, i.e., they were too cheap to rent an air-conditioned hall, and while <u>they</u> are in the shade of that pine, <u>we</u>, the obligated audience of friends, or friends of friends, are standing in the sweltering sun... that's bad enough, but now we have to listen to a fucking religious preacher.

In the Bible, Paul wrote beautifully about the power of love in his first book of letters to the Corinthians, chapter thirteen, where he said: If I speak in the tongues of men and of angels, but have not love, I am a noisy gong or a clanging cymbal. And if I have prophetic powers, and understand all mysteries and all knowledge, and if I have all faith, so as to remove mountains, but have not love, I am nothing. If I give away all I have, and if I deliver my body to be burned, but have not love, I gain nothing. Love is patient and kind; love is not jealous or boastful; it is not arrogant or rude. Love does not insist on its own way; it is not irritable or resentful; it does not rejoice at wrong, but rejoices in the right. Love bears all things, believes all things, hopes all things, endures all things. Love never ends; as for prophecies, they will pass away; as for tongues, they will cease; as for knowledge, it will pass away. For our knowledge is imperfect and our prophecy is imperfect, but when the perfect comes, the imperfect will pass away. When I was a child, I spoke like a child, I thought like a child, I reasoned like a child; when I became a man, I gave up childish ways. For now, we see in a mirror dimly, but then we shall see face to face. Now I know in part; then I shall understand fully, even as I have been fully understood.

So, faith, hope, love abide, these three, but the greatest of these is love.

*   *   *

Ricardo read what he has written. "Interesting," he thought. "I wonder how it will end." But he liked it. It was good to be writing again.

He took another sip of coffee and started typing.

-FIN-

ABOUT THE AUTHOR

Over the past 30 years, Robert Rahula has published dozens books of prose and poetry in Spain and in the United States. While he remains relatively undiscovered in the United States, he is revered in Spain as the founder of the "portilla" style of popular Spanish poetry: non-metered fluid verse that deals with love, loss, bisexuality, separateness, and growing older.

Robert was born in Spain to an American father and Spanish mother, but grew up in Virginia on the farm of his paternal grandparents. He returned to Menorca, Spain, in the 1960s to pursue his writing career. These days he travels in Europe, Central and South America for several months a year, giving readings and lectures, and spends the rest of his time writing, dividing his time between Spain and the United States.

All of Robert's English books are available, including his groundbreaking erotic novel *Messieurs*; his second English novel *Panamaniac;* his erotic murder mystery *Island of Misfits*; his surreal novel *Day Another Paradise In;* his acclaimed supernatural novel *One Last Fling;* his "sexistential" novel *Conversations in a Belgian Bar;* as well as his "Dan Landes Mystery" novels: *Bathhouse Stories, All the Yage in Reno, Exigent Circumstances,* and *Uninvited Guest.*

Eight volumes of Robert's English poetry are also available: *Trigger Points; Inside the Locked Heart; Camino; Migration; I Sing the Body Politic; Wonderland; From Whose Bourn; Expat Poems;* an anthology of his English poems and short stories, *Half-Life;* and a collection of his most famous Spanish poems, *Poemas Españoles.* Other poems, along with his blog on writing and his tour itinerary, appear on his Facebook page and on his website robertrahula.com.

www.ingramcontent.com/pod-product-compliance
Lightning Source LLC
Chambersburg PA
CBHW071507110726
47908CB00003B/752